WITHOUT DUE PROCESS

WITHOUT DUE PROCESS

J. A. JANCE

THORNDIKE
WINDSOR
PARAGON

This Large Print edition is published by Thorndike Press, Waterville, Maine, USA and by BBC Audiobooks Ltd, Bath, England.
Thorndike Press, a part of Gale, Cengage Learning.

A J. P. Beaumont Mystery.

Thorndike Press® Large Print Famous Authors.
The text of this Large Print edition is unabridged.
Other aspects of the book may vary from the original edition.
Set in 16 pt. Plantin.
Printed on permanent paper.

LIBRARY OF CONGRESS CATALOGING-IN-PUBLICATION DATA

Jance, Judith A.
  Without due process / by J. A. Jance.
      p. cm. — (Thorndike Press large print famous authors)
  "A J. P. Beaumont Mystery."
  ISBN-13: 978-1-4104-1549-3 (alk. paper)
  ISBN-10: 1-4104-1549-X (alk. paper)
  1. Beaumont, J. P. (Fictitious character)—Fiction. 2. Police—Washington (State)—Seattle—Fiction. 3. Seattle (Wash.)—Fiction. 4. Large type books. I. Title.
  PS3560.A44W5 2009
  813'.54—dc22   2009003354

BRITISH LIBRARY CATALOGUING-IN-PUBLICATION DATA AVAILABLE

Published in 2009 in the U.S. by arrangement with Avon Books, an imprint of HarperCollins Publishers.
Published in 2009 in the U.K. by arrangement with HarperCollins Publishers Inc.

U.K. Hardcover: 978 1 408 43043 9 (Windsor Large Print)
U.K. Softcover: 978 1 408 43044 6 (Paragon Large Print)

Printed in the United States of America
1 2 3 4 5 6 7 13 12 11 10 09

To the Teddy Bear Patrol,
people who give small comforts to small
people

AUTHOR'S NOTE

Seattle and King County's Teddy Bear Patrol is sponsored by area merchants and spearheaded by Radio Station KLSY. Anyone interested in starting a similar program in another location is welcome to contact the station in care of: Teddy Bear Patrol, 12011 N.E. 3rd Street, Bellevue, Washington 98005 for background and how-to information.

J. A. Jance

CHAPTER 1

Back in the not-so-distant and not-so-good old days, I remember staying up until all hours every April 14 finishing up my income tax returns. It wasn't because they were all that complicated because there was never that much money. No, the difficulty was always nothing more or less than an almost fatal tendency to procrastinate where income taxes are concerned. Once I had completed the dirty job, likely as not I'd reward myself with a couple of stiff belts of MacNaughton's.

A few things have changed since then, some of them for the better. For one, I'm trying, one day at a time, to keep away from Demon Rum. For another, thanks to Anne Corley, there's a hell of a lot more money in my life, and as a consequence, a much more complicated income tax problem. These days, my relations with the IRS are handled by a CPA firm hired and supervised by my attorney and friend, Ralph Ames, whose presence in my life I also owe to Anne Corley. The only thing that hasn't changed is my tendency to procrastinate.

That's why, on the evening of April 14, Ralph showed up around eight o'clock, bringing with him my completed but unsigned returns. The ink was still wet. Ralph, who has been through this exercise with me now a time or two, had held a gun to my accountant's head and insisted that, no, we were not going to file for an extension.

I fixed a pot of coffee, and for a while we sat in my living room window seat, visiting and watching the nighttime boat traffic crisscrossing the black expanse of Puget Sound. Finally, though, Ralph cleared his throat, switched on the table lamp, and handed me the weighty manila envelope. "Time to go to work," he said.

As I read over the return, I knew better than to expect to get anything back, but when I hit the bottom line and saw that the amount due equaled 80 percent of my annual take-home pay as a homicide detective for the Seattle Police Department, I about hit the roof.

"You've got to be kidding! That's how much I owe?"

Ralph Ames nodded and grinned. "Can I

help it if you're making money hand over fist? We lucked into some very good invest-ments this last year. Stop complaining and write the check, Beau. You can transfer in enough money to cover it tomorrow or the next day."

First I signed the return, then I reached for the checkbook. With pen in hand I paused long enough to verify that astonish-ing figure one last time. "What's the point in working then?" I demanded irritably. "Why bother to show up down at the de-partment day after day?"

Ralph waited patiently for me to finish writing the check. When I handed it over to him, he put both the signed return and the check on the coffee table.

"Good question." He smiled. "Seems to me I've mentioned that very thing to you a time or two myself. You need to lighten up, Beau. Work less, learn to have some fun, maybe even find yourself a woman. That's an idea. Whatever happened to Marilyn? I haven't seen her around here for some time."

Marilyn Sykes, the former chief of police on Mercer Island, had been a sometime thing, someone to chum around with and take to bed occasionally until she up and turned serious on me. With a lucrative job offer from Santa Clara, California, in hand, she had come to me with an ultimatum to either get with the program as in marriage or else forget it because she was leaving. She took the job in Santa Clara.

"She got married," I said. "Just before Christmas last year. To some big-time electronics wizard down in California. She sent me an announcement."

"You'll get over her eventually," Ralph said.

I shrugged. "It wasn't that big a thing, really."

Ralph shook his head. "I wasn't talking about Marilyn Sykes," he said carefully.

Without another word, I got up and went to the kitchen to get more coffee. Ralph Ames was one of the few people who knew just how big a hole Anne Corley's death had torn in my heart. It's not something I like to advertise. Years later, I still don't much want to talk about it. Not even with Ralph.

For a few minutes I avoided the subject by dinking around in the kitchen and making one more pot of coffee. Then, just as the coffee finished, I was saved by the bell in the guise of a timely phone call that cut off all further discussion.

The familiar voice on the other end of the line belonged to Sergeant Watkins, the day desk sergeant in Homicide. My partner, Detective "Big Al" Lindstrom and I were on call that night, so the phone call was no particular surprise. What was surprising was for Watty to be making the call rather than the nightshift sergeant. Not only that, he sounded genuinely relieved to hear my voice.

"Glad you're okay, Beau," he said. "I'm more worried about the guys who don't live in secure high rises. Big Al's all right too, by the way. I just checked. He's coming in from Ballard right now. I told him to stop by and pick you up. We need you both down at the department ASAP. I'll meet you there."

That meant Watty had called me from home. His coming back into the department at night was more than slightly out of the ordinary, so something was definitely up. "What's going on?" I asked.

"A call came in to nine-one-one about forty minutes ago. The guy claims to have killed a police officer and wiped out his entire family. The chief has all supervisors checking with individual squad members by phone. Wherever we get no answer, we're sending out cars to check."

"It must have sounded pretty legit," I said.

"You'd better believe it. Enough to get everyone moving in high gear. So far nothing's turned up, but my guess is not every-one's been called yet, either."

"What about us?"

"The chief wants detectives lined up and ready to move at a moment's notice. That's where you and Detective Lindstrom come in. The night shift told me you two were on deck."

"Right," I said. "Can you give us any more information? What exactly was said? Where did the call originate?"

King County's Enhanced 911 system shows a visual display of the originating ad-dress for all emergency phone calls. This al-lows the operators to have accurate address information to forward on to police, fire, and medic personnel.

"Not now," Watty replied. "No time. I'm not done with my calling yet. I'll finish briefing you once we're all down at the of-fice. Gotta go."

The call-waiting signal on my own tele-phone buzzed impatiently, announcing that I had another call on the other line. "Me, too," I told him. "That's probably Big Al now, calling to say he's downstairs."

I switched to the other line and heard the bearlike Detective Lindstrom growling into the receiver. "I'm here, Beau. Hurry it up,

14

will you? Watty's climbing the walls on this one."

Big Al didn't sound any too happy about being out and about. As far as partners go, he's not bad, but he tends to be surly when he's short on sleep. After buzzing Big Al into the lobby, I put the phone down and went back into the living room, where Ralph was finishing licking the flap on the official IRS envelope. He looked up at me as I slipped on my bulletproof vest and fastened my shoulder holster in place.

"Duty calls?" he asked. I nodded.

"Want me to see that this gets in the mail?"

"Thanks, Ralph. That would be great. Send it certified, return receipt requested. I don't trust those guys any further than I can throw them, and I sure as hell don't need Uncle Sugar on my butt for missing the deadline."

"When will you be back?"

I knew that if the anonymous 911 caller had told the truth and that we really were dealing with a multiple homicide, it was going to be a long, terrible night.

"Don't wait up," I said. "There's no telling. Some asshole claims he's killed a cop and several other people besides. With any

15

kind of luck it's somebody's idea of a bad joke."

"I hope so," Ralph said.

"Me too," I added grimly.

He followed me to the door as I made my way into the elevator lobby and pushed the down button. "Sorry if I upset you a minute ago," he said. "I didn't mean to pry, but when the two of us are together, it seems like I can't help thinking about her."

Until that very moment, it hadn't occurred to me that I wasn't the only one who hadn't managed to get past the pain of Anne Corley's death. And I wasn't the only dummy she had led around by the nose, either.

"Don't worry about it, Ralph," I said as the elevator door swished open. "It's no big deal."

He was still standing there looking at me, when the door shut and the elevator started its descent. I usually use the twenty-five-story elevator ride as a pressurization chamber, a place to switch gears from home to work and vice versa, but I was still thinking about Anne and Ralph and me when the door opened and I saw Big Al striding back and forth across Belltown Terrace's marbled lobby while the building's uniformed doorman cowered nervously behind his rosewood writing desk and pretended to read a book.

One look at Big Al's impatient face told me he for one believed the 911 call was the real McCoy. There had been a total changing of the guard in the top echelons of Seattle PD, and the honeymoon period had been brief enough to be almost nonexistent. The new chief was rumored to be a closet racist, while word was out on the streets that someone somewhere was taking payoffs. In previously scandal-free Seattle, community relations had plummeted. Verbal abuse and threats against police officers were up as were outright physical attacks. Maybe the top brass weren't directly affected by all this, but it was no surprise that the middle managers, people like Watty and Captain Powell, were taking this latest telephoned threat in dead earnest.

"Come on," Big Al said, heading for the door as soon as he saw me. "Let's get going."

"You don't think this is just some kind of a kook?"

"Are you kidding?"

I followed him out to the curb and clambered into the car with a knot of apprehension solidifying in the pit of my stomach. If Big Al was right, if Watty was, somewhere in the city of Seattle, a police officer was dead. Chances are, whoever he was, that cop was someone I knew.

"Where are we going?" I asked as we started down Second Avenue.

"To the department. Watty says they have a car waiting for us in the garage. We're supposed to call in as soon as we're back out on the street."

At night, there's hardly ever a shortage of on-street parking outside the Public Safety Building. We left Big Al's Ciera parked half a block away and hoofed it into the garage. Marty Sampson, the nighttime garage supervisor, was standing in the guard shack along with the attendant. They both seemed so mesmerized by something that they didn't even see us until we were directly on top of them. It turned out they were staring at their radio.

"Hey, guys," Big Al said, jarring them awake. "What's happening? Which car is ours?"

When Marty looked up at us, his face reminded me of someone awakened from a terrible nightmare. "That one," he said, pointing. "And hurry. An officer-down call came in a few minutes ago. Watty wants you there, pronto."

"Where?"

"Down in the south end someplace. The street's Cascadia. I don't know the exact address. You can get that once you're on your way."

Big Al and I sprinted to the car, climbed in, and shot out of the garage with lights and siren both going full blast. With Big Al driving, I ran the radio, giving our position and letting Dispatch know we were on our way.

It was several moments before a harried-sounding dispatcher radioed back to us directly. The people who work in Dispatch, officers and civilians alike, pride themselves in maintaining professional composure no matter what, but this one was having a tough time of it. She was so choked up I could barely make out the street name, Cascadia. Once again the exact address got lost in the shuffle while she plunged on with the rest of the transmission.

"Officer down. We've got uniforms and emergency vehicles on the scene. They've called for detectives. That's all I can tell you so far."

No doubt that was all she could say over the air due to the many unofficial ears that routinely monitor official police channels, but her emotion-charged voice allowed my imagination to fill in some chilling blanks.

By then we were careening down the far side of First Hill. "Repeat that address," Big Al said forcefully into the radio. "We didn't catch it the first time."

This time the numbers came through clear as a bell, and I thought I was a dead man.

"Dear God in heaven!" Big Al roared, simultaneously slamming on the brakes. By a mere fraction of an inch we avoided rear-ending a hapless taxi whose oblivious driver had meandered into our path.

"Hey, watch it," I yelped, grabbing at the dash with an outstretched arm. "You could get us killed."

"No," Big Al said.

"What the hell do you mean 'no'? You missed that guy by less than an inch."

But Big Al Lindstrom didn't seem to be listening. "Son of a bitch!" he exclaimed, pounding the steering wheel with both gigantic hands, which meant that he wasn't holding on with any. The whole car seemed to shudder from the force of the blow. The idea of Big Al pitching a temper tantrum at any time is daunting enough, but having him do it in a car which he was supposedly driving at the time was downright terrifying.

"What the hell's going on?" I demanded.

"What's the matter with you?"

"It's Ben. They got Gentle Ben. That's his address."

The lump in my gut turned to solid ice. "Are you sure?" I asked, all the while knowing he was.

"Yes," Big Al replied in a snarl of rage. "I know it as well as I do my own."

Maybe for some people the words "Gentle Ben" evoke only memories of an old, forgettable TV series, but in the parlance of Seattle PD, they referred to just one person — Benjamin Harrison Weston, known to friend and foe alike as Gentle Ben.

Years earlier, Big Al and Ben had worked together when they were both new detectives in the Property division. Except for the distinct difference in skin color, they might have been twins. Massively built yet easygoing, plodding but amazingly thorough, the burly Norwegian and his African-American colleague always left a singular impression on those who had any dealings with them. After six months of working together, diverging career paths had led them in different directions — Big Al into Homicide and Ben into Patrol, but a genuine affection existed between them. Through the years the former partners had stayed in touch.

"They just said officer down," I suggested, trying to inject some hope into the situation. "Maybe he's not dead."

"It wasn't a 'help the officer' call," Big Al pointed out. "That means it's too damn late for help, and you know it."

He was right. There was no arguing that point. While Allen Lindstrom drove us through the city with terrifying, single-minded ferocity, I tried to quell the tide of unreasoning anger boiling up inside me.

Murder investigations don't allow any room for rage. The beginning of a homicide case demands total focus and clearheaded logic. Anything else is an unaffordable luxury. Outrage would have to come later, along with grief. In the meantime, we would both have to shove aside all personal considerations and start asking the stark, necessary, and routine questions about who had killed Ben Weston and why?

The human psyche can assimilate only so much bad news at one time. For a few moments as we raced, siren howling, through the night-lit city, I thought only of Ben. Then I remembered the rest of Watty's phone call — that the killer had bragged of killing a police officer and his entire family. In that mysterious unspoken communication that happens sometimes between husbands and wives or partners, Big Al reached the same conclusion at almost the same moment. He grabbed for the microphone.

I knew exactly what was on his mind. "Don't bother asking," I said. "Dispatch isn't going to tell you what you want to know over the air."

With an oath that was half English and half unprintable Norwegian, Big Al heaved the microphone out of his hand as though it were a piece of hand-singeing charcoal. They make radio equipment out of pretty tough materials these days. The microphone bounced off both the windshield and the dashboard without splintering into a thousand pieces.

"How many are there?" I asked.

"Five," he said. "Ben, his wife, and three kids, two from his first marriage and then the baby, Junior."

"How old?"

"Bonnie's the oldest. She must be fourteen or fifteen by now. Dougie is twelve. Junior's what? . . . maybe five or six. I forget which."

"And the wife's name?"

"Shiree. She's good people," Big Al declared. "I don't know what Ben would have done if she hadn't been there to help out when his first wife died. Ben was all torn

up, and Shiree sort of glued him back together."

I glanced across the seat in time to see
Big Al swipe at a damp cheek with one of
his huge, doubled fists. "Want me to drive?"
I offered.

"Hell no! You wouldn't go fast enough.
I'm gonna get there in time to kill the
bastard myself!"

He meant it too, and I didn't blame him.
I shut up and let him drive. When we finally
reached the general area, we found that an
eight-block area around the Weston family
home on Cascadia was cordoned off. It was
lit up like daylight by the massed collection
of emergency vehicles surrounding it. Big
Al snaked his way through the crush as far
as possible. After that, we got out and
walked.

A grim-faced Captain Lawrence Powell,
head of our Homicide division, met us on
the front porch and barred the way, stopping Big Al in his tracks.

"You probably shouldn't go in there,
Detective Lindstrom," the captain cautioned. "It's real rough — five dead so far."

Big Al's huge shoulders sagged and he
lurched visibly under the weight of Powell's
words. Five dead? That meant that along
with Ben his entire family — his wife and

all three of his children — had been eradicated from the face of the earth!

"I know you and Weston were friends," Powell continued, reaching up to place a restraining hand on Big Al's massive chest. "I'll assign somebody else . . ."

Impatiently, Big Al shook off the captain's hand as though it wasn't there. "Everybody who ever met Ben Weston was his friend," Lindstrom countered doggedly. "Sergeant Watkins assigned me to this case, and I'm taking it."

"Are you sure?"

Detective Lindstrom is a good six inches taller than the captain, and he outweighs him by a minimum of seventy-five pounds. Big Al stared down at Powell, his face contorted by grief, his skin pulsing an eerie red in the reflected glow from the flashing lights of an ambulance parked just outside Ben Weston's gate.

"Yes," Detective Lindstrom replied fiercely. "I'm sure." With that, he stomped off and disappeared into the house.

Captain Powell turned to me. "You keep an eye on him, Beaumont. If Big Al can't handle it, if he needs to be pulled from this case, I expect you to let me know immediately."

"Right," I said, but that wasn't what was

going through my mind.

Like hell I will, I thought as the appalling death toll continued to explode in my head. Five! Five! Five! If Captain Powell thought he could count on me to spy for him and report on the correctness of Big Al's behavior in this case, he was on the wrong track. I wouldn't do it, and nobody else would either. The death of Gentle Ben Weston was everybody's business.

Concerned about public image and letter-of-the-law proper procedure, Captain Powell might very well pull Big Al from the case, but being taken off officially didn't mean the detective would stop working the problem. Not at all. Assigned or not, every homicide detective in the city of Seattle would be walking, talking, and breathing this case twenty-four hours a day until it was over and the killer was either dead or permanently behind bars.

Cops are people too, you see. When faced with the slaughter of one of our own, we all take it very, very personally.

CHAPTER 2

Through some mysterious fluke of fate I happened to be out of town at the beginning of two of Seattle's most notorious murder cases. I was fortunate enough to be in D.C. attending a homicide convention when eleven people were massacred in a downtown supper club. Several years later, I was vacationing in California with my kids when a certified crazy used an ax to murder his psychiatrist as well as the psychiatrist's wife and two young children.

I was involved in those two cases only on a limited, peripheral level. My connection was primarily in dealing with the mountain of departmental paperwork that is the inevitable accompaniment of any multiple murder. To my great good fortune, I wasn't embroiled in any of the immediate crime scene aftermath. My luck in that regard ran out completely when it came to the family of Officer Benjamin Harrison Weston.

When the Westons failed to answer Ben's supervisor's call, two uniformed officers were dispatched at once to check on the family. They arrived sometime after eleven and were, as a consequence, first on the scene. They walked us through the area and gave us a chilling guided tour of the Weston family's senseless slaughter.

The killer's trail was as easy to follow as the set of muddy footprints that marched unwaveringly up the back porch, through the blood-spattered kitchen, dining room, and living room, down the long carpeted hallway, and into two of the three bedrooms.

The first victim was evidently the faithful family dog, a big black-and-white mutt which, according to Big Al, had been unimaginatively but appropriately named Spot. We found Spot in the far corner of the backyard with his throat slit. The patrol officers theorized that the girl might have gone outside after the dog since the first sign of struggle — an overturned chair and a broken flowerpot — were both located on the back deck outside the kitchen door. I made a note to check and see if any of the neighbors might have heard noises from that deadly struggle, but the chances were good that the killer hadn't given her the opportunity to make any noise.

We found the girl herself just inside the kitchen door. She was lying on her side in a pool of blood. Her mouth had been taped shut with duct tape. Big Al looked down at her and shook his head. "Her name's Bonnie," he said gruffly. "Short for Vondelle. Same name as her mother's."

Bonnie Weston may have grappled with her assailant on the back porch in an initial encounter, but in the kitchen itself we found little evidence of her continued fight — no broken dishes or upended chairs that indicated that a life-or-death, hand-to-hand combat had occurred in that incongruously cheerful and homey room. Perhaps, faced with her attacker's superior strength, she had decided to comply with his wishes in hopes of somehow appeasing him. Unfortunately for Bonnie Weston, appeasement had never been part of her killer's agenda.

Mr. and Mrs. John Q. Public, reading headline-grabbing newspaper stories over their morning coffee, may delude themselves into thinking that having your throat slit isn't such a bad way to go, that it's a reasonably quick and relatively merciful way for someone to meet his or her maker. One look at that gore-spattered kitchen floor would convince them otherwise. In her convulsive, drowning death throes, Bonnie Weston had floundered desperately across the yellow tile, leaving behind a muddy brown spatter of stains in which several footprints remained clearly visible.

I turned to the two uniformed officers. "Did either of you leave these tracks?"

The younger one, Officer Dunn, fresh from the academy and barely into his probationary thirteen-week Field Officer Training Program, answered quickly for both of them. "No, sir. We were real careful about that. I came up over there." He pointed to a clean spot on the tile. "I got close enough to check her pulse and then . . ." He shrugged. "She was already dead. Nothing we could do."

I glanced at Big Al. With his face a gray mask, he stood staring down at the dead girl. "This guy's one mean son of a bitch," he said grimly, "a real sicko."

In some politically correct quarters, Big Al's instant assumption that the killer was male might have been regarded as sexist, but I agreed. Homicide is not yet an equal opportunity occupation, although the numbers are gradually coming up as far as female perpetrators are concerned. But women don't usually kill with that kind of wanton brutality. And they usually don't leave that kind of mess either.

"At least she's still got her clothes on," Officer Dunn observed helpfully.

What he was trying to say in his own clumsy fashion was that Bonnie Weston had most likely been spared the further indignity of sexual assault, but that knowledge did nothing to mitigate the ruthless butchery of the young woman's death. I don't think Big Al even heard him.

"How come nobody came to help her?" he asked. "Couldn't anybody hear what was going on? Where were Ben and Shiree?"

Again Officer Dunn was quick to answer. "The parents?" Big Al nodded. "In the bedroom at the far end of the hall. I doubt they heard a thing. When we got here, the stereo in the living room was playing fairly loud, tuned to some hot rock station, and the TV set was on in the parents' room. We switched them off by pulling plugs. We couldn't hear ourselves think."

I nodded, glad someone else had thought to turn off the noise, but grateful that the uniformed officers hadn't touched any of the radio or television controls. I left Big Al to process the kitchen, and I followed Officer Dunn down the hallway to a small bedroom. There, on a two-tiered bunk bed lay two small African-American males, both dead. Both lay on their sides, facing the

31

wall, and both might have been asleep except for deep puncture wounds at the base of each small skull.

Nothing in the room seemed to be disturbed. Little-boy litter, toys and clothes, lay scattered about, but it appeared as though the two children had died without the slightest advance warning of their impending doom.

Without touching anything, I left the room. I found Officer Dunn waiting outside. "Whatever you do," I told him, "don't let Detective Lindstrom set foot inside that room."

Dunn looked at me quizzically. He was far too new on the force to have any inkling of Big Al and Ben Weston's mutual history, but he didn't argue or question my order. "Right," he said. "I'll see to it."

I went back to the living room and discovered my partner standing there, turning slowly, taking in everything there was to see. Except for faint traces of bloodied footprints on the beige carpet, the living room showed no other sign of tragedy. Nothing in that room had been disturbed. A single floor lamp glowed near the end of a long comfortable-looking couch. A soft green afghan was piled in the middle of the couch, looking as though it had been tossed aside by someone momentarily abandoning a cozy reading nest. A book bag sat on the floor near the afghan while an assortment of school paraphernalia — a stack of textbooks, pens and pencils, and an open notebook — littered the oak coffee table. Nearby was a partially filled ceramic mug with the name "Bonnie" printed in cheerful blue script on the outside.

Big Al leaned over and sniffed the mug. "Tea," he said.

"Tea?" I asked. "At her age? Why not Coke or Pepsi?"

"Vondelle, Bonnie's mother, always drank tea. Only tea. No coffee, no sodas. Bonnie must have picked up the habit. Kids do that, you know. It's a way of hanging on to the past."

Big Al swung back toward Officer Dunn. "Exactly how long ago did you two get here?"

I think the terrible reality of what had happened was just beginning to hit home with Officer Dunn. His color had faded to a sickly yellow. Perhaps the younger man was beginning to question his own culpability over those five deaths. He seemed to misread an accusation into Big Al's straightforward question.

"We came as . . . as . . . soon as we could,"

he stammered. "I'm sorry as hell we didn't get here sooner. We were on another call, a domestic, when Dispatch asked us to come here. We didn't dawdle, but we didn't burn up the car, either. We didn't think it was that . . ." He broke off, ducking his chin, his voice choked with emotion.

I felt for him, knew firsthand the impotent frustration of arriving at a crime scene or automobile accident too late to do any good or make any real difference. This might be Officer Dunn's first such gut-wrenching experience. If he made it through his probationary period, it wouldn't be his last.

"You couldn't have saved them," I said consolingly. "They were probably dead long before you took the call." He nodded, but it didn't seem to make him feel any better.

We started toward the hallway only to encounter King County's medical examiner, Dr. Howard Baker. He nodded in my direction. "What do you want us to photograph first, Beaumont, the kitchen or one of the bedrooms?"

I pointed toward the room where the boys were. "Do that one," I said.

Doc Baker headed for the bedroom and Big Al started to follow. Officer Dunn and I both stepped forward to stop him. "The boys?" he asked.

I nodded. "You don't need to see it, Al. Not right now."

He shook his head helplessly. "No," he agreed. "I suppose not."

Without another word, he continued on down the hallway, leading the way into what had been Ben and Shiree Weston's modest master bedroom. I caught him by the arm before he had a chance to step inside.

"Are you sure you want to do this?" I asked. "Sure you're all right?"

"Ja," he said, slipping into Ballardese. "I'm okay." He didn't sound terribly convincing but we went on inside anyway.

The room looked as though it had been through a major earthquake. A six-drawer dresser had been shoved away from the wall with its drawers askew and clothing spilling out. A small television set had fallen on its face beside it. The mirror behind the dresser was a splintered wreck.

Avoiding the scatter of furniture, I moved toward the bed. A bedside lamp with its glass base broken lay in a shattered heap on the carpeted floor along with the usual debris that surfaces daily from male clothing — a wallet, some loose change, a small maroon cowhide Day-Timer, a couple of receipts, and a ticket stub from a dry cleaners. Looking at Ben Weston's leavings, I was struck by the fact that he had emptied his pockets with no inkling that he was doing it for the last time.

That's the irony of what we call "home invasion" cases, where the victims, presumably safe in their own homes, carry on with their normal lives until the precise moment when their killer comes to call.

But looking at demolished furniture, examining the items on the floor, and philosophizing was nothing more than a delaying tactic, a way of putting off the inevitable necessity of examining the murdered man himself. It's bad enough to encounter victims who are total strangers. This one was much worse than that. Benjamin Harrison Weston was no stranger to any of us. Not only was he an acquaintance of long standing, he was a cop besides.

He lay facedown in the exact middle of his king-size bed. Sometimes the dead seem to cave in upon themselves, to shrink. Not so Gentle Ben Weston. In life he had been a mountain of a man, and he remained so in death. He too had died of a single stab wound to the neck. Like that to the two boys, Ben's damage was limited to a single deep puncture right at the base of his skull.

Unknown to me, Doc Baker and both uniformed cops had trailed us into the room. "I believe what you're seeing here and with the two boys," Doc Baker began explaining, presumably for Officer Dunn's benefit, "is something the military refers to as a silent or screamless kill. They teach this kind of thing in hand-to-hand, combat-type training. There are several variations, but for a man sleeping on his stomach, this one would have been by far the simplest. My guess he was attacked without warning. He never had a chance to defend himself or even cry out. If the knife blade is placed exactly right, the result is instant and total paralysis."

"So whoever did this wanted to make sure he didn't have to handle Ben in a fair fight?" I asked. Baker nodded.

"Me neither," I added. "Ben Weston would have swept the floor with me if I'd ever given him a reason."

"Probably some cowardly little shit Ben could have beaten the crap out of if he'd been awake," Big Al added bitterly.

Baker gave Big Al a sidelong glance. "You two were friends?"

Al glared down at his shoe. "You could say that," he said.

Officer Dunn continued to stare at Ben Weston's still body. "I never heard of screamless kills before," he mumbled softly.

Doc Baker stood towering beside the bed, with his shock of white hair standing on end, in a stance designed to strike terror in the hearts of the inexperienced. He resembled nothing so much as a demented polar bear, and I knew he was enjoying Officer Dunn's discomfort.

"Then obviously you've never been in the Marines," Doc Baker observed condescendingly.

"You're right," Officer Dunn returned shakily. "I never was, and I don't think I want to be, either. Mind if I step outside?"

With that, he and his partner left the room. Big Al, too, seemed shaken. Turning away from the bed, he faced the bathroom doorway, but that door only opened onto further evidence of the brutal carnage, for the bathroom was where the killer had left his final victim — Shiree Weston.

"From the looks of it," Baker said, moving in beside him, "the woman must have had some advance warning of her danger. I believe she may have emerged from taking a shower and encountered the intruder, caught him in the act of murdering her husband and tried to stop him. I'll say this much for her. She put up one hell of a fight."

No doubt a fierce battle had been waged all over the demolished bedroom, but inarguably the final confrontation had occurred in the bathroom, where the doorjamb had been splintered around the lock. An examination of the doorknob itself revealed that the lock was still engaged although the door stood wide open.

"She locked herself in trying to get away?" I asked.

Baker shrugged. "Maybe. My guess is she hoped to summon help through the open bathroom window, but it didn't work. He mowed right through the door and got to her before she had a chance."

I stood over a naked Shiree Weston and looked down with a real sense of sadness at a woman I had never met during her lifetime. I knew from Big Al that younger than her husband by a good fifteen years, she had been a vital, vibrant woman, one who had taken a widowed and grieving Ben Weston in hand. She had showed him a way to go on living in the aftermath of his first wife's death.

"Look at her hand," Big Al said quietly, nudging me out of my reverie.

I looked. Her doubled fist was rolled into a solid ball with tufts of hair sticking out between her tightly gripped fingers.

"DNA fingerprints are going to nail this bastard," Big Al vowed, "or I'll know the reason why. Let's get out of here," he added. "I need some air."

With that, he stalked out of the room. I followed him into the hallway. Outside the bedroom, Big Al's slim margin of control evaporated. He covered his eyes with both hands as if to shut out the horror we had both just witnessed.

"I can't believe it," he mumbled, shaking his head. "With Ben and Shiree, it's bad enough, but at least the two of them had a chance at life. They were happy together, but the kids . . . My God, those poor little kids . . ."

He stopped talking then and stood there gulping air like some kind of huge landed fish. A stranger might have thought he was witnessing a heart attack in progress. Instead, it was only Big Al Lindstrom, one of the world's original cool macho dudes, doing his level best not to cry in public.

"Look, fella," I said sympathetically. "Captain Powell was right. These people were all your friends. This is too hard on you. Get your ass back home to Molly and let somebody else handle this case. You don't have to."

"I sure as hell do," Big Al returned in a strangled whisper. "And that's why — *because* he was my friend. I owe him."

We were standing in the hallway near a pocket door that seemed to cover a linen closet. Just then, there was a distinct scratching from somewhere near the base of the other side of that door.

I don't know if the same thing happened to Big Al, but I can tell you, the hair on the back of my neck stood straight up. We both jumped as though we'd been shot, but the scratching came again, followed by a small, whimpering voice.

"Can I come out now? Is the bad man gone?"

If I hadn't seen it myself, I wouldn't have believed Big Al Lindstrom capable of that kind of lightning movement. He spun around and grabbed for the finger hole. For a moment, he struggled, trying to open it, but the door had apparently fallen off its track. He had to lift the door and drop it back into place before he could finally slide it open. When it did, a small, pajama-clad child tumbled out into the hallway.

"Junior!" Big Al croaked as soon as he caught sight of the boy. "What in the world are you doing in there?"

The little kid took one look at Big Al and held out his short arms to be picked up. Obviously they knew each other.

"Where's my daddy?" Junior Weston

asked, snuggling close to Big Al's thick neck "Where's my mommy? Why wouldn't they come let me out? The door got stuck. I had to go to the bathroom, but they didn't come when I called. I think I wet my pants."

You hardly ever consider the possibility of someone like Big Al Lindstrom being radiant. Brides are radiant. Mothers of newborns are radiant. Men aren't supposed to look that way, but the exultant joy on Detective Lindstrom's face was amazing to behold as he clutched Benjamin Harrison Weston, Jr., in a fierce, breath-crushing bear hug.

"Hey, you guys," he crowed, laughing and crying at the same time, shouting to anyone who cared to listen. "Come see what I found!"

The narrow hallway immediately filled with people, although not one of them stepped on the trail of bloody footprints that marred the carpeting. They all wanted to know what was going on, but no one wanted to risk screwing up the evidence.

"Look here," Big Al gloated. "Here's Junior — Junior Weston, and he's all right, by God. There's not a scratch on him!"

"So who's the other kid?"

I asked the question of the world in general rather than anyone in particular, but it turned out that no one was listening and nobody else answered my question. I myself had seen those two dead boys lying on the bunk beds in that first bedroom, but at that precise moment in time, everyone within earshot was focused on the miracle that Junior Weston was still alive, that at least one member of Ben Weston's family had escaped the scourge. No one else had time to think about that other unfortunate child and his soon-to-be-grieving family.

For a moment, we were all too stunned to do anything, but finally my brain slipped out of neutral. "I'll be right back," I told Al. I fought my way down the crowded hallway, through the living room, and out the front door.

"Hey, Detective Beaumont," Captain Powell yelled after me as I vaulted past him down the steps. "Where the hell do you think you're going? You can't be finished in there already."

"I'm going after the teddy bear," I called back over my shoulder, "and there by God better be one out in the car!"

Years earlier, a local radio station had sponsored a program called the Teddy Bear Patrol. The idea was to put donated teddy bears in all local emergency vehicles — law enforcement, fire, and Medic One — in both the city and county. When confronted with traumatized children, emergency personnel and police officers would then have something besides mere words with which to comfort injured or frightened kids.

At the time I first heard about it, I confess it struck me as a pretty dumb idea. The idea of men getting ready to go on shift and making sure they had their weapon, their cuffs, their bulletproof vest, and their teddy bear seemed a little ridiculous. After all, real men don't eat quiche, and they don't pack teddy bears either. Over the years, however, I've been forced to change my mind, having heard enough secondhand, heart-rending stories to see the error of my ways. That April night, though, was the first time I personally had need of one of those damned bears.

"Teddy bear?" Captain Powell echoed, following me down the sidewalk. "What the hell do you want with a teddy bear?"

"Big Al just found one of Ben's kids, Ben Junior."

Powell stopped in his tracks. "He's still alive?"

The soft, squishy brown bear was right there in the trunk, exactly where it was supposed to be. My groping hand closed around one tiny leg. When I triumphantly hauled it out of the car and slammed the trunk lid shut, I almost collided with Captain Powell, who had stopped directly behind me.

"He's alive all right. He's fine. He was hiding in a linen closet. Got stuck in there. I think he just woke up and recognized Al's voice."

"You're kidding!"

"The hell I am! Come see for yourself."

"Hallelujah," Captain Powell breathed. "I can't believe it!"

I left him standing there and hurried back up the sidewalk with that precious teddy bear crushed against my chest. Holding that soft, cuddly creature even helped me that night, made me feel better. I knew holding it would help Junior Weston too.

Back in the hallway, Big Al hadn't moved. He still held the child, although the crowd of onlookers had thinned some as people returned to their various assignments. I caught Big Al's eye and held the bear up high enough so he could see it. He nodded gratefully as I handed it to him.

"Look here," Big Al said to the child in his arms. "Look what Detective Beaumont found for you. A teddy bear."

Benjamin Harrison Weston, Jr., couldn't have been more than five years old. As far as we knew, he was totally unaware of what had happened to his parents. He had no idea that his entire family had been wiped off the face of the earth and that he himself was an orphan. He saw only the lovable brown teddy bear and knew that, for whatever reason, he was being given a gift.

"For me?" he squealed delightedly, hugging the bear to his pajama-clad chest. "Really?"

For a few moments, there wasn't a dry eye anywhere within earshot, mine included.

CHAPTER 3

It seemed important to have Junior Weston well away from the house before Doc Baker's helpers began wheeling gurneys loaded with body bags out the front door and into waiting vans. We bundled the boy into a jacket over his pajamas and then took him along downtown. Some kids might have balked at or been terrified by the prospect of a trip to the Public Safety Building, but because Junior was a cop's kid, for him it was nothing more than a trip to his dad's office.

After a quick but necessary visit to the bathroom, we brought him back to our crowded cubicle on the fifth floor. There he settled easily into Big Al's lap, clutching the teddy bear. A steaming cup of cocoa sat at the ready on the detective's cluttered desk.

Genetically linked stubbornness has necessitated a long learning curve, but now when I'm wrong, I can come right out and

47

admit it. In regard to Detective Lindstrom and the Weston family murders, I'm happy to report I was absolutely dead wrong. During the next few minutes Big Al reverted almost totally to type. By dint of pure Scandinavian hardheadedness, he set aside his own feelings of grief and outrage and functioned flawlessly as the consummate investigator questioning a vulnerable but essential eyewitness.

In dealing with witnesses of any kind — young or old, willing or not — that initial questioning session often offers the best chance of gleaning really useful information. With young children especially, those first few moments are critical. It's important to hear what the child himself has to say before his memory is colored or diluted by the preconceived notions of those around him. Well-intentioned adults — relatives, friends, or social workers — may inadvertently or deliberately encourage him to forget or change what he remembers, thinking that by doing so they will somehow lessen the trauma of what the child has experienced.

In the case of Benjamin Harrison Weston, Jr., there was no other detective in the Seattle Police Department who could have worked with the five-year-old boy the way

Big Al did. Already a known and trusted adult in the Weston family sphere of influence, he dealt with the child in a straightforward, no-nonsense manner that gave the kid credit for having a good head on his shoulders. The detective's whole approach, caring but devoid of condescension, was no doubt good for the boy, with the reverse also true — Junior Weston's trusting innocence gave courage and purpose to the man.

"Do you know what dead is?" Big Al opened the discussion with a quiet but throat-lumping question.

Junior nodded, his eyes focused intently on the man's face. "My granny's dead," he answered slowly, "and so's Bonnie's mama. She died before I was born. Mommy told me that when people die, they go to heaven."

Big Al faltered, his voice cracking slightly. "They're dead, Junior. They're all dead — your mommy and daddy, your sister and your brother."

The child was quiet for a moment, assimilating the words. "Does that mean they're in heaven now, with Jesus?"

Big Al blinked. "Yes," he said. "I suppose they are."

"Can I go too?"

"No, Junior. You can't. You'll have to stay here."

"Alone?"

"Yes."

The boy turned away while two gigantic tears slipped down his round cheeks. "The bad man did it, didn't he," Junior said softly. "He hurt Bonnie. I saw him do it."

"You saw him?" Big Al asked with a meaningful glance in my direction.

"Yes. In the kitchen. He had a knife, a big knife. He started to come after me, too, but I ran and hid in the closet. I closed the door so he couldn't find me."

The bearers of bad news can also issue a rousing call to arms. Big Al, after delivering his devastating news, now wisely offered Junior Weston the opportunity to do something about what had happened to him. "We've got to catch that bad man, Junior. Will you help us?"

The boy's huge, unblinking brown eyes met the detective's searching gaze. "It's what my Daddy would have done, isn't it," he said gravely, making a statement, not asking a question.

Big Al nodded. "Yes," he said. "It's exactly what your daddy would have done."

For a moment Junior Weston nuzzled his small, tear-stained face against the top of the fuzzy teddy bear's head. "I want to catch him," he whispered.

I didn't know Big Al was holding his breath until he let it out in a long, grateful sigh.

"Try to remember everything you saw and heard, Junior. Tell us whatever you can about the man, about how he looked and acted and sounded, about how big he was. Anything at all that you remember. Will you do that?"

"He was wearing sweats," the boy said at once. "Red sweats, and his arm was bleeding."

"Which arm?" Big Al asked. "Right or left?"

Junior shook his head. "I don't know. I can't remember right and left."

"Was it the one that was holding the knife?"

"No, the other one."

"Tell us some more about his clothes. You said sweats. Both top and bottom?"

"Yes. The top had a zipper."

"What about his shoes?"

"High tops, like Reeboks. The kind my daddy doesn't let us get because they cost too much money."

Busy taking notes, I forgot myself and asked a question of my own. "What was the man doing when you first saw him?"

Butting in like that was a serious tactical error, and the moment I opened my mouth I was sorry. Junior Weston stared at me blankly as though I had spoken to him from outer space in some strange, indecipherable language. Totally tuned in to the man who was holding him, he would answer questions from no one else.

"Can you tell us what was happening?" Detective Lindstrom asked, quietly resuming control of the interview.

The boy swallowed hard before he answered. "They were fighting. Bonnie and the man were fighting. He was bigger than she was, and she couldn't get away."

"Did either one of them say anything to you?"

"Bonnie saw me, and she shook her head like for me not to come any closer. The man saw me too, I think, but I ran away before he could catch me."

"What did he look like?"

Junior shrugged. "I dunno. Just a man, I guess."

"Was he tall or short? Taller than your mommy? As tall as your daddy?

"Tall, but not as tall as my daddy."

Big Al looked at me. "Ben was six five,"

he said before turning back to Junior. "Was he fat?"

"No, he was kinda skinny."

"Was the man black or white, brown or yellow?"

"White," Junior answered at once.

"What kind of white?" Big Al asked.

Junior Weston regarded Big Al with his head cocked to one side. "Not like you," he said seriously. "You're kinda red. More like him," he said, pointing at me, "and his hair was brown."

"Long or short, straight or curly?"

Junior leaned back. "It wasn't curly," he said. "Definitely straight."

"Had you ever seen him before? Is he maybe someone from right around here, someone from this neighborhood?"

"No. I never saw him before." Junior hunkered against the detective's chest. "I'm tired. Can't we stop now?"

Big Al shook his head. "It's important to go on. You might forget something."

"Okay," Junior said.

"Do you know what time it was?"

The boy shook his head. "No. We were in bed. We were supposed to be asleep, but Dougie and Adam started telling ghost stories. They do that sometimes, just to scare me 'cause I'm littler than they are.

That's when I went out to sleep in the closet in the hall. It's my secret hiding place. I go there when Dougie and Adam start acting mean or picking on me. I closed the door almost all the way so they couldn't find me. When they got quiet, I was going to go back to bed, but I heard a noise. I went into the kitchen. That's when I saw the bad man."

"Did Bonnie say anything to you?"

"No, she couldn't. She tried, but there was something over her mouth. He was behind her. When she shook her head, he looked up and saw me."

"What did you do then?"

The boy ducked his head and bit his lip. His answer was little more than a whisper. "I ran away."

"You went back to the closet?"

"Uh-huh."

"Where did the bad man go?"

"I don't know. I heard some doors opening and closing. I think he was looking for me. I think he went into our room."

"Why didn't you call your daddy?"

"I was too scared to make a noise. I heard him getting closer, going past. Then, after that, I wanted to get out, but I couldn't. The door was stuck. It got really quiet."

"But you did hear noises?"

This time, instead of answering aloud,

Benjamin Harrison Weston, Jr., buried his head against Big Al's chest and sobbed into it. The detective didn't bother to ask him what he had heard — there was no need. We both had a pretty good idea what the horror outside must have sounded like to a terrified child hiding in a darkened closet, wondering if the monster would come after him next.

"I knew he hurt them. He was bad," Junior Weston said finally. "Before you even told me, I thought maybe he killed them. Like on TV."

"Ja," Big Al said softly. "I thought maybe you did. You're a smart boy, Junior, and you were real smart to stay hidden. Your daddy would be proud of you."

At the mention of his father, Junior's eyes once more clouded with tears. "But I wanted to help . . . what if . . ." he began, then he broke off. For the next several minutes he sobbed brokenly into Big Al's massive chest. I couldn't know how a five-year-old would process the end of that sentence. Maybe he wondered what would have happened if, instead of hiding, he had warned his father, just as Officer Dunn had wondered what would have happened if the patrol car had somehow arrived on the scene sooner.

In the aftermath of death, "what if" becomes a haunting question, a philosophical imperative dictating the lives of survivors. Some ask themselves variations of that question for the rest of their lives. I've done it myself on occasion, especially in regard to Anne Corley, a woman I loved and who I thought loved me — right up until she tricked me into killing her.

Actually, over the years I've almost managed to convince myself that she did love me with the same kind of life-changing ferocity I felt for her. I've wondered if the force of that love didn't somehow bring her face-to-face with the reality of the fiendish monster she'd become. I don't blame her for not being able to live with that reality, but I've often wished she had committed suicide with her own hand instead of mine.

Still, though, I've asked myself countless times what if I had done something else? What if I had taken some other action? Would it have caused a different result? Would we somehow, somewhere have managed to live happily ever after? I don't know. I doubt it.

It was painful hearing Junior Weston, sitting there on Detective Lindstrom's lap in our little cubicle, ask himself those same questions for the very first time. Finally, having cried himself out, the boy grew still.

"He was way bigger than you. You did the best you could at the time," Big Al said reassuringly. "Now you're helping us. We'll have an artist work with you on a composite, a picture drawn from your description. Do you know about those?"

Junior nodded. "I saw one once when Daddy brought me down here on a Saturday morning."

"We'll do that later on, tomorrow or the next day," Big Al added. "In the meantime, we have to talk to the other boy's family, to Adam's family. What's his last name?"

"Jackson. Adam Jackson. He slept over because his mama had to work all night."

"Where does she work?"

"In a hospital."

"Where? Which one?"

"Somewhere," Junior said vaguely. "I don't know the name of it."

"What's Adam's daddy's name?"

"He doesn't have a daddy."

"Does his mother have another name, a first name?"

"Her name is Mrs. Jackson," Junior responded firmly. "That's what my mommy said to call her."

Ben and Shiree Weston had taught their son to respect his elders, but that respect wouldn't make our job any easier.

Big Al took another tack. "Where does she live? Somewhere close to you?"

"No. They live all the way over on Queen Anne. You know, that really steep hill, but Adam and Dougie go to the same school. McClure. They're in junior high. I'm only in kindergarten now, but I'll be big enough to be in first grade next year. Did you know that?"

Hearing the ingenuous certainty in Junior Weston's voice made me wish I could be a little kid again myself. No matter what terrible disasters might befall, kids exist in a plane where much of the future is known and predictable. At least children were free to believe it predictable. Junior Weston's parents, siblings, and friend had been wiped out in the course of a single catastrophic night, but the boy moved forward with every confidence that next year he would shift automatically from kindergarten to first grade. And he was probably right.

"Will I get to see my mommy and daddy?" Junior asked. "I saw Grammy after she was dead. She was in a long box with her good black dress on, her best church dress. There were lots of flowers. I thought she was sleeping. That's what it looked like."

I doubted any amount of mortician's art

would ever restore the appearances of Shiree and Bonnie Weston. They would certainly need closed coffins. As a consequence, the others probably would be too. As if reading my mind, Big Al spoke. "No," he answered firmly. "I don't think so."

"Oh," Junior Weston said. He rubbed his eyes. "I'm tired. Can I go home now? I want to go to bed."

The shift was abrupt but not surprising. A five-year-old's attention span is only so long, and his understanding of the tragedy was as yet only skin-deep. It was fine to talk about people being dead and in heaven, but Junior Weston still had no real grasp of the fundamental changes that had transformed his young life. He was tired, with good reason, but he couldn't go home and go to bed, not to the home and bed he had known, not ever again.

"Someone's gone to get your grandpa," Big Al told him. "When he gets here, you'll have to go home with him."

"Grampa's coming here?" Junior asked incredulously. "How can he? He can't drive, and it's too far to walk. Besides, he doesn't like this place."

"We'll bring him here and then someone will take you both wherever he says."

"Oh," Junior said again. "Okay."

He leaned back against Big Al's shoulder and chest. Like a worn-out puppy, the boy closed his eyes. Within seconds he was sound asleep with one arm wrapped firmly around the teddy bear's comforting neck.

I had been taking notes fast and furiously. "You did a hell of a job with him, Al," I said.

Big Al Lindstrom nodded sadly. "Thanks," he said. "He's a pretty sharp kid. What's next?"

"You sit there with him for the time being and I'll see what I can do about locating Adam Jackson's mother. I'd like to get to her before someone else does."

"Right," Big Al said. "I suppose I should call Molly, too."

But before either one of us had a chance to do anything, we heard a jumble of voices coming down the corridor. I looked up as Sergeant Watkins escorted a tall, stoop-shouldered black man into our cubicle. I would have known him anywhere as Ben Weston's father. Harmon Weston was a thinner, older version of his son.

"I've come for the boy," he said without preamble, looking hard at Big Al Lindstrom through Coke-bottle-bottom glasses. "Has anybody told him yet?"

"I did, Mr. Weston," Big Al said. "I'm so sorry."

Harmon Weston nodded. " 'All they that take the sword shall perish with the sword.' That's what the Good Book says."

At first I didn't understand that the old man was talking about his own son, but Big Al Lindstrom had been far closer to the Weston family, and he immediately recognized the scriptural quote as an attack on Ben. He fairly bristled.

"That's not fair," he said quietly. "No matter what you think, Mr. Weston, your son was not a violent man. He wore a gun, but he didn't use it. He never had to."

"My son is dead," Harmon Weston said stiffly. "I didn't come here to argue about what he did or didn't do. I came for the boy. Wake up, Benjy. Let's go."

Junior Weston fought to rouse himself. For a moment, he looked around, dismayed by the strange surroundings, then his eyes focused on his grandfather's familiar face.

"It's true, isn't it, Grampa? It wasn't a bad dream, was it?"

"No," Harmon Weston answered, reaching out and taking the boy's pudgy hand. He pulled the boy to him and held him close. As he gazed down at his grandson's curly hair I glimpsed the terrible hurt behind the old man's outward show of bitterness and rancor. "It's no dream at all,

61

Benjy. It's a nightmare. Come on now."

"Do you need a ride?" Big Al offered.

"The car's waiting downstairs," Watty said quickly. "We've already got that handled."

Harmon Weston let go of Junior and started toward the door. The boy took a tentative step after him before turning back to Big Al.

"I've gotta go now," Junior said.

Big Al Lindstrom nodded. "I know. Goodbye, Junior. Thanks for all your help."

At that, the boy darted back long enough to give Big Al a quick hug around the neck. Then, clutching his teddy bear, he followed his grandfather into the hallway. Accompanied by Sergeant Watkins, the two of them disappeared from view, leaving Detective Lindstrom staring at the empty doorway behind them and shaking his head.

"Stubborn old son of a bitch," he muttered. "He and Ben were at war for years, and now Harmon's all Junior Weston has left in the world. I wouldn't want to be in that poor little kid's shoes for nothing."

CHAPTER 4

With Junior safely on his way to his grand-father's house, Big Al and I headed back toward the Weston family home in Rainier Valley. Without lights and sirens, it's a ten-minute drive from downtown. For a good part of that time we were both pretty quiet. Big Al finally broke the silence.

"What do you think?" he asked. "Was Ben the real target, or is the killer somebody with a grudge against every cop in the known universe, and Ben was just a stand-in?"

That in a nutshell was the crux of the matter. Should the investigation head off after every crazy who had ever voiced a grudge against the Seattle PD? Regardless, I knew we'd go searching through Ben Weston's catalog of past and present acquaintances both on and off the job. The problem was, Gentle Ben Weston hadn't been given that moniker for being some kind of bad-ass cop.

The last I heard, he had been working a desk job in Patrol. Of all the possible jobs in the department, a desk position in Patrol seemed least likely to create long-term, homicidal-type grudges.

"What would somebody have against a guy like Ben?" I asked. "I can understand how a crook might build up this kind of rage against somebody in Homicide or Vice, but why have such a hard-on for a poor, pen-pushing desk jockey from Patrol?"

"He wasn't in Patrol," Big Al returned quietly, "not anymore."

"That's news to me. Since when?"

Lindstrom shrugged. "Six months? A little longer, maybe. Don't you remember? He took a voluntary downgrade and transfer into CCI."

In Seattle PD jargon, CCI translates into Coordinated Criminal Investigations. In departmental politics, it's currently synonymous with hot potato. CCI started out as the unit nobody wanted to have, doing the dirty work with gangs that no one across the street in City Hall wanted to admit needed doing. CCI's desirability waxes and wanes, depending on the fickle barometer of public relations.

In the past few years, Seattle has received a lot of good press and has turned up on more than one "most livable city" list. Livable cities evidently exist in some kind of fantasy world, and they're not supposed to have any problems, most especially not gang problems. For years the brass upstairs wallowed in denial despite reported gang-type shootings that came in as regularly as One-A-Day vitamins. When other cities started gang units, Seattle didn't because starting a unit would have meant admitting it had the problem. When a new unit was finally created, it was given the innocuous and hence less threatening name of Coordinated Criminal Investigations.

A rose by any other name may smell as sweet, but CCI's whole purpose is to combat gang-related criminal activity, a problem the city still isn't wild about acknowledging. Not surprisingly, the guys in CCI don't always get a whole lot of respect, and a posting to that unit isn't regarded as a plum assignment. If Ben Weston had taken a voluntary downgrade and transfer from patrol supervision to a lower position as a CCI investigator, it was as good as admitting that his career path was way off track and in a downward spiral.

"When did all that happen?" I asked. "I don't remember hearing anything about it."

"There was plenty of talk at the time,"

Big Al answered. "Maybe it was while you were down in Arizona."

Any number of things had slipped by me the previous fall when I spent the better part of two months in doctor-ordered attendance at an alcoholism treatment center near Wickenburg. In the world of work, two months is a considerable period of time. Most departmental gossip doesn't have a two-month-long shelf life. Talk about Ben Weston had evidently run its course well before I came back to work.

"That's probably when it happened, all right," I admitted. "Nobody said word one to me."

"There was quite a stink about it," Big Al said, "with all the usual crap about how he got as far as he did because of quotas and affirmative action and not because he was any good at what he did. Some people claimed Ben couldn't measure up in Patrol and that he transferred out before they caught on to him."

Big Al had known Gentle Ben Weston far better than anyone else in the department. If anyone knew the truth of that matter, he would. "What do you say?" I asked.

There was another pause, longer this time. "I don't know," he said at last. "I just don't know."

"What do you mean, you don't know?"

"His transferring didn't make any sense to me. He was already on the promotion list for lieutenant, but one day for no good reason he just up and says piss on the whole damn thing. Even took a cut in pay because there were no openings at his level. What kind of crazy idea is that with a wife and three kids to support?"

"Did you talk to him about it? Did you ask him why?"

"He told me he had to."

"That's all he said?"

"That's it."

As he answered, Big Al turned off Genesee onto Cascadia and into Ben Weston's immediate neighborhood. The surrounding streets were still jammed with law enforcement vehicles. Adding to these were the media's multiplicity of transportation. We had to park and walk from almost two blocks away. Naturally, someone recognized us, and a group of reporters attached themselves to us like so many hungry leeches, snapping pictures of our backsides and shouting questions behind us.

Maybe familiarity breeds contempt, but most reporters remind me of demanding two-year-olds. No matter how often you tell them you aren't allowed to comment on current investigations, they can't remember it from one time to the next. They still ask the same damn stupid questions. Or, if by chance you do screw up and answer, someone else will ask the same thing over again two minutes later as though they had turned stone-cold deaf the first time you answered.

On this occasion neither Big Al nor I said a word. I was looking forward to ditching the reporters and getting on with the investigation right up until I saw Detective Paul Kramer standing next to the door on Ben Weston's front porch, talking earnestly to Officers Dunn and Wyman.

"Where'd he come from?" I asked.

Big Al sighed. "Out from under a rock," he answered.

Kramer caught sight of us about then. "There you are. Captain Powell sent me out here to snag you when you came back. There'll be a task force meeting starting in five minutes in the Mobile Command Post van in the alley out back. He wants you two there along with everybody else."

"Task force?" I asked. "What task force?"

He looked at me and grinned. "This is a big case, Beaumont. You didn't think you and that square-head partner of yours would get to run the whole show, did you? Come on. Get a move on. Powell wants to talk to both of you before the actual meeting starts."

Kramer motioned for us to follow him and started away without seeing the look of undiluted rage that washed across Detective Lindstrom's face. By and large, Al isn't the excitable type. I would say he's even-tempered and fairly slow to anger, but Kramer's little byplay had an amazing effect that brought Big Al straight to the boiling point. He strode after Kramer, caught him by one arm, and spun him around.

"Get one thing straight, bub," Big Al said without raising his voice. "It's no show! A good man is dead along with most of his family. If you think that's a show, then you can kiss my ass!"

The kind of menace in Big Al's voice usually comes from someone holding the business end of a loaded weapon. Kramer's jaw dropped. "Sorry," he said, with only the slightest hint of sarcastic exaggeration.

"You'd oughta be," Big Al returned coldly. "Now take us to Captain Powell."

For a moment the two men stood staring at one another, and I was afraid they were going to mix it up physically. If anyone tried to break up that confrontation, the guy in the middle would get the short end of it. Finally, Kramer dropped his eyes and started away while I breathed a quick sigh of relief. The incident startled me every bit as much as it did Detective Kramer.

I had worked with Big Al off and on for several years without ever seeing him fly off the handle that way. I wondered if this wasn't the kind of thing Captain Powell meant when he had threatened to pull Big Al from Ben Weston's case. If the captain got even the slightest wind of it, he wouldn't hesitate to make good his threat.

"You'd better cool it before Powell sees you," I suggested. "You know what he said."

"I know very well what he said," Big Al replied, "but if that bastard Kramer so much as looks at me sideways, I'll knock his block off."

What was it Simon and Garfunkel used to say about bridging troubled waters?

"Besides, you know that's the whole idea anyway, don't you?" Big Al continued.

"What's the whole idea? What are you talking about?"

"You heard him — the task force. Powell's already figured out a way to pull me off the case. If they're going to turn this into a task force operation, it'll be nothing more than a group grope. You know how those work. People run around like so many chickens with their heads cut off getting in each

70

other's way. It'll be impossible to get anything done."

I knew Big Al was right. Task forces are notoriously inefficient and cumbersome, but they sound good on paper, make for better public relations, and that was something Seattle's new police chief needed desperately.

"Come on," I said. "Let's go. The captain's waiting."

But Big Al stood without moving, seemingly lost in thought.

"We'd better get going," I urged again.

Big Al Lindstrom seemed to shake himself out of some kind of trance. "You go on ahead," he said, waving me away. "I'll be there in a minute."

He turned his back and lumbered off in the opposite direction. "Hey, wait a minute. Where are you going?"

"If he's going to pull me, I want to go back for one more look. I might've missed something important."

I let him go. For one thing, Big Al is bigger than I am, and there was nothing I could do to stop him. For another, I figured it was probably wise for him to give himself a few cool-down moments before facing either Detective Kramer or Captain Powell.

"Don't take too long," I cautioned.

I headed for the Mobile Command Post in the alley. It's nothing more than a glorified RV that once belonged to a snowbird drug dealer whose delivery route consisted of driving up and down the I-5 corridor. He had a well-heeled clientele that stretched all the way from Canada to Mexico, and he sold drugs in RV parks from the back of a very upscale Winnebago. When a Seattle narcotics unit got lucky and busted him in a parking lot near Northgate, the dealer went off for a stretch in Monroe. The Winnebago, already equipped with a tantalizing array of electronics gear, switched sides and came to work for the Seattle Police Department.

Janice Morraine, a criminalist who's worked her way up to second in command in George Yamamoto's crime lab, was standing outside, smoking a cigarette. Despite insistent warnings from the Surgeon General and despite state laws outlawing smoking on the job, Janice continues to chain-smoke. "Don't go inside any sooner than you have to," she warned. "It's a sardine can."

"How many people are in there?"

"More than should be. It's like Noah's ark except only the Homicide dicks come two by two. One each from everywhere else."

"Sounds great."

Janice Morraine nodded. "That's what I thought. There's nothing like a middle-of-the-night meeting to keep everybody from getting the job done," she grumbled. "I should be back in the house working, not out here cooling my heels."

She stood up on tiptoe and peered over my shoulder. "By the way, where's Detective Lindstrom? As I understand it, we're all waiting for you two to show up."

"He'll be here in a minute. I'd better go tell the captain."

Leaving her alone with only her glowing cigarette for company, I forced my way into the press of people crammed into the RV. Winnebagos may be spacious enough for some little old retired couple traveling the highways and byways to visit their grandkids, but this one was far too small for the group Captain Powell had assembled. People stood shoulder to shoulder.

Powell glanced up at me briefly as I opened the door and worked my way inside. "Where's Detective Lindstrom?" he asked.

"Making a pit stop." That sounded plausible enough. "He'll be here in a minute."

Kramer cleared his throat, but I ignored

him and so did Powell. "We'll start as soon as he gets here," the captain said.

I glanced around the room and discovered quite a gathering. Captain Powell edged his way back into the crowd, where he huddled in a hushed consultation with Captain Norman Nichols, the young, newly appointed head of CCI. With them was Lieutenant Lea Dunkirk, a special projects liaison officer who works directly out of the chief's office. Nearby but not part of the quiet conversation were several others, among them Dr. Mike Wilson, one of Doc Baker's special assistants, and Lieutenant Gilbert McNamara, the ranking officer in Media Relations.

In the background I saw a collection of several somber Homicide detectives — Manny Davis; his partner, Ray Chong; Sue Danielson, whose great misfortune it was to be Paul Kramer's newest partner; and, of course, Kramer himself, who stood with his arms folded smugly across his chest. He glowered in my direction as if to say it was all my fault that Big Al Lindstrom still hadn't answered his summons.

I had started to work my way over to the detectives when the door opened. Ducking to keep from hitting his head on the metal doorframe, Big Al inched his way inside

74

while Janice Morraine squeezed in behind him. Al seemed to have regrouped, to have gotten himself back under control.

"Sorry I'm late, Captain," he mumbled to Powell, who nodded.

"That's okay. We'll go ahead and get started now. Does everybody here know each other?"

We all looked around, checking faces. Detective Danielson, a recent transfer to Homicide from Sexual Assault, was new to the unit, but not to the department. Everyone else was pretty much a known quantity.

"Good," Powell continued, "I'll make this quick. As of now, you are all, with the exception of Detective Lindstrom, part of what will be known as the Weston Family Task Force. For the time being and until further notice, each of you is assigned to this case on a full-time basis. All direct contact with the media is strictly prohibited. Information on this case is to be filtered through Lieutenant McNamara here or one of the other Media Relations officers. All of it. Do I make myself clear?"

We all nodded. It was business as usual only more so.

"What about me?" Big Al interjected.

"I'm coming to that, Al. Detectives Beaumont and Lindstrom were the ones originally assigned to this case, but due to the identity of the victims, and since Detective Lindstrom especially has very close personal connections to the Weston family, we've been forced to make some changes in assignments. Detective Beaumont will still be officially assigned to the case, but his area of responsibility will focus primarily on the second boy — John Doe for now, a victim who is evidently not a part of the Weston family proper."

"Wait a minute . . ." Big Al began, but Powell silenced him with an impatient wave of his hand.

"Obviously, this case will be conducted under intense media and public scrutiny. We can't afford any screwups or any appearance of ignoring due process. Everyone in this room knows that as soon as a police officer is killed, there's an automatic assumption among the media and among the population at large that the entire department turns into a bloodthirsty vigilante committee. Considering your personal relationship with Ben, Detective Lindstrom, I'm sure you can understand why I deem it necessary to remove you from the case. It's no reflection on your professionalism, Al, but you'll be assigned alternate duty for the time being. Any questions?"

If Big Al had questions, he wasn't able to voice them. His face flushed a brilliant red from the top of his shirt collar to the roots of his hair while an incredible array of emotions marched in rapid succession across his broad features.

"No . . . sir," he stammered at last. "Can I go now?"

"Sure," Powell returned sympathetically. "That's probably a good idea. Take the rest of the day off too, why don't you, Al. Get some rest. I'll be in touch with you tomorrow."

To the captain's credit, I knew he had wanted to speak with Big Al prior to the meeting. A private conference in advance might have spared the detective the public humiliation of being pulled from the case in a roomful of his peers. By coming late, Big Al himself had robbed Captain Powell of any more diplomatic alternative.

Without another word, Big Al stalked out into the night, slamming the flimsy metal door behind him. The rest of us waited in uncomfortable silence. I don't think there was anyone in the room, with the possible exception of Paul Kramer, who thought Captain Powell was doing the wrong thing, but we all wished it hadn't come down quite the way it had.

Kramer started to make some off-the-wall comment, but Captain Powell's reprimanding stare shut him up. "As for task force organization," Powell continued, "with this many victims, we're going to need a clearinghouse for personnel and reports both. Sergeant Watkins from Homicide will be taking over as director. He will be assisted by Detective Kramer, who has in the past shown a certain facility for organization and reports. Detective Kramer will work directly under Sergeant Watkins and help delegate assignments.

"We want this thing handled, people. We want it handled right, and we want it done soon. Any questions?"

Paul Kramer favored me with the smallest of smirks. It was lucky for him that Big Al Lindstrom had already left the room.

CHAPTER 5

When the meeting broke up, Janice Morraine and I left the Mobile Command Post together and walked back through the early-morning darkness toward Ben Weston's house, where Janice's crime scene investigators were still hard at work.

Long before anyone ever heard of DNA fingerprinting or even just plain fingerprinting for that matter, a smart French criminologist by the name of Edmond Locard came up with the theory that bears his name. Locard's exchange principle says, in effect, that any person passing through a room will unknowingly leave something there and take something away. This principle forms the basis for most modern crime scene investigation.

Criminalists, as they're called these days — the term "criminologist" evidently disappeared right along with Edmond — take charge of the hair and blood samples, semen and saliva traces, fingerprints and clothing fuzz, carpet lint and dust balls that often form the backbone of evidence in today's criminal prosecutions. Forever focused on physical minutiae, criminalists are a tightly knit group. Without necessarily saying so, they generally look down their collective noses at mere detectives who specialize in the inexact and somewhat messy study of such unscientific things as motive and opportunity.

My opinion is that we're all fine as long as everybody sticks to his or her own area of expertise. It's probably a safe bet that I'll never write a scholarly treatise on the technicalities of DNA fingerprinting, which Janice Morraine could do in a blink, but as far as I'm concerned, she'll never make detective of the year either. Don't misunderstand. I like her, a lot, but not when she veers into my territory.

"What exactly went on between Detective Lindstrom and Ben Weston?" she asked as we walked along. "Did they ever have a falling-out?"

"You mean a fight?"

"Yes, a fight. Did they quarrel about something?"

"Not so far as I know. How come?" I wondered. "What makes you ask that?"

She shrugged. "After what happened in there . . ."

"After what happened? You mean after Captain Powell kicked Lindstrom off the case?"

"Yes well . . ."

For a moment, I thought she didn't understand exactly why that had occurred, so I tried to clarify. "Powell pulled Big Al because he and Ben Weston were good friends, had been for years. No other reason. So why are you asking me about a fight?"

"I was just wondering," she said innocently.

It used to be when a woman gave me that kind of ingenuous nonanswer, I fell for it and really believed they were "just wondering," but I'm older, now, and wiser. Janice's bland response put me on notice that something was up.

"Look, I didn't just fall off the turnip truck yesterday," I told her. "This is your old pal J. P. Beaumont, remember? What gives? What are you driving at?"

"I think a cop did it," she blurted.

My jaw dropped. "A cop? Killed all these people? You're kidding!"

We had stopped on the front porch just outside the door. "I am not kidding," she declared. "Didn't you see how the girl was tied up?"

Actually, I hadn't. For one thing, during our initial kitchen walk-through, I had been on the wrong side of the body. Then, once we discovered Junior in the linen closet, Big Al and I hadn't stayed around long enough to see anything more before racing off to the department with the child in tow.

"Flex-cufs," she informed me. "The girl in the kitchen was bound with Flex-cuf restraints, the very same brand all you guys at the department use every day."

Although metal handcuffs are still more commonly used, Flex-cufs are a high-tech, lightweight substitute. I think of them as a variation on a theme of plastic tie-ups for garbage bags or maybe a hospital ID bracelet for two hands instead of one. Once you put the plastic coil through the hole and tighten it down, the only way to take it off again is to cut it off.

But from this one small piece of evidence, Janice Morraine was making a very premature, very shaky assumption. "Let me get this straight. Because of the presence of Flex-cufs, you've decided that the killer is most likely a cop and further, since Captain Powell threw him off the case, that the cop most likely is none other than Detective Lindstrom, right?"

"It was just an idea," she countered. "Al was acting real strange tonight, or didn't you notice?"

I almost blew up in her face. "Strange? Let me tell you about strange, lady. You'd be acting funny yourself if you showed up at a homicide scene and discovered that the victims are almost the entire family of one of your very best friends. You walk in and find them one after the other, slaughtered in cold blood. Detective Lindstrom's been through a hell of an ordeal tonight, including being told by his supervisor that his services aren't needed or wanted. How the hell would you act?"

"You don't have to get so hot under the collar," Janice returned sulkily. "All I did was ask a question."

I was hot all right. "Why don't you leave the questions to the detectives and go find some lint to pick up?"

A little professional jealousy is to be expected now and then, especially in such circumstances, but I could see from the look on Janice's face that my comment had come off sounding a whole lot more insulting than the situation warranted.

"Up yours, Detective Beaumont," she returned coldly, and marched off into the house, leaving me looking after her in frustrated consternation.

How could someone as smart as Janice Morraine be so dumb? I wondered. How could she even seriously consider the idea that Big Al Lindstrom was capable of murdering his best friend and his family besides? The whole preposterous notion would have been downright laughable if it hadn't made me so damn mad.

Where the hell did Janice Morraine get off? The killer had been loose in Ben Weston's house for a considerable period of time. Maybe Ben had a few Flex-cufs stashed at home someplace, and the killer had used those. Had Janice ever considered that possibility? The thought that I too might be jumping to conclusions never entered my mind, for the idea that a fellow officer — any fellow police officer — might also be a cold-blooded killer was totally unacceptable. I dismissed it out of hand.

Still standing on the porch, I glanced out at the street. At four in the morning, the parking places around the Weston house were gradually emptying. With the bodies all hauled away to the medical examiner's office, most of the law enforcement and emergency vehicles were gone. The Minicam-and microphone-waving reporters had also driven away to meet their various deadlines. By sunrise, except for the yellow crime scene tape that would eventually be strung all the way around the Weston house and yard, the neighborhood would be returning to normal — as normal as it was ever going to be.

Fatigue was catching up with me, and the bone spurs on my feet were killing me. With a sigh, I went inside to go to work. For a while anyway, Paul Kramer was there as well, throwing his considerable weight around, bothering Janice's investigators, and asking questions when he should have been listening. I stayed out of his way as much as possible. My assignment was Adam Jackson — John Doe, as Captain Powell still thought of him. With Big Al's invaluable help I at least knew the boy's name and was that much further along in the investigation. It wasn't a lot, but it was a start.

I prowled around the house, hoping to stumble across something that would be of assistance. In the kitchen I found a push-button address directory. When I pushed the *J* button, I thought at first I had hit the Jackson jackpot, and indeed I had — too well. There were no fewer than six Jacksons listed on a page that slopped over into the *K*'s. Unfortunately, there was no clue as to which was which. None of them had a

85

Queen Anne exchange. I jotted down all the numbers, home and work, knowing that if push came to shove, I could compare all the work numbers and see which one would lead me to a hospital switchboard. That was the long way of doing it.

Still hoping for a shortcut, I left the kitchen, heading for Ben and Shiree Weston's bedroom, where I remembered seeing another phone. Maybe there I would find a forgotten note jotted on a little yellow sticky pad that would give me the information I needed. While I was busy searching, a silent clock ticked continuously in the back of my head, for I was locked in a race against time. If I didn't get to her first, Adam Jackson's mother would inevitably learn of her son's death through other than official channels. Professional pride and compassion mixed fifty-fifty made me want to prevent that from happening.

Walking through the living room, I discovered that, with the exception of a single uniformed officer seated near the front door of the house and another stationed in back, only Janice Morraine and her crime scene specialists remained in the house. The Crime Lab folks acted every bit as frazzled as I felt. By now, I'd been up for twenty-two-plus hours straight, and I sure as hell wasn't as young as I used to be.

I was just crossing the threshold into Ben and Shiree's demolished bedroom when the clock radio beside the bed came on automatically at four-thirty. The soft, mournful wail of a country and western lady singer stopped me in my tracks. The familiar "he done me wrong" lyrics left me with an eerie sense of loss, allowing the finality of what had happened in that house to seep into my consciousness once and for all.

As the music went on and on, I realized how, the night before, Ben Weston had matter-of-factly set that alarm, expecting to get up early the next morning — this morning — and be about his business. Whatever he had planned to do had been important enough to be worth getting out of a warm bed three and a half full hours before he was due in at the department at eight.

But morning had come without him. Ben Weston would never again charge out of bed. He would never again hear the mournful music that was now crooning softly in the background. He wouldn't see Ben Junior play his first Little League game or graduate from high school. Gentle Ben Weston was, literally, history.

I stood there listening, transfixed by the music, struck by the awful senselessness of it all, and then a funny thing happened. A new sense of resolve and purpose seemed to settle over me, washing away my all-nighter fatigue and filling my body with bone-hard determination. Captain Powell may have sidetracked me on to the Adam Jackson end of the investigation, but every one of us, even that worthless Kramer, were all working the same problem, searching for the same killer, and find him we would. I searched the room over but found nothing that would help locate Adam Jackson's mother.

Motivated, ready to do something else positive, I decided to check the place where Big Al had parked to see if, by some lucky chance, he had left the car there for me when he went home. I was almost at the front door when the doorbell rang. In the meantime, the patrol officer on the couch, a guy by the name of Simmons, mumbled something to me. I opened the door, but I leaned away long enough to ask him to repeat it.

No doubt those mumbled words saved my life, because the .44 slug that crashed into the mirrored wall directly behind me shattered the glass right at chest height. Whoever fired it hadn't expected to miss, and at that range, chances are my bulletproof vest wouldn't have done much good. Like Ben Weston, I, too, would have been all through listening to country music.

Stunned, I hit the floor, my ears ringing. Then, as fast as I could, I scrambled back to my feet and fumbled for my automatic while Simmons bounded over me. We both reached the door in time to see a car door open and close as someone leaped inside a waiting, dark-colored vehicle. Leaving behind a spray of gravel, the car, with headlights and taillights both doused, sped away down the still night-black street.

Simmons's partner, a guy named Gary Deddens, had been left to guard the back door. He sprinted up behind us. "What the hell is going on?" he demanded.

The two of them must have arrived at the Weston house at about the same time I did, the second time around. Their car was parked a good block and a half away. While Simmons raced after it, his partner started up the street after the long-gone vehicle. I paused long enough to explain to an ashen-faced Janice what had happened, then I too darted up the sidewalk. We flagged down Simmons as he drove past. The wheels on his patrol car were back in motion before the doors closed.

"You all right, Detective Beaumont?" he asked.

"Yeah. I'm fine. A little shaky, but fine."

"You handle the radio," he said to Deddens. "Did either of you see what kind of car it was?"

"No," we both answered together.

"Shit!" Simmons muttered. "Neither did I."

Within minutes of our call, all of Rainier Valley was crawling with a bunch of very spooked cops. Word was out that someone had declared open warfare on officers of the Seattle Police Department. With Ben Weston and his family dead, and after my narrow escape, we were all feeling mighty vulnerable. And mortal.

Unfortunately, nothing Simmons, his partner, or I could tell our fellow searchers was of any help. In the next hour and a half, a careful dragnet of the neighborhood turned up a few moving violations, including one DWI, but there was no trace at all of our missing gunman and his getaway car.

With Simmons still driving, we had searched as far as the western shore of Lake Washington when the sun came up over the still snowbound Cascades later on that morning. I don't know if this happens in other parts of the world or not, but it was one of those special Washington mornings when, as the natives say, the mountains were out, their rugged profiles shining brilliantly in the early-morning sun without their usual cloak of cloud cover. It was the kind of morning when Seattle's cross-bridge commuters get regular traffic advisories warning them to watch out for the unaccustomed glare of sun off Lake Washington. It was a morning when, shootings aside, Seattle really is one of the most livable cities on the face of the earth.

Believe me. I was happy as hell to be alive to enjoy it.

CHAPTER 6

Simmons and Deddens offered to give me a lift back downtown to the Public Safety Building, and I would have been more than happy to accept, but Watty sent a message through Dispatch that I was to return to the Weston house for a debriefing. When I got there, Detective Kramer was sitting on the front porch waiting for me, notebook in hand. He was not a happy camper.

"I was just crawling into bed for a nap when Watty called and told me to come back here and take your statement. I feel like so much dogshit."

"Well pardon me all to hell for getting shot at," I returned. "Remind me to schedule the next one at a more convenient time, would you, Kramer? I hate to think that I'm causing you to miss your little nappy."

"Cut the crap, will you, Beaumont? Just tell me what happened so we can both get out of here."

So I told him, as briefly as possible, while he took notes. No doubt I'd have to do some paper on the assault, but it seemed fair enough that someone else should have to do so as well. After all, I'm a taxpayer too, I thought, remembering, for the first time since writing it, the sizable check to the IRS that I had left in Ralph Ames's charge.

"The crux of the question, then, is did someone plan to hit Ben Weston, or were you the target this time?" Kramer asked finally.

"I have to assume the bullet was meant for me. Why kill a dead man?"

"Maybe they didn't know he was already dead. Who all knew you were here tonight? Anyone at home?"

"No, I have company from out of town, but at the time the call came in and I left the house, Big Al and I had no idea where we were going or when we'd be back."

"Anybody follow you?"

"Are you kidding? Even if they were, who would notice? Do you watch the rearview mirror when you're on your way to a crime scene?"

"Hardly ever."

"I rest my case."

"Have you been in any kind of a beef with

someone here at the department?"

I hesitated for a fraction of a second before I answered, remembering Janice Morraine's blurted theory that a fellow cop might have killed Ben Weston. But I couldn't think of anyone at Seattle PD who would be that happy if J. P. Beaumont was no more.

"You mean other than you?" I returned.

Kramer glared at me. "Yeah. Who else other than me? I'd already gone home, remember?"

"I don't know of anyone."

"The place was crawling with reporters. I know you don't like them. Is the feeling mutual?"

"Most likely, but I can't think of any of them who'd have balls enough to take a shot at someone they didn't like. Besides, the ones I know are mostly opposed to guns as a matter of principle."

Kramer made another note. "Who all was still here when this happened?"

"Janice Morraine and the rest of her crew from the Crime Lab. And there were two officers from Patrol who were left on duty guarding the front and back doors. They're the ones who brought me back here, Officers Simmons and Deddens."

"And nobody got a good look at the car?"

"No. It was dark — maroon or black maybe, but I can't be sure. It was too far away to get even a glimpse of the license."

It was morning now. People leaving their houses on their way to school and work slowed and stared openly at the two men sitting on the steps of Ben Weston's house — at the two men and also at the grim-looking yellow tape that had been wrapped around the outside of the yard.

Kramer got up stiffly and stretched. "I'm going to go take a look at that hole in the wall. Is the slug still in it?"

"No, Janice Morraine had one of her guys dig it out. They're gone now, but they said they'd have it whenever anybody needed it."

I let Kramer go by himself to examine the bullet hole. He certainly didn't need me holding his hand while he looked at the shattered mirror and the crater in the wallboard. I was waiting for him to come back out on the porch when a beater of a BMW stopped in the street, and a tall black man got out. He started toward the gate. He stopped at the barrier created by a strand of yellow crime scene tape.

"You can't come in here," I called. "It's off limits."

"Who are you?" he asked.

"I'm a police officer."

"Oh," he said. "Good. You're just who I'm looking for." With that he ignored what I had said, stepped easily over the tape, and came on into the yard anyway.

Knees creaking, heels yelping in pain, I got up and limped forward to head him off. "I tell you, you can't come in here. Who are you?"

When he stopped next to me, I realized he dwarfed me. He held out his hand. "Johnson," he said. "Carl Johnson. I'm the principal of McClure Middle School."

If I hadn't been two thirds brain-dead, I would have made the connection without him having to draw me a picture, but I was too slow on the uptake.

"Douglas Weston attends my school," he explained. "One of my parents called me at home and told me something had happened, that police cars had been here during the night. I'm always concerned about anything that affects one of my children, so I came by to see if I could be of any help. What's going on?"

For a moment, I didn't know whether to hug the man or what. His appearance was an answer to a prayer. "Do you happen to know how to get hold of Adam Jackson's mother?"

"Adam? He's here too?"

I nodded. Carl Johnson frowned. "I don't know her number right off the bat, but I'm sure I could get it for you from the office. If Adam spent the night here, it probably means she's on call."

"On call?"

"Emma Jackson is doing her residency with University Hospital. She told me about it at the beginning of the year. She has trouble getting a sitter for those thirty-six-hour shifts, so Adam often spends the night with the Westons. You still haven't told me what's going on."

I reached in my pocket and pulled out a card. He read it, then met my eyes over the top of the card. "This says Homicide." I nodded. "Has someone been killed?"

"Several people," I answered quietly. "Maybe you'd better have a seat here on the porch so I can tell you about what happened."

Carl Johnson shed real tears when I told him, but he jumped up as soon as I finished. "I'd better get back to school," he said urgently. "I need to alert the faculty and the counselors. The district has a team of people who come in to help in situations like this, but I'd better hurry. I want to be there when word gets out."

He started away, then stopped and turned back. "Where will you be?" he asked. "I'll call you with Emma Jackson's phone number as soon as I get back to my office."

I gave him my home number. "I'm going to race home, take a shower, and change clothes. It'll only take a few minutes. If there's no answer, leave the number on my machine, but please don't make any effort to contact Emma until after I do."

"Of course," Carl Johnson agreed. "I wouldn't think of it."

"And I'd appreciate it if you'd hold off making any kind of official announcement, again at least until after I get in touch with her."

"You'll let me know?"

"Yes," I said. "Go ahead and start gathering up the people you need. Just don't give out any names until you get an official go-ahead."

"Right," he said. "I understand."

Carl Johnson strode away from me, his broad shoulders straight, his chin set. Again he stepped over the yellow tape. His ancient Beamer sputtered and backfired before he was able to start it on the third try.

Educators like him seem to be rare these days — old-time teachers who put kids first and everything else second. From the looks of the car he drove, making money sure as hell wasn't Carl Johnson's first priority. No matter what the salary schedule, we'll never be able to pay the Carl Johnsons of this world a fraction of what they're worth.

Janice Morraine came out on the porch just as Carl was driving away, his car coughing and choking. "Who was that?" she asked.

"His name's Carl Johnson," I told her, "and he's a national treasure."

She leveled a hard stare at me, as though I were some kind of raving maniac. "You don't seem to have a car here. Would you like a ride back downtown?" Detective Kramer had taken off while I was dealing with Carl Johnson, and only now did it occur to me that I was totally without transportation.

Considering my previous behavior, I was a little surprised Janice Morraine made the offer. Maybe the fact that someone almost killed me had softened her bony little heart. "I'd appreciate it," I said, meaning every word. "So would my bone spurs."

"It won't take much longer," she said. "I've got one more load of gear to take out to the van."

She turned down my offer of help with the loading. While waiting for her to finish

99

stowing equipment in her state-owned Aero-star, I stood off to one side and thought about Paul Kramer's questions. It seemed unlikely to me that anyone so apparently inoffensive as Gentle Ben Weston would have two entirely different sets of enemies out to kill him, both on the same night. I suffer from the homicide detective's natural aversion to coincidences, and two entirely separate murder plots at once was a bit of a stretch. That being the case, then the second scenario was far more likely — a vicious murderer was out to do in any number of Seattle's finest and their families as well.

Which brought me abruptly to the question of why me? Out of the fifteen hundred or so police officers in the city of Seattle, why had the gunman shot at me? It seemed likely that fate alone had cast me as a potential victim since Simmons, the officer left guarding the front door, would have been far more likely to open it.

I remembered how we had sprinted down the sidewalk after the gunman's car disappearing in the early-morning darkness. Almost all the law enforcement vehicles in the neighborhood had been gone by then, and the crime scene tape had not yet been strung across the gate. If it had been, Simmons, Deddens, or I would have stumbled over it in our race to the car. With that in mind, it was conceivable, then, that whoever did the shooting still believed that Ben Weston was the only possible person who would open his own door at that ungodly hour of the morning.

Which brought me full circle and right back to Ben being the target of two totally separate murder plots at the same time — unless, as Janice Morraine had suggested, the killer really was a cop who knew full well that Ben Weston was already dead, who understood exactly what was going on, who had an accurate count of who was still inside the house, and who could make a pretty good guess which of those was most likely to open the door.

Around and around I went, my thoughts chasing themselves like so many stupid dogs, endlessly pursuing their own tails.

Janice Morraine climbed into the van and started the engine while I jolted myself out of my reverie and settled into the rider's seat. "Where to?" she asked. "The department?"

"Sure. That's fine. I need to pick up a car."

We drove in silence for a few blocks. "Sorry about tonight," I said. "I was out of line."

"We were all tired," she returned. "When

people are running on nerves like that, you can't expect everyone to be on their very best behavior."

"You may be right," I said quietly. "Not about Big Al, but about the murderer being a cop out to kill other cops."

"Forget it," she said. "I've changed my mind about that, too."

"You have?"

"We found six Flex-cufs in Ben Weston's nightstand drawer and two in the kitchen. Maybe he was collecting them. God knows how many others he had stashed here and there around the house, but a cop wouldn't have made all the mistakes."

"What mistakes?"

"The footprints, for one thing. If we once find that pair of shoes, believe me, we won't have any trouble matching them up. And the hair for another."

"The hair stuck between Shiree Weston's fingers?"

She nodded. "That's right. Any cop in his right mind would have noticed and had brains enough to get rid of those."

"What about fingerprints?"

Janice shrugged. "Naturally, we found those all over the house, but until we have a record of all the family members' prints, there's no way to tell which ones, if any, are strays."

By then we were pulling into the garage at the Public Safety Building. "Thanks for the ride," I said.

"No problem."

"And no matter what I may have said before, for a criminalist, you're not bad."

She grinned back at me, and I knew I'd been forgiven. "You're not bad either," she returned lightly, "for a boy."

Touché.

I went upstairs long enough to pick up my messages and to receive a hug from Margie, my clerk, who seemed delighted that I hadn't been shot to pieces. Then I hurried back down to the garage, checked out a car, and went home.

It was only eight o'clock. I could smell the coffee and bacon as soon as the elevator door opened on the twenty-fifth floor. Obviously, Ralph Ames was making himself at home. I don't know what kind of metabolism the man has, but he eats like a horse and never seems to have a problem with his weight. It probably has something to do with swimming daily laps at his pool there in Scottsdale.

"Hey, you're just in time for breakfast. Want some?"

"No time. I came home to grab a shower and change clothes. Pour me a cup of coffee and let it cool. I'll be out in a minute."

By the time I got back out to the dining room, Ralph handed me a message from Carl Johnson. "Rough night?" Ames asked.

I knew from looking in the mirror that I had dark circles under my eyes. "Pretty rough, all right," I said. "Five people dead and I ended up having someone take a potshot at me before the evening was over."

"You're in a tough line of work," Ames said. "Sure you won't try some eggs?"

The food smelled wonderful and I was famished. I allowed myself to be persuaded.

"Try some of the salsa on your eggs," Ames suggested. "It's the real McCoy, straight from Phoenix. I brought it up special."

I tried a daub of the green salsa on my eggs and it instantly cleared every sinus cavity in my head. I bolted my food, toast and all, and pushed my chair away from the table.

"Where to this time?" Ames asked.

"I've got to do a next-of-kin notification. In feet, I should be on my way right this very minute."

I was headed out the door when the phone rang. Expecting new marching orders from

Watty or Captain Powell, I picked it up. Instead, it was Curtis Bell, a guy I knew vaguely from the department, who, now that he was moonlighting as a life insurance salesman, was renowned throughout Seattle PD as an A-number-one pest. He had been hounding me for an appointment for months.

Without allowing me a word in edgewise, he administered the usual appointment-getting canned speech about when could we get together to talk over some ideas that had proved helpful to other officers like myself. Personally, I liked it better back in the old days when moonlighting cops mostly worked as security guards. Security guards usually don't try to sell products or services to their friends. And I remembered the prospecting lessons from my old Fuller Brush days — call everyone you know and ask for an appointment. But I also know what it's like to be a young cop and not make enough money to cover all the bases. I understood what Curtis Bell was trying to do and why he was having to do it.

I tried to be polite. "Look, Curtis, I appreciate your thinking about me, but I'm working a case. I'm real busy right now. In fact, I was just on my way out the door."

"That's all right," he said. "My schedule's

flexible. Are mornings or afternoons better for you, or how about early evening, right after work?"

"Really, none of the above."

I kept saying no, and he kept not listening. After being up working around the clock, the very last thing I needed would be to spend the evening with some boring life insurance puke. I took one more stab at getting rid of him.

"Curtis," I told him as nicely as I could manage. "I'm financially set. I'm divorced and my kids are grown. Why the hell do I need life insurance anyway?"

"That's exactly what I wanted to talk to you about," Curtis returned. "Would tomorrow night be better?"

He had worn me down. The customary ten no's hadn't worked. Sooner or later, he and I were going to talk insurance. "Tell you what, Curtis, I'll get back to you on this. Right now, I've got to go."

I put down the phone and turned around only to find Ralph Ames studying me with a puzzled expression on his face. "What was that all about?" he asked.

"One of the guys from the department who's got a second job selling life insurance. I don't know why, but he thinks I'm a likely prospect."

"Maybe you are," Ames said thoughtfully. "What company is he with?"

"Beats me. How the hell should I know? And anyway, I don't need any life insurance."

"Wait a minute," Ralph said. "You're thinking about leaving the department, and that means you'll be walking away from a whole lot of fringe benefits. There may be some things about insurance that we'll want to consider. My main worry would be about a rating."

I took a moment to consider what he'd said. Evidently, the idea of my leaving the department was something Ralph Ames had been considering even if I hadn't. But instead of thinking about giving up my life's work, I focused in on the last word he'd mentioned.

"Rating? What's a rating?"

"Remember, you're fresh out of alcohol treatment," Ames explained. "Of course, that would have to be disclosed in the medical part of any application. If the underwriters offer you insurance at all, most likely they're going to charge you an extra premium added on to the regular one. They call it a rating."

"That's not fair."

"What's not fair?"

"You mean I have to give up MacNaughton's and pay extra besides?"

"Beau," Ames responded reasonably enough. "They have to charge you an extra premium to cover the extra risk."

"Like hell they do. If Curtis Bell calls back, tell him to go piss up a rope. If I can't have insurance at regular rates, I won't have any at all."

With that, and without bothering to thank Ralph Ames for cooking my breakfast, I slammed out of the apartment and went looking for Emma Jackson.

Extra premium my ass!

CHAPTER 7

Armed with Emma Jackson's name and place of employment, I left Belltown Terrace and drove to University Hospital only to learn that she had already gone home for the day. Thanks to Carl Johnson's phone call, I already had her home address in hand. I headed back downtown, to an address on the lower east side of Queen Anne Hill.

There are matches made in heaven and ones made in hell. My initial meeting with Dr. Emma Jackson was definitely one of the latter. Prejudice on both sides was the root cause of the trouble.

In this day and age, the word "prejudice" naturally conjures up racial difficulties, but between Dr. Emma Jackson and me, race was not necessarily the critical issue. My main bone of contention was the doctor part. Years ago, when my mother was in the hospital dying of cancer, I had a nasty run-in with a particularly arrogant young resident who knew, far better than the patient herself, exactly how much pain Mom could and should tolerate. Ever since then, I've had a bad taste in my mouth for all those not-quite-ready-for-prime-time doctors who are practicing to practice.

No doubt, some early and equally damaging experience had soured Emma Jackson on men in general and male cops in particular. The battle lines between us were drawn from the moment she answered my knock.

Emma lived in an aging, three-story Victorian, a formerly sizable single-family dwelling, that had been converted into a triplex. People from outside the downtown core assume that Queen Anne Hill is uniformly yuppified, gentrified, and scenic, but Emma Jackson's daylight basement apartment at Sixth and Prospect would have given the lie to that notion. The only view from the yard of the Jackson place was of noisy traffic tooling up and down Aurora Avenue North. The place was ramshackle and run-down. The only door, an old-fashioned wooden one with a pane of clear glass at the top, was fast losing its cracked coat of oil-based paint, which was peeling off in long, narrow strips.

Finding no sign of a bell, I knocked.

Initially, no one answered, but a diesel VW Rabbit parked nearby convinced me that someone was home. I knocked again, harder this time.

Finally, a woman wearing a blue sweatshirt and matching sweatpants came to the door. She peered out at me through the window and then pulled down the rolling shade over the inside of the window. The door opened, but only three inches or so, as far as the end of the latched security chain allowed.

"Who are you and what do you want?"

"My name's Beaumont, Detective J. P. Beaumont. I'm a police officer. Are you Emma Jackson?"

"Dr. Emma Jackson." There was a certain injured reproof in the way she emphasized the word "doctor." She had evidently worked hard to earn the title of doctor, and she wanted me to know it.

"Dr. Jackson, I need to speak to you."

She unlatched the chain and opened the door a few more inches, standing in the opening with her arms crossed. "What about? Why would a police officer need to speak to me? Did my license tabs expire? Is my front bumper hanging too far over the parking strip?"

In the past few years, Seattle area blacks

— I still haven't learned to say African Americans with any kind of consistency — have complained about alleged instances of police harassment, incidents in which law-abiding people have been stopped and questioned by Seattle PD officers for seemingly no other reason than their being wherever they are. Blacks certainly do live and work on Queen Anne Hill, but they're not exactly plentiful.

I heard the undisguised antagonism in Emma Jackson's voice and wondered if maybe she had experienced some similar kind of treatment. Even so, I'm sure she would have found undeserved police harassment far preferable to receiving the painful news I was about to deliver.

"It's your son," I said quietly. "About Adam. Do you mind if I come in?"

Instead of asking me in, Emma Jackson stepped out onto the concrete pavers that constituted the tiny apartment's make-do porch and closed the door behind her. She was a woman in her early thirties, fairly tall, and well built. Her face was attractive but haggard, her dark eyes red-rimmed and bloodshot from lack of sleep.

"What about him?" she asked. "Where is he? Is he all right?"

It didn't seem right, telling her there on

the porch in front of God and everybody. "Really, Dr. Jackson, if we could just go inside . . ."

"I'm too tired to play games. If something's happened to Adam, tell me and tell me now!"

"There's been an incident . . ."

"What kind of incident?"

"Where did your son spend last night?"

"With some friends. Why?"

"Could you tell me their names?"

"Why should I?"

"Dr. Jackson. Please, this is a very serious matter."

For the first time the tiniest bit of alarm seemed to leak into her overriding anger. "Ben and Shiree Weston. They live down in the south end. What's this all about?"

There was no way to soften the blow, and she had refused any suggestion that would have allowed me to tell her in the privacy of her own home.

"Dr. Jackson," I said quietly, "I want you to understand that we don't have a positive ID yet, but we have reason to believe that your son has been murdered, along with Shiree and Ben Weston and two of their three kids."

Emma Jackson's eyes darted back and forth across my face as though trying to read the truth of what I was saying from what she saw there. Both hands went to her mouth.

"No," she said.

"Officers were summoned . . ."

"No," she repeated, a little louder this time. "That can't be true!"

"It is true, Dr. Jackson," I insisted. "I came to take you downtown so . . ."

"No!" This time the word was an anguished shriek that echoed through the relative peace of a pristinely clear Seattle morning. Not only did Emma Jackson scream, but she launched herself at me in an all-out physical attack, flailing at me with both balled fists. I caught her by the wrists and held her at arm's length — far enough away to keep her from bloodying my nose.

"Please, Dr. Jackson," I pleaded. "Quiet down. Listen to me."

But she didn't listen and she didn't stop screaming. "No! No! Please, God, no!"

Anyone hearing that terrible, agonized cry on a city street was bound to assume the worst, that a woman was being viciously assaulted in broad daylight. A neighbor evidently took corrective action and called for help, because the two of us were still standing there locked in struggle when I heard the quick sharp burst of siren from an approaching squad car. The wail of the siren seemed to penetrate through Emma Jackson's pain. She stopped screaming suddenly and stood quivering, her hands limp. I didn't know if I dared let loose of her or not. To be on the safe side, I didn't.

"We need you to do a positive ID," I said into the echoing silence. "On the other victims as well, if you could, since you evidently knew them all."

"It's true then?" she whispered brokenly. "All of them?"

"Yes," I answered. "It's true, all but Junior."

I expected another outburst. Instead, she tugged her hands free of mine just as a blue-and-white squad car pulled up and parked behind the Rabbit. Emma Jackson started inside as two uniformed cops leaped out of the car and came toward us.

"Where are you going?" I asked.

"To put on some other clothes," she answered, her voice fiercely calm and controlled. "I can't go downtown dressed like this."

I've seen some pretty amazing things in my time as a police officer, but Emma Jackson's transformation was downright astonishing. Now that I know her a little better, I suspect that pride kept her from wanting to share pain that was that deep, that intense with a total stranger, but I can't say for sure. In any event, she started into the house.

"Tell your friends here that it's okay," she said over her shoulder. "I'll be right back."

I turned to meet the two patrol officers who were hurrying up the walkway. Rank hath its privileges around Seattle PD, and most of the day-shift officers have been on the force for some time. I knew both these guys, Joe Miller and Fred Keanes.

"Hey, Beau," Joe said, recognizing me. "What's going on? We had a report of a domestic disturbance."

"Not a domestic," I told them. "The woman who lives here is the mother of the child who spent the night with Ben and Shiree Weston."

"The one who's dead?" Joe asked. I nodded. "And she just found out?"

"That's right. I came to tell her what happened and to take her downtown for the ID."

"Jeez!" Joe shook his head. "It's terrible. I hear through the grapevine that whoever it was took a potshot at you too, didn't they? What's the world coming to, Beau? Seattle never used to be like this."

He was wrong there. Seattle always used

to be "like this." That's why people like me have jobs as homicide detectives.

Moments later Emma Jackson emerged from the house. She was wearing a blazer, a blouse, and a pair of well-tailored slacks. Her face was set in a grim mask. "I'm ready," she said flatly. Her voice was low and husky, as though the strain of screaming had somehow damaged her vocal cords. "Where to? The medical examiner's office?"

I nodded, remembering after all that since she was Dr. Emma Jackson, she probably knew the drill.

"Yes."

I led the way. Emma Jackson stood to one side while I held the car door for her. Once we were both inside, I started the car and headed for Harborview Hospital and Doc Baker's office. I glanced at her from time to time, but she remained locked in stoic silence. I felt like I was riding next to a human Mount St. Helens. Emma Jackson was quiet, just like the mountain was for a hundred-and-twenty-odd years, but smart money said she was probably going to blow sky-high sooner or later.

"When did you find them?" she asked eventually.

"I didn't. Not me personally. Somebody else did. Around eleven."

"Eleven?" she demanded. "That long ago? Why the hell am I not finding out about it until almost twelve hours later?"

"The child wasn't wearing any identification," I told her. "At first we had no way of knowing who he was. In fact, we thought he was one of Ben and Shiree's until we found Junior."

"Junior? He's all right?"

"He's fine. He was hiding. The killer missed him. Junior gave us Adam's name, but he couldn't give us an address or tell us where you worked. And your phone number isn't listed."

"It still shouldn't have taken so long," she said. "You said yourself that it's already been on the radio."

"Without any names being mentioned," I told her. "We never release names until after we've located the next of kin."

"Just like good Boy Scouts," she returned sarcastically. "Ben was always a great one for telling us that you guys did things by the book. So who killed him?"

"Who killed your son?"

"No. Adam was just a little boy. The real question is who killed Benjamin Weston, isn't it?"

The hard edge on her question put me on notice that there was something behind it.

"I don't know," I answered. "Do you have any idea?"

She shrugged. "A jealous husband, most likely," she said. "That would be my guess."

I was thunderstruck. Gentle Ben Weston? Screwing around on the side? That didn't square with anything I personally knew about the man, but I wasn't exactly what you could call a friend of the family either. Emma Jackson was, and she sounded quite certain.

"Do you know something about that," I asked, "something we maybe should know too?"

"You tell me. For months now Shiree's been complaining to me about him going to work early and coming home late with no apparent explanation. You figure it out. What's the usual answer when that kind of thing gets started? I told Shiree that in this day and age she was stupid as a stump to look the other way and let him get away with it."

"Shiree Weston discussed the situation with you?"

"Shiree Garvey and I go back a long way. We discussed everything. I hated him for what he was doing to her."

The shrinks call it transference, I believe. It works the same way radar jamming does.

By keeping her mental signals full of other angers and issues, Emma Jackson avoided the terrible subject at hand — the senseless death of her son. It's a form of denial, and denial is common in the people I deal with. Nevertheless, I couldn't afford to ignore the fact that this woman might be presenting me with both a possible motive and hence a possible suspect.

"Did she mention any names?"

"No, but it won't be hard to find out. Men are never nearly as clever about these things as they think they are."

"I assume Garvey was Shiree Weston's maiden name?" Emma nodded. "How far back do you two go?" I asked.

"Grade school."

Both my question and Emma's initial answer seemed innocuous enough, but then she added an afterthought. "About the same age Adam is now. Was," she whispered.

Suddenly Dr. Emma Jackson's steely reserve shattered. She began crying quietly into her hand while I kept driving. By the time we arrived at Harborview, Emma had pulled herself together again. I would have gone around and opened the car door for her, but she beat me to the punch. She led the way into the building as though she knew it well.

"You seem to know your way around," I commented.

"I've been here before," she replied without explanation.

The lower floor of Harborview Hospital, occupied by the King County Medical Examiner's Office, is dedicated to the dead rather than to the living. There Dr. Howard Baker reigns supreme over a small corps of dedicated employees and an ever-changing and always deceased clientele. As a Homicide detective bringing in victims' relatives to make identifications, I'm used to taking charge at the receptionist's desk. This time, however, Emma Jackson handled it herself.

"I'm Dr. Jackson," she announced. "I'm here to see Dr. Baker about my son, Adam."

The receptionist, bleary-eyed from being called in during the middle of the night, blinked in recognition at the name. "Oh, of course. Wait right here. Dr. Baker's busy in the back right now."

"In the back" is a medical examiner's office euphemism that means either that Doc Baker's really out playing golf or else he's up to his armpits in an autopsy, a word that is seldom if ever uttered aloud in that grim little waiting room.

The receptionist jumped up and hurried through the swinging door that opened into

121

the lab. She returned moments later with Doc Baker in tow.

Emma had walked over to the window and was standing with her back to us looking outside when the M.E. came into the room. "Hello there, Beau," he said, nodding in my direction. "I understand you brought the mother along?"

Emma Jackson whirled around and faced him. At once I saw a look of shocked recognition cross Doc Baker's face. "Why, Emma. It's not your boy, is it?"

"That's what he told me," she said grimly. "I'm here to find out for sure, one way or the other."

Clearly Drs. Baker and Jackson knew each other, although I had no idea how. He held out his arm, and she took it. "This way," he said solicitously, leading her toward the swinging doors.

Maybe up until then Emma Jackson still had some hope I was wrong. But of course, I wasn't.

CHAPTER 8

In the years I've worked homicide, I've been through plenty of identification ordeals. Seeing your own child dead in some cold, stainless-steel-furnished morgue has to be one of the worst trials a parent ever endures. The emotional devastation of that encounter strikes both men and women pretty much equally. I've seen more than a few men faint dead away and have to be carried out of the room. Hysterics, explosions of anger, and racking wails of despair are common occurrences that know no gender divisions at a time like that. Men and women, fathers and mothers, are both identically susceptible to grief.

Even though she'd pulled herself together so well back at her apartment, Emma Jackson's reaction still surprised the hell out of me. It was like she slipped out of the role of mother, put on her doctor suit, and was totally professional about doing what had to be done. When Doc Baker lifted the sheet that covered her son's face, she swallowed hard and nodded.

"Yes," she said. "That's him. That's Adam."

I excused myself long enough to call Carl Johnson at McClure Middle School. When I came back, Doc Baker was leading Emma from one victim to another. Each time he lifted the sheet, she spoke quietly for several minutes while the M.E. took copious notes. Their exchanges were conducted in guarded undertones, totally inaudible to me or to anyone else in the room. Whatever information she imparted was delivered with a quiet dignity that I found absolutely mind-boggling considering the circumstances.

Subconsciously keeping count, I was surprised when, after Ben and Shiree Weston as well as the three dead children had all been identified, Doc Baker led Emma Jackson to yet another gurney. Beneath the sheet on that one lay Spot, the Weston family's dog. That was the first and only time I ever knew of a dog being accorded the medical examiner's office's full, deluxe postmortem treatment.

After that, we left the lab and retreated to Doc Baker's private office. This, too, was highly unusual. After making the IDs, victims' relatives are usually hustled away from Harborview as quickly as possible. They are generally excluded from any debriefings between the M.E. and the Homicide detectives working the case. When Baker ushered us into his office, I naturally assumed he was just being polite and that conversation would be strictly limited to sympathetic small talk.

"Coffee?" he asked, motioning us into chairs.

The stuff they call coffee in the M.E.'s staff lounge bears a startling resemblance to battery acid with just a hint of formaldehyde on the side. When Emma Jackson nodded and said, yes, she'd like some, I figured she simply didn't know any better. I did, but I was desperate. The beneficial effects of Ralph Ames's refueling breakfast were fading fast. My back hurt and so did my feet. My eyes burned from lack of sleep. Even terrible coffee was bound to help a little.

"I'll have some too," I said.

"Still drink it black?" Baker asked.

I thought for a moment he was talking to me and was surprised and gratified that he remembered, considering the number of Homicide dicks that pass through his office on a daily basis, but it turned out he was asking Emma.

"Black will be fine," she said.

That set me back on my heels. Theirs had to be more than a nodding acquaintance. "How is it that you two know each other?" I asked.

"Emma didn't tell you? She used to work here. Upstairs, I mean, in the hospital trauma center. Whenever she lost a patient, she's the only one of the whole bunch who ever bothered to follow them down here to find out what exactly went wrong. A lot of doctors never figure out that even dead patients can teach you something. Sometimes especially the dead ones."

Doc Baker smiled a proud mentor's smile which Emma Jackson did not return. Instead, she picked up the steaming cup of coffee the receptionist had placed on the desk in front of her.

"Tell him about the dog, Howard," she urged.

"What about the dog?"

Baker seemed unhappy that she had turned the conversation away from his reminiscing. "Spot's the only one we've had a chance to work on so far. He's told us a little, but not much."

"For instance?"

"He bit somebody," Emma Jackson blurted, answering my question before

Baker had a chance.

"Really?" I asked.

Baker nodded. "Tried to anyway. Just before he died. I found traces of material, a thread or two, still stuck to his teeth. Unfortunately, we haven't been able to determine whether or not he actually drew blood."

"He did," I said.

Both Doc Baker and Emma Jackson sat up and took notice. "How do you know that?" Baker asked.

"The boy told us," I replied. "Junior Weston. He told me the man's arm was bleeding. I thought maybe he'd cut himself with his own knife in the struggle with Bonnie, but I'll bet the dog nailed him at least once."

Baker nodded and began writing himself a note, talking as he did so. "We'll have to analyze all those bloodstains very carefully. We may have some of the killer's blood mixed in with that of the victims. As for the bite itself, the killer may have been bitten, but it's hard to say how badly. It might be worthwhile to check with the emergency rooms around town and see if they treated any dog-bite victims overnight."

I was shocked to hear Baker strategizing in front of a civilian, a victim's mother yet, without seeming to care whether or not she was authorized to hear those kinds of case-specific details, but it wasn't my place to tell him to shut up, not when he was essentially giving me marching orders. The possibility of finding a dog-bite victim somewhere among the metropolitan area's myriad hospitals didn't amount to much of a lead.

"There are a lot of emergency rooms in this town," I said.

Baker glowered at me with a look that meant don't look a gift horse in the mouth. He said, "It's more than you had before." Which was undeniably true.

"Now tell him about the hair," Emma Jackson urged.

"The hair we found in Shiree Weston's hands?"

Doc Baker opened his desk drawer, carefully removed a pile of paper clips and began to toss them thoughtfully into the vase in the windowsill. "Actually, we found two distinctly different hair samples — the ones in Shiree Weston's hand and on her body and some with the daughter as well. Naturally, the Crime Lab will be doing a detailed analysis of all samples, and there may be some other explanation for their presence at the crime scene, but my initial reaction is that we have two distinctly separate individuals here."

"Two?"

Baker nodded. "Two. One would be a . . ." I'm sure Doc Baker started to say "black," but he corrected himself in time. ". . . an African American. The second is definitely Caucasian."

I remembered what Junior Weston had told us about the bad man he had seen struggling with Bonnie, about his skin color being similar to mine. So the child had seen only one of his family's attackers, not both of them. It was a chilling thought. What the hell had Ben Weston been up to that so many people wanted to see him dead?

For a moment or two, we were all three quiet. "So what do you think?" I asked at last. "Gang warfare of some kind?"

Considering Ben Weston's position on the CCI unit, that was the most logical question, and one the whole city would be asking the moment the story hit the papers. Emma Jackson and Doc Baker both shook their heads in instant unison.

"No way," Baker answered at once. "Not their style unless they went out and hired a pro to do the dirty work. Those kids are all playacting at being big-time gangsters. They all want to be Al Capone or some other mafioso hood. If gangs decide they're going to kill somebody, they usually assign it to somebody as an initiation kind of thing, a rite of passage, or they want to do it in style and make like the St. Valentine's Day Massacre. This isn't right."

"What isn't right?"

"You know yourself, Beau. Drive-by shootings or the guy who took a shot at you from outside on a porch. Those sound like gang activity. This is something else. Those kids may all have street names and guns, and they don't think twice about blowing somebody off the face of the earth, but they aren't trained killers. They don't do silent kills. At least one of the perpetrators involved here is a highly trained professional killer."

"What do you mean professional?" I asked.

"Military most likely. Marines maybe? Whatever, he's dangerous as hell."

"And I want him," Emma Jackson added softly, almost under her breath. "Hanging's too good for a monster like that."

It was the only time in the whole process that Dr. Emma Jackson's professional demeanor slipped, and it caught Doc Baker off guard. She may have been a colleague of his, a sometime insider of the M.E.'s office, but right that minute she was just another mother of a homicide victim, someone interested in vengeance, not justice.

If anyone was to be faulted in that situation, it was Doc Baker for forgetting that Emma Jackson was a mother first and a doctor second. Doc Baker's rash disclosures in her presence had been indiscreet to say the least. In my opinion, she was a victim, and she, by God, should have been treated as such.

"You put that idea right out of your mind, Emma," he ordered indignantly. "We're talking about very dangerous men here. You stay out of it and let Detective Beaumont and the others handle it. I'm sorry. I shouldn't have discussed any of it in front of you."

"Don't worry about me, Howard," she returned coldly. "I can take care of myself. Now, if you don't mind, I think I want to go home."

Dr. Emma Jackson walked out of the room and closed the door behind her, leaving Baker and me staring at each other across the stacks of papers on his messy desk.

"Thanks a whole hell of a lot," I said. "When you screw up, you do it all the way. What in God's name do you expect me to do with that woman now?"

In all the years I'd known him, I had never seen Dr. Howard Baker so chagrined. In a matter of minutes he seemed to have aged a good ten years. His ran his fingers through his hair, leaving his unruly white mane standing even more on end.

"Do what you can to keep her out of it," he said.

"Right," I said. "I'll do my best, but thanks to you, right this minute she has more information than I do."

Standing up abruptly, Doc Baker glowered down at me. "I already said I'm sorry, and I am, but I can't take it back, now can I? So we'll just have to make the best of it. You go do your job and I'll do mine. One down and five to go."

With that, he stalked out of his office, heading back for the lab. I followed Baker as far as the reception area, but Emma Jackson wasn't there. I found her out in the parking lot, pacing back and forth beside the car. She was understandably agitated and upset, but I wondered if there was more to it than that.

"Look," I said, once we were in the car, "I know how awful all this is for you, but I hope you're not thinking about turning yourself into a one-woman posse. Forget it."

"Why should I?"

"Why? Because it's dangerous, just like Doc Baker said. If you tangle with these creeps, you could be killed too."

"So?" she asked.

She didn't say, "What's the big deal?" but the thought was there, hanging heavily in the air between us. I glanced across the seat. Her slender jaw was set. A single tear glistened in the corner of her eye. The idea of being killed herself didn't seem to offer much terror to Emma Jackson right about then. In fact, death may have seemed like a reasonable alternative to the ordeal she was facing.

"Things'll get better," I said, hoping to offer some comfort. "Don't think you've got nothing left to live for."

"That's easy for you to say, Detective Beaumont," she declared reproachfully. "Your son isn't lying back there on a stainless steel slab. Mine is."

There wasn't a hell of a lot I could say to counter that remark. If Dr. Jackson made up her mind to become personally involved in solving the case, there wasn't a whole lot I could do about that either. My best tactic was to try to derail her by embroiling her in some innocuous aspect of the case. I needed to give her a task assignment so she'd feel as though she was accomplishing something, making a contribution.

"You have connections with all the hospitals around town, haven't you?"

She shrugged. "I suppose. Why?"

"The first thing you need to do is to get some rest and then you'll probably need to work on funeral arrangements. But after that, I'd like to ask you to help me."

"Doing what?"

"By calling each of the hospitals and checking with the various E.R.s to see if any dog-bite victims came through last night."

"If I find anything out, what makes you think I'll tell you?"

"You're not stupid, Dr. Jackson," I told her bluntly. "If the killers were tough enough to handle Ben Weston, they'd certainly be more than a match for you."

She seemed to think about it for a moment or two. "I suppose I could do that," she said eventually. "Check for you, I mean."

"Good."

We came to a stoplight. I dug out one of my cards and scribbled my home number on the back of it. "Call me any time of the day or night and let me know whatever you find out."

"All right."

"The department has created a task force to handle this," I continued. "I'm only assigned to Adam's part of the case. Later on, I'll need to interview you in detail and, most likely, so will other members of the team."

She nodded. "Right," she said. "I understand."

"But do me a favor, would you?"

"What's that?"

"If you talk to someone named Detective Kramer, don't mention to him that I have you checking with the hospitals for me, would you? He's a lot more territorial about that kind of thing than I am."

"I won't mention it," she said.

We headed straight back toward her house on Queen Anne Hill. We were turning off Denny Way onto Fifth North when Emma Jackson jumped as though she'd forgotten something important.

"What is it?"

"You said Junior's all right, but you never told me where he is."

"With his grandfather," I told her, "Ben Weston's father. We turned Junior over to old Mr. Weston early this morning. He came down to the Public Safety Building and picked him up."

"Really," she snorted. "Wonders will never cease."

"Why do you say that?"

"Because Ben Weston's father hated everything about the Seattle Police Department. I'm surprised he'd set foot in that place, even to pick up his grandson."

"But why?"

"Who knows?" she returned. "I gave up trying to figure out men years ago. There's no percentage in it."

The reverse is also true, I almost told her, but I didn't. Because Emma Jackson had what kids playing tag used to call King's-X so they couldn't be caught by whoever it was. Her son was dead and mine wasn't. She had full permission to say any damned thing she pleased and get away with it.

After dropping her off at her place, I headed back home. It was close to noon. I'm too old to work all day, all night, and all the next day without stopping long enough for a nap. There was plenty to do, but nothing that wouldn't wait until I caught a couple of hours' worth of shut-eye.

I walked into my apartment and went straight down the hall to my bedroom. Kicking off my shoes, I flopped across the bed fully dressed while my back and feet heaved heartfelt sighs of relief.

Tired as I was, I didn't fall asleep instantly. There was too much about this case that hit close to home, too many crossed and re-crossed connections — Ben Weston and Big Al Lindstrom, Emma Jackson and Doc Baker. Everyone involved seemed to be involved twice over, and at least one of the people who had killed Ben Weston had tried to kill me as well. The slug that had smashed into the wall behind me had come far too close for comfort.

Then, just as I was telling myself I was being jumpy for no good reason, I heard the door of my apartment open and close. My heart pounding, I eased my way off the bed, gasping at the pain in my feet. I limped across the room to the closed bedroom door and stood there listening.

"You're sure he won't come in and catch us?" a woman's voice asked.

Relief flooded through me when I heard Ralph Ames's answering laughter. "He won't, not when he's busy working a case. We've got hours. Come on. Let's get started. Can I get you something to drink?"

The voices moved away from the entryway into the front end of the house, the living room, dining room, and den. Every once in a while I could hear the sounds of low voices and muffled laughter. I was uncomfortably aware that Ralph and his female companion were under the erroneous impression that they had my apartment all to themselves. No telling what they were up to.

There I stood, trapped in my own bedroom, while the impeccable Ralph Ames carried on with a lady friend just down the hall. I didn't know if I should be more embarrassed for him or for me, so I finally gave up, undressed, and crawled back on the bed. Into it this time, covers and all.

If I was going to have to take an enforced nap anyway, I might just as well be comfortable.

CHAPTER 9

My pager woke me up an hour or so later.
Lack of sleep left me feeling as rummy and
miserable as any honest hangover I've ever
encountered. The call, when I returned it,
was from none other than the Weston Family Task Force commander, Sergeant Watty
Watkins himself.

"Beau, where are you?"

"In bed. Asleep actually. I was up all night,
remember?"

"You and everybody else. You're not the
only one whose tail is dragging. I'm headed
home myself in a few minutes, but I wanted
to touch bases with everyone first. I heard
from Doc Baker that you got the positive
IDs handled. Good work. Anything else
turn up that I should know about?"

I tried to sweep some of the cobwebs out
of my poor, befuddled brain.

"Did Doc Baker mention the two separate
hair samples and the possible dog bite?"

"He told me about both of those," Watty acknowledged. "Anything else?"

Only one other item stood out in my mind as being important enough to mention. "Emma Jackson, the one boy's mother, believes Ben Weston might have been screwing around on the side. She thinks his death may be somehow related to that."

There was a pause while Watty mulled over what I had told him. "No kidding. That doesn't sound like Ben Weston to me. What exactly did this Jackson woman say?"

"Remember, she's a long-term friend of the family, a childhood chum of Shiree Weston's. She claims that in the past few months Ben's been coming and going at all hours of the day and night. She says Shiree assumed it was another woman and had talked to her about it, complained about it."

"What do you think?" Watty asked.

"I think there are a whole lot of other possibilities besides another woman. Besides, a jealous husband might have a beef with Ben, but not with the entire rest of his family. It just doesn't add up."

"Maybe not," Watty replied, "but you'd better check it out anyway and see if there's any truth to it. If there does turn out to be another woman involved, then we'll look for a possible connection."

Watty paused. Through the receiver I could hear the scratching of pen on paper as he made notes. "Do you want to mention all this to Detective Kramer or should I?" he asked.

"It'll all be in my report when I get around to writing one, but be my guest. You go right ahead and tell him if you want to," I said. The less I had to talk to Paul Kramer, the better I liked it.

"Will you be coming back in to the department?"

"Eventually, I suppose. I had planned on getting a little more sleep first. Anything important going on that you think I should know about?"

"Everybody's in pretty much the same shape you are — worn-out and barely upright. Several of the guys are trying to catch a little shut-eye while we wait for some of the preliminary test results. Both the Crime Lab and Doc Baker's crews are hard at work. Kramer has a squad of officers out surveying the Weston neighborhood to see if anyone saw or heard something out of the ordinary last night."

By rights, I should have been part of the neighborhood survey, but considering the number of people involved, I supposed dividing up the investigative territory made sense.

"I've scheduled the first official task force meeting tomorrow morning at eight," Watty continued. "Don't be late, but don't push yourself to come back in tonight, either. We'll all be better off if everybody gets some rest and takes a fresh run at this thing in the morning. In other words, do what you can, but don't kill yourself."

"Right," I replied. "I'll make a point not to."

"By the way," Watty added. "Speaking of which, we lucked out on that score, didn't we. I'm real happy that slug didn't have your name on it."

"That makes two of us," I told him, and meant it.

After Watty hung up, I lay there on my back, unable to fall back asleep and wondering what to do next. How long did discretion dictate that I stay out of the way and give Ralph Ames and company clear sailing? Were they up and dressed and out, or would I walk down the hall and stumble across something indiscreet that would embarrass us all?

But then I remembered Ralph's totally nonjudgmental response a few months earlier at his home in Arizona when the shoe had been firmly on the other foot, when Rhonda Attwood, Ralph's other overnight guest, had unaccountably turned up in my room at breakfast time.

Totally unflappable as usual, Ralph had fixed coffee and juiced a bunch of oranges, serving both juice and coffee without so much as a single snide editorial comment. If Ralph Ames could be that cool, that cosmopolitan, I decided, so could I. Determined to be totally blasé about the whole situation, I staggered out of bed and headed for the kitchen, where I had plenty of Seattle's Best Coffee but absolutely no tree-ripened oranges.

I banged around in the kitchen, making as much noise as possible. Despite the rattling and clattering, no one emerged from the guest room. Ralph Ames and his lady friend were evidently either dead to the world, or they had vacated the premises while I was asleep.

On the dining room table I discovered an early-afternoon city edition of *The Seattle Times* with its full, three-column-wide, front-page account of the tragic Weston family murders. While I waited for the coffee, I scanned through the article. There wasn't much in the story that I didn't already know.

Various luminaries in city government as well as prominent members of the African-American community were quoted expressing their shock, dismay, and outrage. Speculation was pretty evenly divided between those who regarded the murders as racially motivated hate crimes and those who saw in the deaths the specter of escalating gang warfare. Neither possibility did much for Seattle's much-vaunted national reputation for livability.

The coffee still wasn't finished when a key turned in the lock and Ralph Ames sauntered in, grinning broadly from ear to ear. He was clearly inordinately pleased with himself, and I was discreet enough not to let on that I knew the real origins of that grin. Remembering Rhonda Attwood, I offered him coffee without even so much as the smallest sarcastic remark.

"Been here long?" he asked.

"Nope. Just walked in a few minutes ago."

"Oh," he said. "Good. I see you found the copy of the paper I left you. I figured you'd want to see it. How's the case going?"

"Not bad, I guess. Things are always slow at this stage of the game while we wait for results from the various labs. Detective Kramer supposedly has a bunch of detectives out canvasing the nearby neighborhood. So far as I know, nothing much has turned up. I'll find out more once I get back down to the department."

"You must be beat," Ralph said. "Aren't you going to try to sleep for a while?"

I didn't want to tell him I'd already done that. Hurrying to the counter after the coffeepot and another cup, I hoped my face wouldn't give me away. Lying has never been one of my long suits.

"No," I said. "I'm in pretty good shape, all things considered. I just came home to put my feet up for a few minutes and to have some decent coffee."

That was true as far as it went, but it was also somewhat dishonest. Next to Ron Peters, Ralph is probably my best friend, but I couldn't bring myself to tell him that I knew what he'd been up to at lunchtime. I'm not the type to whack somebody on the shoulder and congratulate him for getting lucky in my guest room when he thought I was safely at work. I noticed he didn't mention it to me either. Men may have the reputation for bawdy locker room score-keeping-type talk, but in my experience we're a whole lot more reticent about personal disclosures than women are — Emma Jackson and Shiree Weston being prime cases in point.

I stood by the counter lost in thought, staring down at the two newly filled coffee cups sitting there steaming in front of me.

"What's going on?" Ralph asked. "Is something the matter?"

"Nothing," I told him, bringing the cups back to the table. "Nothing important."

The phone rang just then. The caller was none other than Detective Paul Kramer himself, sounding excited.

"Beaumont, give me that Jackson woman's phone number, will you," he said. "Watty told me you had it. I need to talk to her right away."

I knew from his voice that Detective Kramer was on to something. "Why? Did you find something to corroborate her story?"

"Not exactly," he returned, suddenly turning coy. "I just want to hear whatever it is she can tell us about him."

Like hell he did. "What exactly did you find, Kramer?" I insisted. As the one person at Seattle PD in sole possession of Emma Jackson's phone number, I had myself some bargaining room and I was prepared to play hard to get.

Kramer paused, pondering whether or not to let me in on his little secret horde of knowledge. When someone's that wound up, a few seconds of silence is the best ploy in the world.

"Did you know Shiree Weston worked for the Mount Zion Federal Credit Union?" he asked.

Of course I didn't know that. I had been unofficially benched from the real investigation, sidetracked into something that should have been a dead end, but maybe my part of the job wasn't such a dead end after all.

"So?" I said, unable to fathom how Shiree Weston's job with a credit union might have anything at all to do with the price of peanuts.

"After I talked to Sergeant Watkins this afternoon," Kramer continued, "I decided to take a look at Ben Weston's desk here at the department. What I discovered was very interesting."

"What?"

By then I knew nothing would keep Paul Kramer from blabbing his news to the world. Even to me, although under most circumstances, I would have been his very last choice of audience.

"Loan applications!" Kramer crowed.

At first I thought lack of sleep was screwing up my hearing. "Loan applications?" I asked. "What's the big deal about that?"

"So far I've found he cosigned on three different student loans, and they're not with his wife's credit union either. Plus there's another one that's filled out but not signed. Does the name Ezra T. Russell mean anything to you?"

"Not that I can think of."

"How about Knuckles Russell?"

That one did ring a bell. Knuckles Russell was a rising young star in the ranks of the Black Gangster Disciples, an upstart gang that rivals both the Bloods and the Crips when it comes to pieces of Seattle's gangland turf.

"You mean Knuckles Russell of the BGD?" I asked, using the accepted shorthand for the Black Gangster Disciples.

"You got it. And the application lists Ben Weston's address as Russell's home address. Same way on the other three. I've got someone checking rap sheets on the others right now."

"So what are you saying?"

"That Ben Weston got himself into something heavy, something that had nothing to do with screwing around behind his wife's back. Gambling maybe, drug payoffs of some kind. Who knows? Whatever it was, I figure he ran short of cash and borrowed money to make ends meet. By doing it with student loans, nobody would come after him right away to start making payments.

Sounds like a hell of a scam to me. What do you think?"

What I was thinking was how grateful I was that Big Al Lindstrom was nowhere within earshot. Kramer should have been too.

"So give me that woman's address," Kramer continued. "I want to find out if she knows anything about all this."

"You're right," I said. "We should see what she has to say. Where are you, the department?"

"Yes, but . . ."

"Be down in front of the Third Avenue entrance in fifteen minutes," I told him. "I'll stop by and pick you up."

"Wait a minute. Can't you just give me the address? I'll go talk to her myself."

That was exactly what Kramer was angling for — to see Emma Jackson alone. I was equally determined not to give in, not to be cut out of the picture any more than I already was, but I didn't come straight out and tell my supposed cohort that I didn't trust him any further than I could throw him.

"No," I said reasonably enough. "Emma Jackson's already been through hell today. She's not the easiest person to deal with in the first place, and she already knows me.

I'd better come along."

"If you insist," Kramer allowed grudgingly. "See you in fifteen."

Ralph Ames was still sipping his coffee when I got off the phone. "Heading back out?" he asked. I nodded. "Any plans for dinner?"

"Not that I can think of. After last night, I'll be lucky if I'm still on my feet come dinnertime. Why?"

"There's someone I want you to meet," he said, "and if you don't mind, I thought I'd whip up something on the barbecue."

I tried my best to suppress a knowing grin. So he was going to bring the lady in question out from under wraps and introduce her around after all. That might be worth struggling to stay awake for.

"Make it early," I said. "I'll try to be home by six. If we eat by seven or so, it won't matter if I crash right after dinner, will it?"

"No," Ralph replied, poker-faced as ever. "I don't suppose it will."

I started toward the door. "By the way," he said. "I hope you don't mind. I took the liberty of calling that life insurance agent back. I left a message for him to get in touch with me. I'm not certain he's the best man for the job, but it seems to me we ought to be exploring some of your options. After all, he did call to ask for an appointment."

"I already told you. If I've got to pay a rating or whatever the hell they call it, I'm not buying a dime's worth of insurance no matter what you say."

"The least we can do is give him a fair hearing."

"I'll tell you what. You give old Curtis Bell all the fair hearings you like. I'm going to work."

Ralph and I both know that on less than two hours' worth of sleep I'm never going to win any congeniality awards. Fortunately, he isn't the kind of friend who holds grudges.

By the time I was back out on the street, the afternoon had turned blustery and cold with a chill wind blowing in off Puget Sound. When Kramer and I got to Emma Jackson's place, a half dozen cars were parked nearby. We were about to knock on the door when it opened and a broad, imposing man barred our way. His face seemed familiar, but I couldn't quite place him.

"May I help you?" he asked in a bass voice that sounded like it was coming from a loudspeaker instead of a human chest.

"I'm Detective Beaumont," I answered, "and this is Detective Kramer from the

Seattle Police Department. We're here to speak to Dr. Jackson."

"I'm not sure Emma's up to seeing anyone just now," he told us. "Wait here. I'll go check."

He turned back into the apartment and left us standing on the little concrete porch. "Wasn't that Reverend Walters?" Kramer asked.

"Reverend Walters?" I repeated.

"You know. Reverend Homer Walters of the Mount Zion Baptist Church."

Reverend Walters of the Mount Zion Baptist Church is almost as much of a Seattle institution as the church itself. No wonder he looked familiar.

A few moments later he reappeared in the doorway, shaking his head. "No," he said gravely, peering at us across the tops of his silver wire-rimmed glasses. "Emma's on her way to bed now. We've been here doing a little planning for the funeral. With this many people involved, we have to get started right away."

"What do you mean, this many people?"

"We have a very full schedule this weekend, so we'll be funeralizing them all — Ben and Shiree and all those poor little children — at two o'clock on Saturday afternoon. They're all members of the Mount Zion

152

Church, you see, so we'll be sending them off together. If we do it on Saturday, people who want to come won't be missing any work."

Detective Kramer cleared his throat. "Excuse me, Reverend Walters, but these are all homicide cases. It might be better if you made your plans for later, say sometime next week. That would give us a little more time for lab work, that kind of thing."

Reverend Walters was already shaking his head.

"Even Sunday might be better," Kramer said.

The Reverend Homer Walters pulled himself up to his considerable height. "Sunday is a day of worship, young man. I don't do funerals on Sunday, and people have to work on Monday. Saturday will be just fine."

Kramer seemed taken aback and for good reason. In homicide cases there are often innumerable delays before bodies can be released to families and funeral homes for preparation and burial.

"Have you discussed this with anyone down at Seattle PD?" Kramer asked, trying to move the burden on to someone else's shoulders.

"I have not," Reverend Walters declared,

"and I don't intend to. Emma Jackson, Harmon Weston, and I have discussed the situation with the Lord. He's the only one who matters, you see. I am sure He will provide whatever laboratory time is necessary between now and then. The Lord does provide, you know."

With that, the Reverend Homer Walters gently closed the door and went back inside, leaving a perplexed Detective Paul Kramer looking as though he had been run over by a truck — a gentle, Christian truck maybe, but a Mack nonetheless. It did my heart good to see it.

Amen, brother, preach on.

CHAPTER 10

Kramer was ripped, both because of the speed of Reverend Walters's funeral arrangements and also because we had missed out on the chance for him to talk to Emma Jackson. He grilled me on the way back to the department, trying to learn if there was anything I had gleaned from my talk with her that might give him a handle on how to approach her.

Now that he knew how to reach Emma himself, I was sure he would cut me out of any subsequent interviews, but that was hardly anything new and different in my dealings with Detective Kramer. Every time I have any contact with the man, he always acts as though we're working for opposite teams. Come to think of it, maybe we are.

To give the devil his due, however, Kramer wasn't the only one angling for information. If he wanted data from me, the reverse was also true. Those possibly fraudulent student loans that Kramer's part of the investigation had turned up might bear some pretty unsavory fruit by the time the investigation was over.

According to law enforcement ethics, cops aren't supposed to have any kind of business dealings with members of the criminal element. The idea is to avoid both the appearance of evil as well as the actuality of it. Owning jointly held businesses or taking out personal loans with crooks qualifies under the broad heading of conduct unbecoming an officer, and the offenses would cast a major blemish on Ben Weston's previously flawless record.

I wanted to learn everything I could about those loans while Kramer and I were still trading tit for tat. "How did you find out about the loans?" I asked. "What tipped you off?"

He shrugged with uncharacteristic modesty. "To begin with, going through his desk was just routine, but when I found the set of bank statements, that got my attention. If somebody starts keeping financial records at work instead of at home, what does that usually mean?"

"That he's got something to hide," I replied. "And most likely he's hiding whatever it is from his wife."

"Exactly," Kramer agreed. "So when I stumbled on the file folder with all the loan applications in it, I was already on point, already looking. It didn't take me two seconds to figure it out. There are four separate bank loans all together, four different banks, and four different names, but all the cosigners share the same home address which also happens to be Ben Weston's address. What does that say to you?"

"It does raise a question or two, doesn't it?"

Kramer glared at me. "More than one or two, if you ask me. Several in fact. I've got Sue Danielson checking for rap sheets on the other three names. I turned up Russell's on my own."

"What about the schools?"

"Schools?" Kramer asked. "What schools?"

"Don't student loan applications indicate where the student is enrolling? Have you checked with the registrars to see whether or not those students are actually there?"

Kramer didn't answer, an omission which was, by itself, an admission. No, he hadn't checked.

"Shouldn't you?" I prodded. "If the students on the applications are actually enrolled just the way the form says they are, then maybe there's no fraud involved, after all."

By then, I was parking the car in the Public Safety Building parking garage. Kramer shot me a withering look as he reached to open the car door. "Believe me," he said, "they won't be registered anywhere. This is the real world, Beaumont, not some kind of never-never land. Knuckles Russell is a two-bit thug with a rap sheet ten feet long. I'll lay you odds the others won't be any different. The only institution of higher learning these guys will ever land in is a federal pen."

On that congenial and uplifting note, we headed upstairs. I think Kramer expected to lose me in the fifth floor maze, but I was determined to see copies of Ben Weston's loan applications. I followed Kramer on down the hall. When we turned into his cubicle, the whole place was a shambles. Multiple boxes, some opened and some closed, were stacked against the wall. A half-emptied file cabinet with the top three drawers opened stood in the far corner. I waded through the boxes to a chair, removed a stack of folders, and made myself at home.

Kramer began shoving file folders into one box. "Looks like you're moving," I said.

He glanced up and seemed surprised to

find me sitting there. "Down the hall," he mumbled, "so I can be closer to Watty. We'll be working together closely on this one, you know."

"Right."

He stared at me in what could only be described as a clear-cut invitation to leave, the old here's-your-hat-what's-your-hurry-type stare. I didn't take the hint. "What do you want?" he asked finally. "Don't you have work to do?"

"This is work. I want to see Ben Weston's student loan applications."

Grudgingly, he picked up a file folder from a stack on his desk, extracted a sheaf of papers, and shoved them across the desk in my direction, but before I had a chance to glance at them, Sue Danielson appeared in the doorway and looked at us across the disarray.

Sue, a single mother with two teenagers at home, is a recent transplant in Homicide. She started out years ago as a 911 dispatcher and has gradually worked her way up. Gravelly voiced, she along with Janice Morraine down in the Crime Lab are two of the Public Safety Building's unrepentant smoking holdouts. They both go downstairs and stand outside in all kinds of weather to have a morning and afternoon smoke.

Sue nodded briefly in my direction, but her real message was for Detective Kramer. "You called that shot," she said, "four for zip. Every last one of them has a sizable rap sheet, and they're all BGD, or at least they were. They've all dropped out of sight in the last three to ten months."

"You're sure they're not in jail someplace?" Kramer growled.

"Not that I can find so far."

"Maybe they're dead then. Maybe Weston had someone knock them off."

"Maybe you should check with the schools," I suggested.

Kramer glowered at me while Sue Danielson looked genuinely surprised. "What's this about schools?"

"What if those students are actually enrolled there?" I continued. "Maybe the applications are just exactly what they say they are and these kids are all back in school."

"Like hell they are!" Kramer said, exasperated.

But Sue Danielson had been paying attention to me, not to him. "That's a good idea, Beau," she said. "I'll do some checking on that, if not tonight, then for sure in the morning. Bye."

Waving, she backed away from the door before Kramer had a chance to say anything

160

more. Pissed, he went on pitching file folders into boxes while I glanced through the set of loan applications.

That's what they were — student loan applications. Despite the rap sheets, these kids were really that — kids, with the oldest barely twenty-two. The largest loan amount was for two thousand a semester for Washington State University over in Pullman. One applicant listed his school of choice as Central Washington with the required loan amount of a thousand dollars per quarter. The third, for the same dollar amount, listed Western Washington in Bellingham. The last one, for an Ezra Russell, was only partially completed. It didn't list a school at all.

If his amount was similar to the others, that would bring the total indebtedness up to around twelve or thirteen grand a year. For a cop with a family of his own to support, thirteen thousand dollars a year would be one hell of a financial burden if one or more of Ben Weston's cosigners defaulted on the loans, but in the drug-dealing world that these gang members formerly inhabited, thirteen thou was small potatoes, not even one night's take — on a slow night. What the hell was going on?

I put the papers back down on Kramer's

desk. "Don't you think these ought to be turned over to Internal Investigations?" I asked.

That got Kramer's attention about the same way a red flag grabs a maddened bull. "I don't think anything of the kind, and don't you go leaking one word of it. Crimes have been committed, Detective Beaumont. Murders to be exact. That already takes this case well beyond the scope of the guys upstairs. I don't want one word of this to go to the Double I's," he said. "This is first and foremost a homicide investigation. Understand?"

I understood all right. As per usual, Detective Kramer wanted to play with all the marbles again, and he didn't want any interference and/or help from anyone else. Regardless of field of endeavor, that's the way it is with fast-rising stars. They can't afford to share the limelight. They're also scarce as hens' teeth when it comes time to take responsibility for something that goes wrong.

"You do whatever you want to, Kramer," I told him, "but if I were you, I think I'd talk this over with Watty before making too many unilateral decisions. He's the one who's really in charge of the task force, you know. He should be consulted."

Kramer stopped loading files into the cardboard box. "You do your job and I'll do mine, Beaumont. Incidentally, I haven't seen any reports on the Adam Jackson end of the investigation. If I were you, I wouldn't show up at that meeting tomorrow morning empty-handed. That would be a real shame."

So the battle lines were drawn. I headed for my own cubicle with my jaws clenched as well as my fists. Paul Kramer has the unerring capacity for bringing out the very worst in me.

Back at my desk, I dialed my voice-mail code and had a message to call Big Al, but when I returned the call Molly said he wasn't home. Just the way she said it sounded funny, as though the words didn't quite ring true.

"Tell him I called," I told her. "I'm here at the office working on paper. I'm due to be home around six. If he misses me here, he can try there."

I started in on the reports, but I kept nodding off. Twice I fell asleep with the pen on the paper and had to start over again to get rid of the stray line of ink that trailed cornerwise across the bottom half of the page. I was out like a light, drooling, with my chin resting on my chest and probably even snoring when the phone woke me up.

"The killer was wearing gloves, yellow rubber gloves," Big Al announced without preamble. "Junior didn't remember that until just a little while ago. I thought you should know. It's got to be somebody in the AFIS files, somebody we could find for sure if we just had a set of prints. Otherwise, why screw around with gloves?"

The Automated Fingerprint Identification System is a new, computerized system that can nail crooks to the wall as long as there's enough money in the budget to feed the file prints as well as the requests for matchups into the system. Big Al almost got me. I was so struck by the presence of gloves on the killer's hands that it took me a minute to wonder how he happened to be in possession of that stray bit of information.

"Hold on. You say Junior remembered that a little while ago? That means you've been over to his grandfather's house talking to him?"

Big Al sounded offended. "Why shouldn't I go there? I'm a friend of the family, remember? I can talk to Junior Weston any damned time I want to, and nobody's going to tell me I can't."

"But how'd you get permission? I got the distinct impression this morning that Harmon Weston isn't exactly wild about cops. Are you telling me he actually let you in to talk to the kid?"

There was a slight pause. "Well, maybe he didn't," Big Al admitted. "Not exactly. The old man was sound asleep, taking a nap. When I showed up at the door, Junior let me in. Why wouldn't he? He knows me. Besides, I had a Nintendo along for him. I figured he'd be better off with one of those instead of a potful of flowers."

"Wait a minute, you went over there while the grandfather was asleep, essentially broke into the house, gave Junior a game, talked to him, and the old man was never any wiser?"

"I didn't break in. Junior let me in," Big Al insisted. "I just wanted to visit with him for a little while to see if there was anything else he remembered. And there was. Like I told you, the gloves."

A dozen alarm bells went off in my head. "Hell with the gloves, Al! Forget about them. Junior's a witness for Christ's sake. He actually saw Bonnie's killer. If you got in and out that easily, so could somebody else!"

For a moment the phone was so quiet I was afraid it had gone dead. "Al, are you there?"

"I'm here," he said, "and I get your drift. If the killer bothered to read this afternoon's newspaper, he knows for sure that he screwed up and missed one kid who is also the only living eyewitness. Shit! They could get to him in a minute. What the hell are we going to do?"

Just as doctors don't practice medicine on their own family members, police officers aren't allowed to work on cases that come too close to them personally. They lose their professional detachment, take unnecessary risks.

"You stay out of it, Al. If Watty finds out you've been within a mile of Junior Weston, your tail will be in a gate for sure. Tell me, would the grandfather hold still for protective custody or a police guard?"

"Not likely. Old man Weston hates cops — all cops — his own son included."

"Then I'd better come up with some better idea."

"Like what? We'd best get on the stick. It'll be dark soon."

"Goddamnit, Lindstrom, you hardheaded lug. I told you we aren't doing a thing. You stay the hell out of it, you hear?"

For an answer, he banged the receiver down in my ear. I hung up too and sat there staring at the phone trying to imagine a solution. Who could I call in to deal with Harmon Weston? From what Al Lindstrom had told me, I knew instinctively that I could haul the mayor or the police chief himself into the melee, and it wouldn't do a damn bit of good.

What I needed was a higher authority, an ultimate authority. When the answer came to me, it was like a bolt out of the blue. It even made me smile. I grabbed the nearest phone book and looked up the number of the Mount Zion Baptist Church. Reverend Homer Walters himself didn't answer the phone, but I was put through to him with only a minimal delay.

"This is Detective Beaumont," I said. "We met briefly earlier this afternoon at Dr. Jackson's place."

"Yes, Detective Beaumont. I remember. What can I do for you? I hope you're not calling to ask me to change the funeral time."

"Oh no," I said. "Nothing like that. I was actually calling to ask for your help. I'm concerned for the safety of Junior Weston, especially since he qualifies as an eyewitness."

Briefly I went on to explain what had happened earlier that afternoon, how Big Al had come and gone from Harmon Weston's place without the old man ever hearing a thing. If I expected my tattling to be news to Reverend Walters, I was wrong.

"That's true," Reverend Walters said when I finished. "Harmon Weston sleeps like a rock, and that includes sleeping in church. If I happen to run on too long of a Sunday morning, he turns off his hearing aid and doesn't hear a thing. Sometimes one of the deacons has to go back and wake him up after the service is over. I can see we're going to have to do something about this."

"What do you suggest?"

"Bring Junior over to our house, of course," Reverend Walters said decisively. "And we'll bring that new Nintendo game along as well. Francine and I can look after him with no trouble, but he'll need games and things to help occupy his time."

When I finally came back home to Belltown Terrace at five forty-five, my tail feathers were dragging, but I was feeling a real sense of accomplishment. Through my intervention, Homer Walters had picked Junior up and taken him, along with his new teddy bear, to the Walterses' gracious home on the back side of Beacon Hill. I stopped by briefly to check on the boy and found him deeply engrossed in a game called Super Mario Brothers, whatever that is. His

Teddy Bear Patrol teddy bear sat on the couch nearby, well within safe touching distance.

I had forgotten all about Ralph Ames and his plans for the evening until I walked up to the door of my apartment and smelled the garlic. Ralph Ames is one of those people who never met a garlic clove he didn't like. He claims that the real secret behind every successful barbecue is layering it on — ground, minced, pressed, or chopped, it doesn't matter. That initial savory whiff was followed by the sound of female laughter coming from behind the still-closed door.

She was there all right. The lunchtime lady had returned for a dinnertime engagement when all I wanted to do was eat a square meal, hit the sack, and let them do the same. I stuck an idiotic grin on my face and opened the door.

Ralph Ames is never so happy as when he's busy demolishing my kitchen. The edible results are always masterful, but the kitchen usually resembles a war zone afterward. This particular meal was no exception.

While Ralph held sway over a smoking Jenn-Air grill with a pasta pot bubbling near his elbow, a woman with a dish towel tied around her waist stood at the far end of the counter breaking up handfuls of romaine.

"Why, Beau," Ralph said heartily. "You're just in time. Let me introduce you to Alexis Downey, Alex for short. Alex, this is my friend J. P. Beaumont. Everyone calls him Beau."

I held out my hand. She dried one hand on the towel and then shook mine. She was in her mid-to-late thirties probably, medium tall with short, auburn hair, a bit of gray around the temples, and a pair of amazingly blue eyes.

She smiled. "Glad to meet you, Beau. Ralph has told me so much about you."

"Alex is the director of development for the Seattle Repertory Theater," Ralph announced, flopping the steaks over on the grill.

"Glad to make your acquaintance, Alex," I returned politely, but secretly I was wondering how much of a donation she had hit him up for. Which only goes to show how naïve I still am.

I mistakenly thought Ralph Ames was the target.

CHAPTER 11

I made it through dinner without falling asleep in my food, but only just barely. Alexis Downey went out of her way to be cordial and include me in the general conversation, but it was all I could do to concentrate on what she and Ralph were saying.

For some reason, Alex was inordinately interested in Belltown Terrace's Bentley which I, along with the rest of my partners, regard as a royal pain in the ass. Intended to be one of the condominium's distinctive amenities, the limo actually had spent far more time in the shop than it had on the street. Finally, sick of repairs and complaints from periodically stranded riders/residents, we leased a new Cadillac for the building and left the aging Bentley covered and more or less permanently parked on the P-1 level of the garage.

"Is it running now?" Alex Downey asked.

"Hard to say," I told her. "It has what mechanics call an intermittent ignition problem. That means sometimes it works and sometimes it doesn't."

"Would I be able to go for a ride in it? I've never ridden in a Bentley, and I've always wanted to."

"Call down to the concierge," I told her. "If the driver isn't all booked up, and if he can get it started, maybe he can take you and Ralph for a spin later on tonight after dinner."

"Wouldn't you like to come along?" Alex Downey enthused. "We could ride over to West Seattle and watch the city lights from Alki Point."

"No thanks. I'm on my way to bed. I was up working all last night."

"Oh really? What do you do?"

Obviously in the "so much" Ralph had told her about me, he had neglected to include anything so basic as information about my work. "I'm a cop," I told her. "A detective down at Seattle PD."

"How exciting."

"It's a job," I returned.

Alex glanced meaningfully around my penthouse apartment, suddenly seeing it with new eyes. "Yours must pay better than most," she said.

"Not that much better," I told her gruffly.

I didn't feel like going into any detailed personal explanations about how I managed to live in Belltown Terrace's penthouse on an ordinary cop's salary. It was none of Alex Downey's business.

During all this repartee, Ralph sat at the far end of the table, grinning from ear to ear. His eyes shifted between Alex and me as though watching a conversational tennis ball being lobbed back and forth. He was up to something, but I couldn't quite figure out what, and I didn't want to.

Halfway through my steak, I gave out completely. "You two are going to have to excuse me," I said, abandoning my plate. "I just hit the wall. If I don't go to bed soon, you'll have to carry me."

Alex Downey stood up and offered her hand. "It's been a pleasure meeting you, Beau. Can I call and talk to you about the Bentley Monday or Tuesday of next week?"

Back to the Bentley again. "You can talk to me about it anytime you please, just not tonight."

With that, I staggered off to bed. I was asleep within seconds, but my last waking thought was something about Ralph Ames's strange taste in women.

I slept for twelve solid hours. The clock

radio evidently came on and went off again without my hearing a thing. Big Al called at ten to eight. "Aren't you supposed to be down here for a task force meeting in ten minutes?"

"Holy shit! I overslept."

With no time to shower, I bounded out of bed and started rummaging for clothes. I was slipping on my shoes when Ralph knocked on the bedroom door.

"Coffee?" he asked. He was already dressed. In his hand he held a steaming mug of coffee which I accepted gratefully.

"I'm late," I told him. "Do you mind dropping me off at the department?"

"Not at all. I'll go get my wallet."

The lights on Second and Fourth Avenues are timed so that, if you hit them just right, you can make it all the way from Denny to Jackson or the other way around without being stopped. Ralph guided my newly repaired Porsche down Second without the slightest hitch, and I dashed into the building at three minutes after. The real traffic jam of the morning was inside the building, where the lobby was crowded with people waiting for elevators. The door of one was plastered with a hand-painted OUT OF OR-DER sign, making a critical problem out of a chronic one. I bypassed the elevators and ran, puffing, up the seemingly endless flights of stairs.

After jostling my way through another lobby, this one crowded with media types, I edged my way into the eighth floor conference room. Sergeant Watkins, standing in front of a chalkboard, fixed me with a hard-edged stare as I tried to slip unobtrusively into the last row of seats.

"Glad you could make it this morning, Detective Beaumont," he said, meaning, of course, that everyone else had managed to arrive on time. "Hope this meeting isn't inconveniencing you." Properly chastised, I stared down at my feet. Only then, in the brilliant glow of fluorescent lights, did I realize I was wearing one brown and one black sock.

Up front, Watty continued his chalk talk. While he spoke, I listened to what he was saying, but my eyes kept straying back to the black ribbon, the department's traditional symbol of mourning, that had been taped over part of his badge. Looking at the badge was a constant reminder that, no matter what Ben Weston may or may not have done, the business at hand was really about a dead cop.

"As I was saying, this task force is a team effort, and I do mean T-E-A-M. Each of you will have focused responsibilities on one aspect of the case or another, but every one of you will be sharing all pertinent information with everyone else. Is that clear?"

Nods of agreement spread through the room. Detective Kramer, seated next to a small table in the front of the room, nodded so hard I'm surprised his teeth didn't fall out — the ass-kissing son of a bitch.

"Through the years, many of you may have had personal dealings with Benjamin Weston," Watty went on. "He was a well-liked, well-respected officer. At this time, however, there's a distinct possibility that this investigation may turn up some wrong-doing on his part. Our responsibility, as officers of the law, is to find the killer and take him off the streets. If Ben Weston's reputation ends up taking a beating in the process, that's life! Our first and foremost duty is to solve these homicides without any kind of whitewashing or cover-up. Again, am I making myself clear?"

There was a second series of nods, this one less general, and it was accompanied by an uneasy shifting of butts on chairs. No one, with the possible exception of Detective Kramer, wanted to hear that Gentle Ben Weston had somehow gone bad.

"Taking all this into consideration, we

have to remember the kind of impact this case is going to have on the entire community. Because Ben was an African American and because the investigation may lead to suspects involved in some of the better-known gangs — the Bloods, Crips, and Black Gangster Disciples — we must be careful that no one involved in the investigation says or does anything to further inflame the situation. There are all the usual restrictions about not speaking directly with the media, but it's not out of line to suggest that we all exercise extra caution in this regard."

Watty paused and glanced around the room, letting his eyes hold those of each officer for a fraction of a second. Finally he nodded. "All right then. Enough cheerleading. Let's get started. Kramer, what have we got?"

With that Sergeant Watkins sat down abruptly while Detective Kramer took the floor and assumed the speaker's mantle. Ever since he showed up in Homicide, I've been one of Kramer's main detractors and not, I believe, without reason. As a partner, he's a damn prima donna at best, but I have to admit that the military-type briefing he delivered that morning was good, very good, in fact.

The first day following a multiple homicide is like the first day of a war — there are so many things happening on so many fronts that it's almost impossible to get a clear overview of any of it. Kramer had done his homework. Starting from the collection of written reports by everyone involved, he broke the whole process down into bite-size pieces, going over in detail the pertinent information about the murder victims themselves, times of death, manner of death, etc. He discussed the preliminary autopsy findings as well as what little had so far been gleaned from Crime Lab analyses. He went on to discuss what avenues were being explored in the immediate neighborhood of the crime scene as well as some of the side issues — the questionable bank loans, the involvement of various gang members, etc. At the very end he even threw in a brief mention of the almost fatal attack on yours truly.

When Kramer finished his formal presentation, he called on the officers present in the room to volunteer any additional information that had turned up during the night. Sue Danielson was the first to raise her hand.

"I've been in touch with all the schools mentioned on the loan applications," she said. "All of them cite confidentiality issues, and they all refuse to confirm or deny the attendance of any of the names listed."

"What do you mean, refuse?" I asked.

She shrugged. "Just that. Evidently, one of the schools gave out unauthorized information on a student years ago and that student ended up as the victim of a serious crime. They all seem to be under orders not to make the same mistake again. The only way we'll get any real information out of them is with a court order."

I tried to catch Watty's attention. "Can we get one?"

He deferred my question to Kramer, who said, "When we get around to it, Beaumont. All in good time."

In other words, don't hold your breath.

A brief silence followed before one of the uniformed officers raised his hand. "I've been down working the neighborhood canvass. This morning I had a callback from the mother of a paperboy, who told her he's seen a couple of strange cars hanging around Ben Weston's neighborhood for the past few days. The kid goes to school at Garfield. I've got his name. Do you want me to go interview him, or should somebody else?"

"Detective Danielson, how about if you

handle that one?" Kramer said. She nodded.

It was neat the way he did it, giving her
something relatively important to do so she
wouldn't have any spare time to go trailing
after the school records of those student
loan applicants. I figured it was a good bet
that Kramer wouldn't authorize me to go
after them either.

"Anything else?" he asked.

I waited to see if someone else would
volunteer. No one did. "I may have something to add," I said.

"What's that?" Kramer asked bluntly.

"Ben Weston Junior has been moved to an
undisclosed location for safekeeping."

Kramer looked surprised to hear that.
"Really. Who came up with that brilliant
idea?"

"I did. It came to my attention that his
grandfather might not be physically able to
protect him properly. Mr. Weston is, after
all, up in years and hard of hearing, while
Junior Weston must be regarded as an
invaluable eyewitness."

"Do you mind telling us where this 'undisclosed location' is so those of us who need
to interview him will actually be able to find
him?"

"He's staying out on Beacon Hill with

Reverend Homer Walters and his wife, Francine."

"I see. Anything else?"

I didn't want to bring up Big Al's part in the proceedings. "Well, actually, there is one more thing. When I was taking Junior over there, to the Walterses' place, he happened to remember that the man, the killer, was wearing gloves of some kind, yellow rubber gloves."

"Do you place any particular importance on this, Detective Beaumont?"

"Only that the killer may be a known criminal with readily identifiable fingerprints."

Kramer gave a half smile designed to put me in my place. "I think most of us already figured that out. Anything else?"

He glanced around the room. No one on the task force seemed to have anything more to add, but now Captain Powell, who had slipped virtually unnoticed into the chair beside me, raised his hand. When Kramer acknowledged him, Powell strode to the front of the room. He too was wearing a badge with a somber black ribbon covering part of its face.

"In a few minutes, Sergeant Watkins, Detective Kramer, and I will be meeting with the Media Relations folks to decide what, if anything, from this meeting can be released to the public. There will be the usual holdouts, of course, so I don't need to tell you again that confidentiality is essential, but there's something else I do feel compelled to add.

"You are all aware that in the past few months there's been an increase in the number of threats made against the police officers of this city. One of our own is dead, and another, Detective Beaumont here, came very close to taking a bullet early yesterday morning. At this time, no firm link has been made between these last two incidents and the other threats, but it is certainly possible that they are connected.

"Therefore, as you conduct this investigation, I ask each and every one of you to exercise extreme caution. We are dealing with some very volatile and dangerous elements here, and I don't want to have to wear more than one piece of black ribbon on my badge at a time. Is that clear?"

It was clear, all right, and also extremely sobering. Twice now, in the course of the task force meeting, I had been reminded that I, too, had been a target. I had been so busy hustling around and being a worker bee that I had almost forgotten the bullet that had slammed into the wall behind me.

Remembering didn't improve my outlook on life, and it didn't change the color of my socks either.

People were fairly quick about clearing the room once the meeting was over. Sue Danielson had been close to the door. I had to push and shove my way through the crush to catch up with her by the time she reached the elevator. "Care to stop long enough for a cup of coffee?" I asked.

"Sure," she said. "Why not? But not in here. There's an espresso cart down on the street."

A few minutes later we found ourselves huddled under the building overhang on Third Avenue, drinking lattes and trying to stay out of a chill wind while Sue Danielson inhaled deeply on one of her Virginia Slims.

"What did you want to talk about, Beau?" she asked.

"Tell me exactly what the schools said when you talked to them."

"You want me to tell you what they said, or do you want my gut instinct?"

"Both."

She shrugged. "All right. You heard what I said upstairs, and that's the official line, but I think they're lying through their teeth. That's instinct, pure and simple. In each case, I didn't get an answer from the little lowly clerk who first took my call. In each case, I got passed on upstairs more than once before someone told me that no, they could neither confirm nor deny that person's presence. My impression, and it's nothing more than that, is that those people are actually there and enrolled in each of the schools, but they are absolutely under wraps and with some kind of flag on their records that dictates special handling. Bottom line, it sounds almost like some kind of witness-protection arrangement, except no one here at the department is willing to say so."

I nodded. That assessment sounded almost plausible. We stood there for a few moments in contemplative silence.

"Supposing that's true," I said finally, "what does it take to pull three or four fast-living, souped-up, hell-bent-for-election gang-type kids out of their home turf and get them back in school, any kind of school?"

Sue Danielson looked at me thoughtfully through an eddying plume of smoke. "Are you asking me?"

"You bet I'm asking you. You've got teenagers, don't you?"

"A club," she answered.

"You mean like Kiwanis or Rotary?"

She smiled. "No sir. I mean club as in baseball bat. A club and a miracle. In that order. Now I'd better get my ass moving and head for Garfield."

I smiled as I watched her go. Kramer may have given her an assignment designed to keep her away from traipsing after the student loans, but by accident he was sending her on another errand for which Sue Danielson was eminently qualified. If anyone could get usable information from an adolescent paperboy at Garfield High School, Detective Sue Danielson was definitely it.

CHAPTER 12

I took what was left of my latte, bought one for Big Al, and went back up to the fifth floor. Big Al makes fun of the numerous outdoor espresso carts that have sprung up like so many weeds all over downtown Seattle. He may joke about them, but he didn't turn down the latte.

"What's happening?" he asked.

On Captain Powell's orders, Big Al had been locked out of the official task force meeting. I knew it was bothering him.

"Nothing much to report," I told him. "Sue Danielson's on her way to interview a paperboy who may or may not have seen suspicious vehicles in the Weston neighborhood over the past few days. Kramer's pissed that we moved Junior Weston to another location without his express knowledge and permission. That's about it."

"Hell with him," Big Al muttered, then sipped his latte in brooding silence.

"Hey, by the way. Thanks for dragging me out of the sack this morning. If you hadn't, I would have missed the meeting completely, but I didn't think you were going to be here at all today. Aren't you supposed to be home? I distinctly remember hearing Captain Powell say something about administrative leave."

"You're right. I'm supposed to be home," he concurred, "but I can't take it. The only thing worse than being here doing nothing is being home doing nothing. At least here I have some idea of what's going on. At home, I'm completely in the dark. Not only that, Molly's in a real state over all this. I don't know what to do with her. She's always been the strong one, you know, thick-skinned and tough. When she bursts into tears every time I look at her, it drives me straight up the wall."

Truth be known, looking at Allen Lindstrom's haggard face was probably pretty hard on Molly as well. No doubt she was just as happy to have him out of the house as he was to be gone.

For a while, the two of us sat there quietly in our dingy little cubicle. A ring of latte had slopped out of the cup onto Big Al's desk top. Idly he ran one finger through the sticky stuff, leaving behind a blurred, milky finger painting on the worn laminate.

"They're saying Ben went bad," Al said eventually.

He left the words hanging in the air between us like an ominous cloud while he waited for me to say it wasn't so, to give him the comfort of a heartfelt denial. Unfortunately, I had seen copies of Ben Weston's loan applications with my own two eyes. I had also read through the voluminous rap sheets on Ben's nefarious cosigners.

"The jury's still out on that," I said noncommittally. "We'll have to wait and see."

Big Al slammed his massive fist onto the desk top while the paper cup with what was left of his latte danced wildly in place, spilling another ring of coffee.

"The hell we will!" he thundered. "Ben Weston's never going to get his shot at due process. He'll never have his day in court, but he'll be tried and convicted in the media anyway. You know that as well as I do. Once somebody gets labeled a bad cop, that reputation sticks. It never goes away, no matter what, not even when you're six feet under!"

He paused for a moment while the voices of detectives in nearby cubicles fell silent. Big Al Lindstrom wasn't the only one thinking those thoughts, but he was the only one voicing them. Aware that other people were listening, Al did his best to regain control.

"Think about it," he said, lowering his voice, forcing himself to speak calmly. "What if Ben didn't really break any rules? What if he just bent them real good? You said last night that Sue Danielson was checking with the various schools to find out whether or not those kids were actually enrolled. What did she find out?"

Big Al was clutching at straws. I didn't blame him, but I couldn't encourage him either.

"Nothing," I told him. "Not a damn thing. She ran into all kinds of bureaucratic tangles with each of the three registrars' offices. No one would tell her anything, one way or the other. They all said she'd have to have a court order if she wanted more information."

"So let's get one."

"Did you say 'let's'? How often do I have to tell you? It's not up to me, Al. That's not my end of the investigation, and it sure as hell isn't yours, either."

"Let me loose for half an hour in those goddamned administration buildings. I'll bet money I could find out."

"No doubt you could, but my advice is

don't. Leave it be. You were given strict orders to butt out, and that's what you'd better do."

"Since when did you become such an observer of rules and regulations, Detective Beaumont? Who appointed you guardian of the world?"

"You're my partner, Al. I don't want to see you do something stupid."

He thought about that for a moment or two and finally nodded. "Thanks," he said bleakly. "I guess."

Allen Lindstrom shoved a roll of black electrical tape across the top of his desk and rolled it onto mine. "Here," he said, "put some of this on your badge."

I tore off a hunk of tape, stuck it across the face of my badge, and then passed the roll back to him. Big Al stood up, pocketed the tape, picked up his latte, and wiped up the remaining spillage from his desk with a hankie.

"Where are you going?"

"Out," he said. "My main job here today is as a dispenser of black tape for the fifth floor. It's not much, but it sure as hell beats staying at home."

What he said sounded innocuous enough, but I didn't quite believe that was the whole story. "Stay out of trouble, Al," I cautioned.

"You betcha," he replied.

I wasn't convinced, but I figured Allen Lindstrom was a big boy, and I didn't take him to raise. I had my own agenda, one that needed attending to, starting with Dr. Emma Jackson. I called her first thing.

"Detective Beaumont here," I said. "Am I catching you at a bad time, Dr. Jackson?"

"Actually, I was on my way out the door. I have to stop by the hospital this morning for a few minutes."

She sounded composed, businesslike. It occurred to me that a doctor's patients don't necessarily stop being sick just because the doctor's child happens to have been murdered. We agreed that after her hospital visit we would meet at the Little Cheerful, a university area hangout known citywide for its homemade, onion-laden hash browns. I was halfway through my breakfast, hash browns included, when Emma Jackson showed up. She ordered black coffee and orange juice.

"Nothing else?" I asked.

"I'm not hungry."

Emma Jackson sat there stone-faced, watching me eat and making me feel terribly self-conscious. "The funeral arrangements are all handled?" I asked, trying to make casual conversation.

She nodded. "Reverend Walters is taking care of most of it, coordinating it really. I'm just not up to it, and neither is Harmon, Ben's father. He wanted to have a joint service."

"How big is Mount Zion?" I asked.

She frowned. "Big enough. Why?"

"Ben was a police officer," I explained. "There will probably be a fairly large contingent of law enforcement people from all over the state in attendance."

"Oh," she said. "I never thought of that. I doubt Ben's father did either."

I was probably way out of line asking the question, but if I did it, Big Al wouldn't have to.

"What about pallbearers?" I asked.

"What about them?"

"Usually, when a cop dies, a contingent of fellow officers carries the casket. We consider it a duty and an honor."

Dr. Emma Jackson's eyes met and held mine above the rim of her coffee cup. "I don't think so," she said. "Not this time. Adam's father was a cop. He was also a rat. I won't have cops for pallbearers and neither will Harmon Weston."

"It'll break my partner's heart."

"Why?"

"His name's Detective Lindstrom . . ."

"He has another name, doesn't he?" she interrupted.

"Big Al."

"I know about him," she said, "and I know he was a good friend of Ben's, but Harmon and I agreed, no cops whatsoever, no exceptions. Now let's get down to business. I don't have much time."

Leaving the last few crisp crumbs of the hash browns languishing in traces of egg yolk, I pushed my plate aside. "Thanks for squeezing me in," I said. "I more than half expected to have to take a number and get in line to talk to you this morning."

Emma frowned, taking umbrage. "Are you being sarcastic because I'm not taking time off, Detective Beaumont? I can't afford to. Medical school rules don't allow for residents' children being murdered. It's not supposed to happen that way."

I flushed in confusion. "That wasn't what I meant at all."

"Maybe you'd better explain."

"I expected you'd be busy with calls from reporters and from some of the other detectives down at the department as well."

"No. No one called except you."

"I don't understand that," I said. "The other detectives should have been in touch with you the minute they got out of the task force meeting."

There was the slightest softening in the anger-hardened contours of her face. She looked at me and shook her head, smiling sadly. "You're really very naïve, aren't you, Detective Beaumont? You don't understand at all."

"Understand what?" I demanded.

"Adam was only a little boy," she said softly, "and African American besides. His death is hardly newsworthy. And I don't expect people down at the Seattle PD to pay any particular attention. In fact, I guess I'm surprised you do."

For the first time since meeting her, I had the smallest glimmer of what made Dr. Emma Jackson the way she was.

"Your son was murdered," I told her. "And I'm a Homicide detective. It's my job to find out who did it, regardless. I care."

She nodded. "I know," she said. "Ask your questions, Detective Beaumont. I'll do my best to answer them."

The waitress stopped by and poured more coffee. The interruption gave us both a break, some emotional breathing space. Once she left I went about getting the interview on track.

"Did you check on the dog bite?"

"I tried to, but I didn't turn up anything

at all. Chances are, if the man was bitten, it was only a superficial wound, one that didn't require stitches or medical attention."

"I'm not surprised. A wound serious enough for stitches might have interfered with the killer's ability to function."

She nodded. "That doesn't seem to have been the case, does it."

Emma Jackson was a curious and puzzling mixture, forever switching back and forth between dispassionate professional and grieving mother. From moment to moment, it was impossible to predict which one of the two would surface.

"No," I agreed.

"If you already had a pretty fair idea that was the case to begin with, why did you send me off on a wild-goose chase? Was the plan to keep me occupied and out of your hair?"

When it comes to dealing with difficult women, especially smart difficult women, it's often best to fall back on some of my mother's sage advice about honesty being the best policy.

"You've got me dead to rights," I admitted. "I wanted to keep you out of my hair, but I've changed my mind about you."

"How so?"

"Some things have surfaced in this investigation that make me think you may be able to be very helpful."

Dr. Emma Jackson eyed me intently. "What kinds of things?" she asked.

"You're going to have to bear with me, Dr. Jackson. To begin with, I'm going to ask some tough questions. Please be patient and don't expect any answers in return, at least not right away." She started to voice an objection, but I held up my hand to stop her.

"I'm going to ask you things about Ben and Shiree Weston's relationship that only someone like you, only a close family friend, would have any knowledge of. Those things may or may not have some future bearing on the case. If they don't, whatever you tell me stays between us. If they do, then I'll do my best to protect you as the source of whatever revelations may be pertinent."

"It sounds as though you expect some of these 'revelations,' as you call them, to be damaging, either to Ben or Shiree."

I nodded.

"And what's in it for me?"

"Not much, I'm afraid. All I can hope to promise you is a better chance at catching your son's killer."

Her eyes narrowed. "Not Ben Weston's killer?"

"I'm the only detective who's been officially assigned to your son's case," I said quietly. "And by solving that one, we'll automatically solve the others as well, but my primary responsibility is to you and to Adam."

She gave me a long, searching look, and it was clear from the expression on her face that my answer to her question had been correct.

"What do you want to know?" she asked.

"Everything, Dr. Jackson. I'll need to know every single detail you can tell me."

"You can call me Emma," she said.

I knew then that I had won big. Emma Jackson was going to be working with me on this one and not with Detective Paul Kramer. Maybe he and I really don't work on the same team.

"Thanks," I said. "My friends call me Beau."

We spent the better part of the next two hours together, drinking cup after cup of Little Cheerful coffee. Gradually Ben and Shiree Weston's story trickled out. At first it seemed like a fairy tale, like something too good to be true, and maybe that was part of what had gone wrong.

According to Emma Jackson, Ben and Shiree Garvey had known each other vaguely from church, but they hadn't really become well acquainted until that critical period of time in Ben's life when his first wife, Vondelle, was dying of cancer. With his wife sick, Ben had struggled desperately to keep all the various balls in the air — his job, his kids, the regular bills, and the medical bills. When he found himself inevitably sinking into a morass of past-due notices, Reverend Homer Walters sent him to Shiree Garvey at the Mount Zion Federal Credit Union for some much needed help and counseling.

Shiree had worked with him and with the creditors through the cash flow crunch, helping to smooth things over until insurance payments and hospital bills coalesced into an understandable whole. With Shiree's guidance, the financial picture began to improve, even while Vondelle's physical condition steadily worsened. Gradually, almost without either one of them really noticing, Shiree Garvey began assuming more and more responsibilities in the Weston household, helping to care for the children while Ben spent long nights haunting hospital corridors. By the time Vondelle died, Shiree had become emotionally indispensable to all of them. She and Ben married six months later.

"That's what hurt Shiree so much, you know," Emma said. "And I don't blame her."

"What?" I had no idea.

"He never ran around on Vondelle, not during all the years she was sick. He was true to her to the very end. He and Shiree were nothing but friends until after Vondelle was dead and gone. So Shiree couldn't understand what was going on when he started messing around behind her back."

"Do you know who with?"

"No, not yet. But I will. You just wait and see. Somebody will spill the beans, and when they do, you and I will know where to go next."

So Emma Jackson was still convinced that the killer was a jealous husband, but then she didn't know anything about the loan applications either.

"Were Ben and Shiree having money troubles?"

"You mean recently? No. No way. Not them. Shiree Garvey Weston knew how to budget and how to squeeze the very last pinch out of each and every penny. Ben never had another moment's worth of money worries from the time Shiree started handling the bills. Why are you asking about money?"

I wanted Emma Jackson's help, but I didn't want to tell her everything I knew. "Sometimes that's one of the reasons marriages go bad," I said evasively.

"Not this one," Emma declared with yet another flare of anger. "Ben and Shiree Weston's marriage went bad because Ben was too damn stupid to recognize a good thing when he had it."

CHAPTER 13

On my way back to the department I slipped into a noontime brown-bag AA meeting in a downtown Methodist church. It's not a meeting I attend often, so I could come and go without being trapped into a long-drawn-out post-meeting conversation as sometimes happens. When I got back to the fifth floor, Curtis Bell was comfortably ensconced at my desk chatting earnestly with Big Al Lindstrom. Curt looked cheerful, Big Al thunderous.

Curt scrambled out of my chair as soon as I appeared in the doorway. "Didn't mean to take over your desk," he apologized, "but I've been playing phone tag with that attorney of yours. I wanted to check with you and see if we'd be able to get together some time over the weekend. The attorney sounded like he wanted to be in on the appointment."

"Watch out for this guy," Big Al warned.

"If you ask me, he's nothing but a god-damned ambulance chaser. He even tried to get an appointment with me."

Curtis shrugged off Detective Lindstrom's comment as though it was nothing more than a good-humored dig, but from the sour expression on Big Al's face I guessed he wasn't really kidding.

"Whatever it takes to get people to listen to reason," Curtis said with an easy grin. "After all, there's nothing like a couple of bullets whizzing past a guy's ears to give him a sense of his own mortality, right, Beaumont?"

"No doubt about it," I said, and meant it.

"So what's this guy's name? Your attorney?"

"Ralph Ames."

"Yeah, him. He said we'd either have to do it sometime over this weekend, or we'd have to wait a whole month."

"That's right. He's only here until Monday or Tuesday this trip. I forget which."

"I don't understand why he has to be included in the first place. What's the big deal? I mean, can't the two of us just get together and talk?"

"Believe me, if it's got something to do with me and money, Ralph Ames is in on it from the very beginning, or it doesn't happen. That's what I pay him for."

"Well okay then," Curtis agreed reluctantly. "When?"

"Hold on," I told him. "I'll call Ralph and ask."

Picking up the phone, I dialed my home number. It was shortly after one, and I wondered if Ralph might once more be entertaining his noontime lady friend. The phone rang, but instead of reaching either Ralph or my answering machine, my eardrum was pierced by a high-pitched, raucous screech. Thinking I must have dialed wrong, I tried again only to have the same thing happen.

"What's the matter?" Big Al asked. "Nobody home?"

"My phone must be out of order."

I dialed the operator and told her about the difficulty on my line. "Before I report the trouble to Repair, sir, let me try it for you," the operator said.

This time, I had brains enough to hold the phone away from my head before another ear-splitting squawk came zinging through the receiver.

"You must have left your fax machine hooked up," the operator told me.

"Fax machine?" I echoed. "I don't even own a fax machine, so how could it be hooked up? There must be some mistake."

The operator's tone grew a bit testy. "Sir," she said, "there is no mistake. If the number you gave me is correct, then, whether or not you own a machine, there is definitely one attached to your telephone outlet at the present time."

Good old "Gadget Ralph" was obviously up to his old tricks again. "No doubt you're right," I told the operator. "It is hooked up, and I probably do own it. I just didn't know I owned it."

"That's quite all right, sir," she returned, sounding slightly mollified. "Glad to be of service."

"Well?" Curtis asked when I put down the phone.

"You'll have to wait for me to get back to you, after I get hold of Ralph and check his schedule. Until then, I can't make any promises. And as far as I'm concerned, if this case heats up over the weekend, my own schedule may go out the window. I could end up working the whole time."

Curtis nodded. "I understand Ben Weston's funeral is tomorrow. It sounds like the brass are treating his death like a line of duty, so I guess the force will be out in force regardless of . . ." Catching sight of the expression on Big Al's face, Curtis Bell backed away from the pun and allowed his voice to dwindle uneasily away.

"Regardless of what?" Allen Lindstrom demanded.

"You know. Everyone's talking about it — about Ben and whatever it was he was up to."

"Get your butt out of here," Big Al ordered. "Who the hell are you to say it wasn't line of duty?"

Curtis Bell looked at the other man appraisingly. "Come on, Al. Lighten up. I didn't mean anything by it. People are talking, that's all. Everybody down in CCI is hoping you guys will find something that will exonerate him. Ben Weston was one hell of a guy. Nobody wants to see his name dragged through the mud."

But Big Al was in no mood to be placated. "Like hell they don't. Get the fuck out of here, Curtis, and quit gossiping. We've got work to do. Besides, aren't there rules against conducting private business on company time?"

"Hey, I'm off duty this morning," Curtis Bell returned, but he edged toward the door all the same. "Call me, Beau. About the appointment, I mean. After you hear from Ralph Banes."

Ralph Banes indeed!

As Curtis took off down the hallway, we heard the sounds of a slight scuffle followed by a mumbled apology. Moments later, Ron Peters and his wheelchair appeared in the doorway. He waved at Big Al and nodded to me. "What on earth did you two say to that guy?" Ron asked. "He almost ran me down."

"I told him to get out of my face," Big Al said morosely. "And he did."

Ron studied Big Al for a long moment. "I probably would, too," he said. "How are you doing, Al?"

Detective Lindstrom dropped his gaze and stared at the floor. "All right, I guess," he said.

"They told me upstairs that you were handing out the tape. I could have gotten it from somebody up there, but I'm a fifth floor kind of guy, Al, and I wanted to wear fifth floor tape. I also wanted to tell you how sorry I was."

Big Al nodded his thanks and reached into his pocket, where he retrieved his somewhat depleted roll of tape. He tore off a hunk and passed it to Ron, who dutifully stuck it to his own badge.

"And as for you," Peters said, turning to me, "I'm real happy that bullet didn't come any closer. If it had, we'd all be wearing two pieces of tape instead of just one."

"That's an old joke, Ron. I've already heard it once this morning from Captain Powell. Let's just leave it at that, shall we?"

Ron Peters looked from Big Al to me and back again. "Well, it's certainly not sweetness and light around here, is it. I take it you two are up to your eyeballs in this Weston case?" he asked.

"Actually, we're not," I told him. "You're looking at the Weston Family Task Force second string. I'm about to write a report on my interview with the mother of the one unrelated victim. That's my part of the case, and I'm expected to stick to it. And, as you've already heard, Al's assignment today is to hand out black tape. He's locked out of the investigation because he was friends with several of the victims, and I'm sidetracked because Paul Kramer hates my guts."

"Sounds almost as political as working in Media Relations," Ron said with a half-hearted grin that wasn't really funny.

Ron and I had been partners in Homicide before a permanent spinal injury put him in his chair. After long months of rehabilitation, he had come back to the department as a Media Relations officer, but I knew he longed to be back home with the detectives on the fifth floor, where the action is. I couldn't blame him for that. For my money, working with murderers is often a whole lot less hazardous to your health than working with reporters.

"By the way," Ron said, "that's another reason I'm here. My job. It seems Maxwell Cole has turned over a new leaf. He says he understands the Weston Family Task Force guidelines. For a change, he's not trying to go around them. He wants me to get a quote from you — a direct quote, if possible — about how it feels to have dodged out of the way of that stray bullet yesterday morning."

Max is an old fraternity brother turned columnist and long-term media adversary. He went to work for the local morning rag, the *Seattle Post-Intelligencer,* about the same time I hired on with the Seattle Police Department. We've been on each other's backs and down each other's throats ever since. He's the least favorite practitioner of my least favorite profession.

"Max wants a direct quote?" I asked.

Ron nodded. "You know him. He wants something short and punchy, but fit for publication in a family newspaper."

"Tell him 'good.' "

"Good?"

"That's right. You asked me how it feels, and you can tell him my answer is 'good.' Period. That should be short and punchy enough for Maxwell Cole."

Ron Peters grinned, a real grin this time. The shadow of a smile even flickered across Big Al's somber face.

"Somehow I don't think it's exactly what he had in mind," Ron said, "but it'll have to do."

I figured that now that he had what he wanted, Ron would head straight back upstairs. Instead, he moved his chair closer to our desks. "Okay, you two," he said. "All bullshit aside, I want you to tell me what's really going on."

"With what?"

"With the task force. Believe me, I know the party line. I'm in charge of disseminating the party line — that Ben Weston and his family died in an apparently gang-related multiple homicide. But scuttlebutt has it that Ben himself is being investigated for some allegedly illegal financial activities — conduct unbecoming an officer, they're calling it. I want to know the straight scoop."

Big Al Lindstrom cut loose with one of his half English–half Norwegian streams of profanity. Having grown up in the Ballard section of Seattle, I may not know enough adolescent Norwegian to be able to cuss fluently in a second language, but I understand it well enough.

"Hold it down, Al," I cautioned. "You don't want Kramer or Watty to hear you carrying on like this."

"But isn't it just what I told you? If this gets out, and it's bound to, they'll end up trying Ben in the press, even though he's the one who's dead, for Christ's sakes! They'll make out like it's all his fault that somebody killed him."

"Maybe gangs did do it," I told Ron, "but, if so, it sure as hell wasn't the usual gang-type hit."

Ron Peters nodded. "That's what I thought," he said. "Unless the gangs have hired some retired Marine Corps drill instructor to do their dirty work."

"You've seen Baker's autopsies then?"

"I probably wasn't supposed to, but, yes, I have. And I've seen some of Kramer's stuff too, and that's what's got me so puzzled. Why's he so hot and bothered about that bank loan stuff? I mean, if I were a police officer who was going to risk breaking the law, I'd sure as hell pick something more lucrative than student loans."

"What are you saying?" I asked.

Ron Peters looked me right in the eye.

"I'm convinced those loan applications are legitimate," he answered. "They're too damn corny not to be. Have any of those kids been found yet?"

"Not as far as I know."

"But I thought Detective Danielson was working on that."

"She was, but she struck out completely when she got as far as the various registrars' offices. They stonewalled her. Now Kramer's pulled her away from that to go talk to some stray paperboy, an alleged witness, down at Garfield."

"And he didn't assign anybody else in her place with the colleges?"

"I doubt it."

"Why not?"

"Because it was my idea, for one thing," I told them. "Like I said before, Kramer hates my guts."

Big Al nodded. "There's always that, Beau," he agreed, "but that's not all. Kramer doesn't want to see his pet theory blown out of the water. Those loan applications are the only chinks he can find in Ben Weston's armor, and he doesn't want to let loose of them."

"Maybe," Ron Peters asserted quietly, "someone will have to pry them out of his hands."

Saying that, Ron reached behind his chair, opened the knapsack that hangs there for ease of carrying things, and pulled out a sheaf of paper — thirty pages or so of continuous-feed computer printout. He handed the papers over to me.

"What's this?" I asked.

"Last summer, a reporter from the Los Angeles Times called and asked me about the gang-related data base he had somehow heard we were working on up here. Supposedly, it was a data base analysis of local and visiting gang members and their various arrests and activities. He wanted to know how much of Seattle's gang problem had been imported from California and Chicago.

"I don't know how a reporter from L.A. heard about it, because I had a hell of a time tracking it down. As far as I could discover, no one had been officially assigned to do that kind of study and Ben Weston wasn't exactly going around bragging about it, but eventually the trail led me to him. It turned out he was working on the project at home, on his own computer, on his own time."

"That was well before he transferred into CCI, wasn't it?" Big Al asked.

Ron Peters nodded. "Right. One of those labors of love, I guess. When I asked him about it, he showed me this — a preliminary copy of what he had done so far — but he told me he wanted to keep a low profile, that he didn't want a lot of publicity on the project. So I squelched the story with the reporter, and since he didn't need it back, I ended up keeping this. I had forgotten all about it until this morning. When I remembered, I had to dig through months of accumulated paper to find it. I've spent the last hour and a half going over it with a fine-tooth comb."

"And?"

"Remember, this go-down is nine or ten months old. Between then and now, Ben transferred into the gang unit and started working on a similar but officially sanctioned project on a full-time basis. I'm sure he must have used the information he had previously gathered as a starting point, but I'm sure he's added a great deal."

"Have you looked at what's there now?"

"No. Just this, but even so, even from way last summer, two of the four names on the loan applications are already here."

"No kidding. Which ones?"

"Dathan Collins and Leonard Washburn."

I scanned through the list far enough to locate Dathan Collins's name. The information on him gave his given name, his parents' names and addresses, his street name, his gang affiliation, his schooling background, his girlfriend's name and address as well as a brief synopsis of his rap sheet. The intelligence Ben Weston had collected was surprisingly thorough. I passed the papers on to Big Al, who studied them in turn before passing them back to Ron.

"This is pretty impressive," I said. "It's like the complete *Encyclopaedia Britannica* analysis of Seattle's street gangs. Where'd he get all his information? Did he do all this on his own before he went to work for the gang unit?"

Ron nodded. "That's right. It's a hell of a lot of work. My guess is that the other two names will show up in the computer along with whatever else he's done since then."

"We've got to get a look at that file," I said.

Ron Peters grinned. "My sentiments exactly. I tried, but it didn't work. Ben's stuff is stored in one of the department's secured PCs. You can't call it up without proper authorization — which I can't get because I'm in Media Relations — and/or Ben's personal identification number — which, of course, we don't have either."

"If it's a number," Big Al chimed in, "we can get it. That's easy."

"Easy? How come?"

"Ben Weston was a smart man, but he

couldn't remember numbers worth a shit. Most people can remember the numbers they use most often off the tops of their heads, but Ben had to have them all written down — his PIN from the bank, his telephone credit card number, even Shiree's work phone number. He kept them all in that little directory in his Day-Timer. If he had to have an ID number to get in and out of the computer, we'll find that one there, too, along with all the others. I'd bet money on it."

"Great," Ron Peters said. "So where's the Day-Timer?"

There's an old saying about how you can lead a horse to water, but you can't make him drink. With Homicide detectives, it's just the opposite. You can kick them off the fifth floor, but you can't necessarily get them out of the habit of being detectives. Ron may have been booted upstairs into Media Relations, but his mind and instincts were still those of a working homicide cop.

"Ask Janice Morraine," I said. "The last I saw, there was a Day-Timer with Ben Weston's initials on it lying on the floor of his bedroom."

"I can't ask Janice Morraine for the time of day," Ron Peters replied. "I'm not a detective, remember? How about if one of you ask her?"

"No can do, either," Big Al grumbled morosely. "I'm aced out of it completely — Captain Powell's orders." He glanced at me. "You're not much better off yourself. You're supposed to be doing Adam Jackson. Maybe you'd better pass it along to Kramer."

"Like hell!" I said. The three of us stared at one another. In our own way, we were all benched second stringers. We had a perfectly good piece of information, but no above-board way of acting on it.

My telephone rang just then, and the caller was none other than Sue Danielson. "Hi, Beau. I wanted to get back to you. I talked to that kid, the one down at Garfield. He really is a witness, at least to your part of the incident, and I thought you'd like to know about it."

"Any information at all is welcome," I said. "Want me to come to you or do you want to come to me?"

"Neither. Not here on the floor, anyway. Detective Kramer would have a fit if he saw us together. I missed lunch today. How about if you meet me at that little Mexican joint on Marion, Mexico Lindo, I think it's called."

After my Little Cheerful threshing-crew-type breakfast, I wasn't quite up to *dos to-*

cos or even *uno* for that matter, but the offer of information was irresistible.

"See you there in ten minutes," I told her, hanging up and standing up, all in the same motion.

"So where are you going?"

"That was Sue Danielson on the phone. She wants to meet so she can tell me what some kid told her about the guy who took the shot at me." As I said the words, the glimmer of an idea came into my head. "Who knows? Maybe we can arrange some kind of trade on this computer thing."

Big Al looked surprised. "Are you sure? She's Paul Kramer's partner."

"It's not a social disease," I countered. "You were stuck with him once for a case or two, and so was I. Remember how it felt?"

Allen Lindstrom nodded. "Coulda killed him myself."

"I rest my case," I returned. "I'm off to meet the lady for lunch. Wish me luck. The rest of us may be benched, but she's not, at least not yet."

CHAPTER 14

It was drizzling lightly as I set out up a crowded Third Avenue sidewalk on my way to Marion and the quaint, upstairs Mexican restaurant frequented by downtown-type Mexican food freaks.

As I walked, I couldn't help feeling a little guilty. Sue had called out of courtesy offering to volunteer information she was under no obligation to share with me. In return, here I was planning to use her for my own underhanded ends. That didn't seem quite fair, but I wanted to be part of learning whatever could be learned from Ben Weston's computer file. Given a choice, Paul Kramer sure as hell wouldn't clue me in. Because she's a straightforward woman, Sue Danielson was the weak link in Kramer's chain of command. By the time I reached the restaurant I had more or less convinced myself that in this case, the ends really did justify the means.

I made good time, but Sue was already there, seated in the smoking section of the restaurant and puffing away like a chimney long before I arrived. A hostess with an authentically thick Mexican accent led me to the table and tried to tempt me with a margarita. Fortunately, I was wearing my margarita repellent.

"So are we having a secret rendezvous?" I asked Sue teasingly, with what I hoped passed for a mischievous grin. "Do you think Detective Kramer had either one of us tailed?"

She didn't laugh. In fact, she never even cracked a smile. "This is no joke, Beau. What's with you two guys, anyway? When I mentioned to him that I intended to tell you what I'd learned from the paperboy, Kramer pitched a fit all over that brand-new private office of his."

"It's just a little personality conflict," I assured her. "Nothing serious, but the animosity cuts both ways, if that's any consolation. I don't like him any better than he likes me."

"Great!" she said, shaking her head in disgust. "Some men never grow up, do they. Is this another one of those locker room mine's-bigger-than-yours situations?"

It pains me to admit that she was probably fairly close to the mark, but I refrained from dignifying her comment with a reply, and she left it at that.

"By the way, I hope you like Mexican food," she added.

"You go right ahead," I told her. "I'll just have coffee. What's up?"

The waitress came by. Sue ordered a combination plate and a Coke. Although close to my limit, I ordered more black coffee. "Tell me about the paperboy," I said. "I want to hear all about him."

"Have you ever had a paper route?" she asked.

It was a typically female way of starting a conversation from way out in left field without directly tackling the issue at hand. Over the years, however, I've managed to develop considerable patience, and I played right along.

"Not me. I worked in a movie theater as a kid — hawking tickets and popcorn and jujubes. I've been a night owl all my life. I never could have roused myself at some ungodly hour to go deliver morning papers, and an evening route would have screwed up my extracurricular activities. How about you?"

"I had one," she replied, "back in Cincinnati. A city's funny at that hour of the morning. It's so still and peaceful when you're the only person out and around. You wander up and down streets and through neighborhoods while cars are still parked wherever people happen to leave them overnight. You know who gets up first, who will already be up and waiting for a paper by the time you drop it on the porch. You see all kinds of things, including some things you shouldn't. Just before the sun comes up, I used to pretend I was invisible."

She paused and studied me with a searching look. "Am I making sense?"

I bit back the temptation to tell her to hurry up and get to the point. "More or less," I said.

"Anyway, this kid from Garfield — Bob Case is his name — has had the same *Seattle Post-Intelligencer* route for three years. He says he used to see Ben Weston out running every morning at the same time, rain or shine. He claims to know most of the cars and drivers that belong in the neighborhood and what times they come and go. He says that in the past few weeks there's been a lot of extra traffic in the early-morning hours."

"What kind of traffic?"

"He mentioned three in particular. One is a late-model Lexus with a cellular radio antenna."

"That doesn't help much. I don't remem-

221

ber the last time I saw a Lexus without a cellular phone, do you? All the ones I've seen do."

Sue glowered at me. "Let me finish. He says he got a real close look at it the morning after the murders. Too close, actually. It almost ran him down just half a minute or so after whoever it was took a potshot at you. He heard the noise and thought it was a backfire until the guy almost ran him and his bicycle off the street three blocks away from Ben Weston's house."

"How come it took him until now to come forward?" I asked.

"He's scared, Beau. He's out on that paper route by himself every single morning. He's afraid if whoever it was hears he's gone to the cops, they'll come back looking for him next. He made the mistake of telling his mother about it, and she called us."

From a strictly survival standpoint, I had to admit the kid had the right idea. Paperboys on bicycles are sitting ducks for drive-by shootings. I took out my notebook. "What's his name again?"

"Bob. Robert actually. Robert Case."

"Well, Bob Case is probably right to be scared. I don't hold it against him. Did he get a look at the driver?"

"Not really. He said it was a young black

man, but he claims he didn't get a good enough look to give us a positive ID."

"That figures. My guess is even if he did, he wouldn't tell us. License number?"

"Negative on that too."

"So we have what is commonly known as a semi-eyewitness. What about the rest of the unexplained traffic you were telling me about? The news about someone seeing that speeding Lexus moments after the shooting is great, but what did he say about other vehicles?"

"Three. One is a Honda CRX driven by a young black male. On several occasions, Case saw this one driving along beside Ben Weston. The driver and Ben seemed to be chatting while Ben jogged, but the last time he saw that one was maybe as long as a month or two ago. The second is a late-model white Toyota Tercel, driven by a Caucasian male."

Sue Danielson stopped talking and made no indication that she was going to continue.

"You said three," I prodded. "What about the last one?"

"A patrol car." She said the words softly and then waited for my reaction. I didn't disappoint.

"A patrol car!" I exploded. "You mean as

in a Seattle PD blue-and-white?"

Sue Danielson nodded grimly. "That's exactly what I mean. One of our own. With a uniformed driver."

"Well," I said, "what's wrong with that? That's not so unusual. There are cop cars in every neighborhood in the city at all hours of the day and night."

I said the words, but even as I voiced my objection, I remembered what Janice Morraine had said about the Flex-cufs and the possibility of the killer being a cop. First the cuffs and now a patrol car. I let Sue Danielson continue on with her story, hoping my face didn't betray everything that was going on in my head.

"According to Bob Case, it's highly unusual in his neighborhood, especially at that hour of the morning. Except for Ben Weston, who happened to live there, other cops tend to show up only when somebody hollers 'cop.' The rest of the time they pretty much leave well enough alone. In other words, there's usually zero police presence."

I didn't like the troubled look in Sue Danielson's eyes or the stubborn set to her chin, and I wanted there to be some reasonably innocent explanation for the appearance of that patrol car, just as there had been for the Flex-cufs.

"Maybe the officers in the car were friends of Ben's from Patrol. Maybe they stopped off now and then to chew the fat for a while before their shifts ended."

Sue Danielson was prepared for that one, and she lobbed it right back at me. "That's what Bob Case thought too, until the morning he saw Ben headed down the street in one direction and the patrol car pulled into the alley and stopped behind Ben's house. The car made zero effort to follow Ben, and the kid thought it was odd. So do I."

"Surveillance maybe? Had Ben or anyone else reported any recent break-ins or car prowls?" I asked.

"No," Sue Danielson responded. "I wondered that myself. I already checked."

"So what do you think?"

"I've been wrestling with it ever since I found out. I figure it could go any number of ways."

I could see several myself. "Maybe whoever was in the patrol car suspected Ben was up to something, and they wanted to catch him at it," I suggested blandly, already knowing that even Patrol would be more subtle than that. "Or maybe they had a tip that something serious was about to go down, and they were trying to protect him."

"You're dead wrong about one thing," Sue

said, "and that's the 'they' part of the equation. According to Bob Case, there was only one person in that car every single time he saw it — a male Caucasian."

"But graveyard uniformed officers only operate in pairs," I objected.

She nodded. "I know. I thought at first that maybe someone had called in Internal Investigations Squad, but they usually operate in plain clothes and in unmarked vehicles, don't they?"

"Most of the time. Did you call up to Internal Investigations and ask?"

Sue Danielson shook her head. "I didn't have enough nerve. I've never talked with anyone from IIS, and I'm still not sure if there's anything here worth bothering them about."

Considering the presence of both the Flex-cufs and the mysterious patrol car, I thought there was, but I wanted to play those cards fairly close to my chest.

"With what we've found out in the past twenty-four hours," I said, "especially the bank loan thing, I'd be surprised if they weren't interested. As a matter of fact, maybe they already were. That would take care of the patrol car problem in a minute."

"Except for what you said before, that IIS

wouldn't send someone out in a blue-and-white."

"So where does that leave us?"

Sue pushed her plate away, flattened her napkin, and pulled out a pen. She reminded me of my old-time Ballard High School football coaches, hanging around Zesto's, drawing *X*'s and *O*'s on innumerable paper napkins.

"We have at least two, maybe three players," Sue said, explaining for her own benefit as well as for mine. "The black guy in the Lexus and the black guy in the CRX who may or may not be one and the same, ditto with the white guy from the patrol car and the one from the Tercel. Since he was fleeing the scene of a crime, it's safe to assume the guy in the Lexus is also a bad guy. As far as the other two are concerned, it's anybody's guess."

I felt obliged to add my two cents' worth. "And is the guy in the patrol car really a cop or is he somebody masquerading as a cop?"

"If he isn't, how would he get hold of the car?" she asked.

"If he's fake, the vehicle could be too."

"I suppose," she agreed reluctantly, but she didn't sound entirely convinced. Neither was I, but the idea of an imposter posing as a cop sounded a lot more acceptable than the other alternative of a police officer perpetrator.

"What do you think?" I asked her.

"Wild-assed guess?"

"Yes."

"I didn't know Ben Weston personally, but from what people have told me about him, if he could go bad, then anybody in the department could go bad, you and me included."

Detective Danielson's bleak assessment wasn't that far from my own. She put her pen down and pushed her napkin with its good guy-bad guy notations in my direction. "Any additions or corrections to the minutes?"

"No, you've pretty well covered it all."

"Any suggestions about what to do next?"

That last question gave me the opening I had been looking for, a way to bring up the question of Ben Weston's computer project.

"It would help a lot if we knew for sure about Ben Weston, wouldn't it?" I suggested tentatively.

In a homicide investigation, sometimes the small and seemingly unimportant answers to side questions lead to answers on the important ones as well. Sue grabbed the bait and ran with it. "It sure as hell would."

"Has anyone talked to you about what exactly Ben was doing in the gang unit?"

"Not specifically, no."

"Doesn't it seem like they should? I found out today, almost by accident, that he's been building a gang profile data base. It includes all kinds of information on the various gang members — where they came from, what their affiliations are, that kind of thing. He was doing it all on the CCI computer."

"Sounds reasonable," she said.

"Maybe. Today I saw a very early version of that data base, something he was doing on his own long before he ever transferred into CCI. Two of the bank loan names were on even that early version. We need to get a look at what he's been doing recently. Maybe then we'll be able to sort out a pattern or see some connection."

"Are you sure Detective Kramer hasn't already done this?"

"Maybe, but I doubt it. Kramer's got his hands full. He might not even have thought of it, but I'll tell you one thing, if I ask him to look into it, it'll be a cold day in hell before it actually gets done. Remember the court orders?"

Sue looked at me warily. "So why are you telling me? Do you want me to go see if I can get you a copy of whatever it is?"

I tried to look as innocent as possible. "You're still supposed to be locating those missing cosigners, aren't you? And having their families' names and telephone numbers couldn't hurt that process, could it? In fact, it might just make your job a whole lot easier."

She smiled then, for the first time since we'd entered the restaurant. "Men are so damn transparent it's disgusting. This is still part and parcel of what's going on between you and Kramer, isn't it? You're afraid to give him the information for fear he'll ignore it. And you think I'm dumb enough to jump into the cross fire."

"Are you?"

She grinned back at me. "I prefer to call it curiosity rather than stupidity, if you don't mind."

"Which is why you're going to be one hell of a detective one of these days, if you aren't already."

I was deliberately baiting her, expecting a little on-the-job male-female give-and-take. Instead, Sue nodded and raised her Coke glass in acknowledgment, ignoring the teasing and accepting my comment as a compliment.

"And what do you suggest we do about IIS?" she asked. "Call them in? Leave them out of it?"

"That's a sticky one. I would imagine they're already looking into the Ben Weston matter. Their concern will be what exactly he was up to and whether or not any other police officers were involved. For right now, though, until we get a better handle on your 'players,' as you call them, I don't think we should call the Double I's in. It would be premature, and it just might backfire."

She nodded. "That's exactly why I wanted to talk to you about it, Detective Beaumont. I figured if anybody could give me the benefit of the long view, it was you."

I'm sure Sue Danielson meant her comment as a compliment — at least I think she did — but there's a certain amount of ego damage that goes along with being considered the ancient, all-knowing, and time-honored dispenser of the long view. When she offered to buy my coffee, I let her, and I left the restaurant feeling more butt-sprung than ever.

We walked back to the Public Safety Building together. Sue headed for CCI while I went back to my little cubicle in Homicide. Big Al was gone, giving me some working peace and quiet for a change. I was just getting a good start on the Emma Jackson report when the phone rang. It was Sue.

I could tell from the sound of her voice that something was seriously wrong.

"What's going on?" I asked.

"Meet me on the eleventh floor," she answered tersely. "We're going to IIS for sure, now, and I do mean now. I tried to get hold of Kramer to tell him, but he's not around, and neither is Watty. I don't think we should sit on this any longer. It's too important."

"For Christ's sake, Sue, tell me what's happening?"

"I had to jump through all kinds of hoops, but I finally got Ben Weston's password and current verification question from the only person who supposedly has it, Kyle Lehman, the department's computer systems operator. Captain Nichols, the head of CCI, woke him out of a sound sleep to do it. We logged into Ben's directory on the computer just a few minutes ago."

I didn't like the way she verbally underlined the word "supposedly." "And?" I prompted.

"Between one forty-five and two-fifteen on the morning of April fifteenth, all but two of the files in Ben Weston's directory were opened and closed."

"What are you saying?"

"I'm saying that within hours of Ben

Weston's death, someone went through his secured computer directory in CCI. The directory shows log-on and log-off times. In each case the file was open for less than a minute."

"Was anything changed?"

"I don't think so."

"But someone was looking for something."

"Someone inside Seattle PD was looking for something," Sue Danielson corrected. "You know yourself. The computer operates on a secured system. You don't get into it without having the proper passwords as well as coming up with all the right answers to the verifying questions."

"What do you suppose they were looking for?" I asked.

"And did they find it?" Sue added.

Of course, that changed everything. If someone had tampered with Ben Weston's files on a secured computer system located in the Public Safety Building within hours of his murder, then it was definitely time for someone to pay a visit to Internal Investigations. High time.

"You're absolutely right, Sue," I said. "See you on the eleventh floor just as soon as that damned slow-boat-to-China elevator can get us there."

CHAPTER 15

In my opinion, the Internal Investigations Section is a whole lot like a plumber's friend — one of life's necessary evils. A bathroom plunger isn't something you're particularly proud of owning. You don't wave it around and brag about it, but when you need one, there's nothing in the world quite like it. As circling water rises ominously and inevitably toward the rim of a backed-up toilet bowl, you're usually damned grateful to have one in your hand.

I wasn't ready to brag about IIS, but knowing that in the aftermath of Ben's murder someone inside the Seattle Police Department had gained unauthorized access to his computer files made me more than ready to go see them. Sue Danielson, still too new at the Detective Division to have rotated in and out of IIS, was edgy about the entire process. I, on the other hand, had done a couple of stints in IIS over the years. Once again, I was able to offer some moral support from that dubiously gratifying vantage point — the long view.

"It's not really an us-and-them situation, you know," I counseled, once we met in the elevator lobby on the eleventh floor. "As a detective, you'll find yourself assigned to work up here from time to time. These folks are mostly just a bunch of regular guys, especially Tony Freeman."

Sue shot me a skeptical glance. "They may all be regular," she countered, "but I still can't see myself ever wanting to join them."

Because IIS is a secured area, we had to stop at the reception desk and log in. "I'm Detective Beaumont," I said to the young woman sitting there. "And this is Detective Danielson from Homicide. We're here to talk to whoever's handling Ben Weston's case."

There must be something about the set of my eyes and nose, or maybe it's the way I comb my hair that brings out the worst in receptionists everywhere. This one was no exception. Busy filing a broken nail, she seemed only vaguely interested in what I had to say.

"Do you have an appointment?" she asked.

I smiled back at her, one of those longview smiles. "We work in Homicide," I told her. "It's hard to schedule those a week or so in advance. Can you tell me if someone in IIS has been assigned to work on the Weston case?"

"I'm not allowed to give out that kind of information."

"Who is?"

"Captain Freeman."

"Can we see him?"

She glanced pointedly behind her at the door with its number-coded lock. A red light glowed above it, announcing to those outside that the room was occupied and no one was to enter without Captain Freeman's express permission. "He's with someone right now," the receptionist replied curtly, "and it's already after four. Maybe you could come back tomorrow morning."

"Maybe we'll wait," I said. "In fact, I'm sure of it."

I motioned Sue into a chair and took one myself. It's the kind of passive/aggressive resistance that universally drives receptionists crazy. This one flushed angrily and slammed the nail file into the top drawer of her desk. She picked up the phone and pounded the keypad.

"Captain Freeman? There are two detectives from Homicide out here. They want to talk to someone about the Weston case. Should they wait, or should I have them come back later?"

After listening for a moment, she nodded. "All right. I'll tell them." Putting down the phone, she allowed grudgingly, "You can wait, but it may be some time."

We must have cooled our heels for a good half hour before the light went off and the inner door clicked open. Captain Anthony Freeman, the tall, ramrod-straight commander of IIS, ushered a young black woman out of his office. She was five six or so and slender, wearing one of those tight, ankle-fitting getups we used to call toreador pants. She wore a red windbreaker with the word "Powerized" printed on the back. Her hair hung down in a mane of shoulder-length, pencil-thin braids. She carried a large leather purse which she held up to her face as they slipped past us, effectively obscuring her features from our view.

Captain Freeman hustled her into the elevator. Only when she was safely inside the elevator and totally out of sight did he stop to shake her hand. "Thank you so much for coming in," he said to her. "You can be sure we'll get on this right away."

There was a murmured but inaudible reply, then Freeman stepped back and the elevator door glided shut.

Who's this mystery lady? I wondered. She must have had something to do with Ben Weston's case, or they both wouldn't have been so concerned about Sue and me not being able to identify her later. Whoever she was, she was important enough that Captain Freeman himself, the head honcho of IIS, rather than one of his investigative underlings, was dealing with her directly.

Now, though, Freeman turned his full attention on us. He came back to where we were sitting. "Won't you come in," he said graciously, as though inviting welcome guests into his own personal living room.

For someone used to the dingy municipal appointments of the rest of the Public Safety Building, IIS can be a real shock to the system. Just to give some scale of value, let me point out that Captain Powell's fishbowl office on the fifth floor has zero windows to the outside world. Tony Freeman has two. Powell conducts his business in his cramped office where everyone who walks by has a clear view of everything that goes on at his desk. Freeman's interviewees are hidden from view beyond that daunting security door with its electronically controlled lock.

Inside, Freeman's digs are almost spacious, with an "art in public places" piece — one of the less-controversial ones — that covers most of one wall. The Scandinavian teak furnishings themselves may not qualify at the corporate executive level, but they're a whole lot better than the Spartan green metal stuff down in Homicide.

Once we stepped inside the room, the lock clicked home and Freeman paused long enough to flip on the switch to the red light. Evidently we were not to be disturbed. Then he hurried over to his desk and turned over the top page of the yellow pad that was lying there before straightening up and looking us in the eye. He proffered his hand.

"Hello there, Detective Beaumont. Good to see you again." He shook my hand and then turned to Sue. "I don't believe I've had the pleasure."

"Detective Danielson," she said quickly, returning his handshake. "Sue." He nodded back at her and sat down behind the desk.

Captain Anthony Freeman is as straight a straight arrow as they come. As Seattle PD's designated Eagle Scout, Freeman has the spit-and-polish look of the military about him. Prematurely bald but with a fringe of reddish hair and a matching bottle-brush mustache, he inarguably counts as one of the good guys. You don't get to be Camp

Fire's Man of the Year two years in a row without making some contribution to the community at large, but he's no pushover either. Despite twenty-two years on the force, he still manages to maintain some of his youthful illusions, but anyone who's broken the rules will tell you that he's hell on wheels when it comes to crooked cops.

He motioned the two of us into chairs. "What can I do for you today?" he asked. "Connie said you wanted to talk to someone about Ben Weston."

Sue glanced briefly in my direction, as though appealing for help, but then she launched off into it on her own anyway. "We've just learned something very disturbing, Captain Freeman. Detective Beaumont and I both thought it necessary to bring it directly to your attention."

"The two of you are on the Weston Family Task Force, aren't you?" Freeman asked. "I believe I remember seeing both your names in the set of reports I've been given."

Sue nodded. "Detective Beaumont is assigned to the Adam Jackson part of the investigation. Since my regular partner, Detective Kramer, is helping Sergeant Watkins run the entire operation, I've been pitching in wherever needed."

Freeman nodded. "Before you begin, let

me ask you a question, Detective Daniel-son. Has whatever it is you've learned, whatever you've come here to tell me, been brought to the attention of either Sergeant Watkins or Detective Kramer or some other member of the task force?"

"I mentioned some of it to Detective Kra-mer earlier today, but I haven't written an official report yet. I haven't had time. The other, the part we found out just a few minutes ago, we haven't told anybody. As I said, we came directly here."

"Good," Captain Freeman said, nodding thoughtfully. "Now, go on."

Sue hesitated. "Is Internal Investigations conducting its own Ben Weston inquiry?"

"I'm not at liberty to say at the moment," Anthony Freeman replied. "Considering everything that's happened in the past few days, it would certainly be reasonable to as-sume that we were; and whether or not we are, I'd be most interested in hearing whatever it is you have to say."

I hadn't warned Detective Danielson about that aggravating aspect of dealing with Tony Freeman. Talking to him is often like dropping so many pebbles into a deep, dark well — a lot may go in, but not much comes back out. Sue didn't catch on to that right away.

"Were you conducting one earlier, before Ben Weston died?"

"Detective Danielson, I can tell you that as of now, Ben Weston is definitely a person of interest as far as this office is concerned. Not his murder, since that is already being handled by you down in Homicide, but certainly his other activities. We're trying to understand what exactly went on, whether or not there was any criminal activity involved, and whether or not there were any other Seattle PD personnel involved as well. As you know, our usual procedure is to investigate allegations of wrongdoing on the part of departmental personnel. If we find evidence to back up those allegations, the inquiry is turned over to the proper squad for further investigation as well as for the filing of charges should that prove necessary."

"You say 'as of now,' Captain Freeman, but I was asking about earlier," Sue insisted. "Were you or any of your people conducting an investigation of Ben Weston prior to his death?"

"No, we were not."

"You're sure no one from your office had Ben Weston under surveillance?"

"Absolutely."

"Somebody from Seattle PD did," Sue

Danielson said quietly.

"Who?" Freeman demanded.

"We were hoping you could tell us. Actually, we were hoping it might be someone from here."

"What kind of surveillance are you talking about?"

Sue took a deep breath. "We have a witness who tells us that a Seattle PD blue-and-white with a single-occupant driver was seen cruising Ben Weston's neighborhood regularly in the early-morning hours in the weeks preceding the murders."

"Always the same car and driver?" Freeman asked.

"Maybe not the same car, but always the same driver, and always in close proximity to Ben Weston's house."

Freeman picked up his pen and started making notes. "Who's the witness?" he asked sharply.

"A paperboy," Sue answered.

"Does he have something to gain by making the police department look bad?"

"I can't see how. He's just a high school kid, and he was scared to death to come forward. His mother forced the issue. If he had been left to his own devices, I don't think we would have heard from him."

"Have you checked with Patrol?" Freeman asked.

Sue shook her head. "Not yet, but my understanding is that Patrol doesn't send out single officers at that time of the night, and, to my knowledge, none of the other units told the task force about the existence of a prior surveillance. That's why we thought it might be someone from here, one of your people."

"A single occupant in a patrol car on the graveyard shift," Captain Freeman mused thoughtfully, as though speaking to himself. "That does narrow it down, doesn't it?"

"That's not all," Sue said grimly.

"What else?"

"A little while ago Detective Beaumont suggested to me that maybe we should look into the project Ben Weston had been working on for Coordinated Criminal Investigations."

"His gang-member profile?" Freeman asked.

"You know about that?"

The captain nodded. "I sure do. It's a good piece of work. Once it's finished, it's going to be an invaluable crime-solving tool. Up to now we've had no systematic way of following all the strings and seeing how all the various street gangs are interrelated, of knowing who is connected to whom and why."

"Was he working on anything else?"

"He may have been, but that's all I know of. Why?"

"Because the morning after his death, between one and three o'clock, someone got into Ben Weston's secured computer file and opened and closed every single file."

Sue Danielson stated her case quietly and then shut up, allowing Tony Freeman to draw his own conclusions.

The captain frowned. "It sounds to me like someone looking for something but they weren't sure if it was there to begin with, and they had no idea what file name it might have been under. You say this was the morning after the murders?"

Sue nodded.

"I wonder if anything is missing," Freeman mused.

His comment seemed to annoy Sue. "It's a little difficult to tell what's missing from looking at the files," she countered. "If a file has been deleted, it's just not there."

Freeman nodded. "What about the floppy disk back-up copy? Everybody's supposed to keep one of those, and that would have been with Ben himself. Does Property show it on the inventory?"

Sue looked questioningly at me. "I never saw one," I said. "In fact, now that you mention it, I remember Ron saying something about Ben working on this gang project at home originally, but I don't remember seeing a computer in his house, either."

"Ron?" Freeman asked.

"Ron Peters, in Media Relations. He used to be my partner before he got hurt. He's the one who brought the gang profile project to our attention in the first place."

Tony turned back to Sue. "All right. Go on."

"That's all we have so far," Sue answered. "It's not much, but . . ."

Abruptly, Freeman spun his chair around and sat for several long moments with his back to us, staring out through the still dripping rain at the moldy green-brown façade of the building across the street. Finally, he turned back toward us, reaching for the telephone at the same time.

"Connie," he said. "Call upstairs and see if the chief's still here. If he is, ask him to come down. Tell him to use the stairs. I don't want anyone to see him punching the button for this floor in the elevator. And see if you can reach Larry Powell down in Homicide and Captain Nichols in CCI. I need to see the three of them and Kyle Lehman too. On the double."

Freeman paused. "Yes, I know damn good and well that Kyle sleeps all day and works all night. Wake him up and tell him it's urgent. Oh, and bring in some more chairs from the conference room, would you?"

I had expected someone from Internal Investigations to be interested in what we had to say, but Freeman's prompt calling of a top-level meeting was beyond my wildest expectations. Assuming Sue and I were being dismissed in favor of a roomful of brass, I got up and headed for the door.

"Hey, wait a minute," Freeman demanded. "Where do you think you're going?"

"Back downstairs. We've got work to do."

He shook his head and motioned me back toward the chair. "No way. We're having a little meeting here in just a few minutes. You and Detective Danielson constitute exhibits one and two. Sit down. Would either of you like some coffee?"

To be polite, I dutifully accepted a cup of coffee from an acrid-smelling pot on a table in the corner of the room. Sue Danielson remained in her chair.

"Is all this really necessary?" she asked. "Do we really need to be here for the meeting? We've already told you everything we know."

Freeman smiled at her. "You don't like all this very much, do you, Detective Danielson? Remember, we're only Internal Investigations, not the Spanish Inquisition."

Sue kept her cool verbally, but two angry splotches of color appeared on her cheekbones. "Don't make fun of me, Captain Freeman. I'm new at this job. I still have lots to learn."

"Sorry," he apologized quickly. "No offense. It's just that people often label IIS in their minds and turn it into something it isn't. All the detectives in the department get cycled through here eventually, including you once you've been around long enough. That keeps the unit from becoming a real power structure which, considering what we do, could be dangerous. Our job is to keep good cops from going bad and to find bad cops and get them off the force. It's that simple.

"I run a tight ship, Detective Danielson," Tony Freeman continued, "and I run it on the basis of the golden rule — Do unto others and all that jazz. That may sound corny at first, but with detectives rotating in and out of here, it really is a matter of what goes around comes around. Somebody who acts like a jerk when he's on the delivery end of IIS may very well end up being on the receiving end a few months down the line. That knowledge helps keep everybody honest."

There was a light tapping on the door. Freeman pressed a button to disable the security lock. The door opened and Kyle Lehman entered the room.

If Captain Freeman is Seattle PD's straight arrow, Kyle Lehman is its ghostly computer guru. A scrawny, sallow-faced, bespectacled nerd who's probably thirty but looks nineteen or twenty, Kyle came to Seattle PD years ago to install our computer system and get it up and running. Afterward, he never left. Legend has it that Lehman is listed as a resident in an apartment over on Eastlake somewhere, but he spends most of his time baby-sitting the department's sometimes temperamental computer system. He sleeps on a cot in his office, showers in the change room, survives on a diet of readily available neighborhood fast food, and spends his spare time playing fantasy quest games on his personal desktop computer.

Not surprisingly, Lehman was the first to show. He arrived dressed all in black — an aging rendition of what teenagers currently call a "bat caver." He wore a single earring, and his reddish hair flopped crookedly over one eye.

"Morning, Tony," he said casually to Freeman, although it was well after four in the afternoon.

"I trust this isn't too early for you," Freeman returned.

Kyle grinned ingratiatingly. "Naw. Somebody from CCI already woke me up. Mind if I have some breakfast?"

"Be my guest," Tony Freeman told him.

Lehman took a seat in the corner. At the same time he bit into a mustard-slathered corn dog. An unopened can of diet Pepsi hung out of the pocket of his frayed houndstooth jacket.

Up to that point, I had never exchanged a word with Kyle Lehman, but that didn't keep me from having an immediate, none-too-favorable opinion of the man. I had seen him skulking around the halls on occasion. The only thing that really pissed me off more than his looks was the common departmental knowledge that Lehman made more money than almost any detective on the force. For that kind of money, it seemed to me we could have hired someone who looked a little more like a regular human being and less like something that had just oozed out from under a hard disk drive.

Next, Connie ushered Captain Powell into the room. Larry glanced at Sue and me, nodded curtly, and kept on walking. He greeted Freeman and sat down on one of the three extra chairs that had been crowded in next to the wall on either side of Tony Freeman's desk.

He exchanged polite greetings with Lehman and then turned to us. "What are you two doing here?" he asked.

Freeman answered before either Sue or I could open our mouths. "Waiting for the rest of our party to show up. Want some coffee, Larry?"

Connie, who evidently was capable of taking a hint once her nails were filed, grabbed the pot along with the rest of its evil-smelling dregs and disappeared into the outer office.

Norman Nichols showed up next. He nodded to Sue as he took a seat next to Captain Powell. Having just helped Sue break into Ben Weston's computer files, Nichols probably more than anyone had a fairly good idea of why we were there.

Time passed. Tony Freeman sat gazing serenely at the artwork on the wall behind us as though he didn't have a care in the world. Kyle munched thoughtfully on his corn dog and sipped his soda while the rest of us waited in uneasy silence. There was no joking or lighthearted banter. The new coffee was halfway through dripping into the pot and Connie had left for the day when the third tap finally sounded on the door. Freeman pressed the button and in walked Chief of Police Kenneth Rankin, flushed and puffing and out of breath.

"Why did you insist I use the stairs for God's sake, Tony?" Chief Rankin growled. "I was all the way down in the Crime Lab. It's a helluva long hike up from the third floor to the eleventh, you know. And what's so damned important that it couldn't wait until tomorrow morning?"

"Have a seat, Chief," Freeman said quietly. "We'll get to it as quickly as we can. Thank you all for coming. Does everyone know everyone else?"

We all did. "Good," Freeman continued. "I've called you here this afternoon to ask for your help and cooperation. It looks as though we have a serious problem on our hands — a rogue cop problem."

Rankin paled. "Don't tell me we've got another one," he groaned. "The business with Benjamin Weston is bad enough."

Lehman, who doesn't regard himself as a cop and finds no horror in the words "rogue cop," chose that moment to noisily open a bag of potato chips. Larry Powell looked stricken but sat up straight, paying absolute attention.

"It's possible," Captain Freeman said softly, "that this one is far worse."

"Worse!" Rankin exploded. "How could it possibly be worse?"

"Unless I'm sadly mistaken, Ben Weston may have been nothing but the tip of the iceberg."

His words grabbed my gut and shook it. Tip of the iceberg? In other words, Tony Freeman was convinced Ben Weston was part of whatever dirty crap was going on. That hurt. It hurt real bad.

"This has something to do with the murders then?" Larry Powell asked after a moment.

Freeman nodded. "Probably. What I'm about to tell you is not to be discussed with anyone outside this room. I've just had a very disturbing visit from someone who's working undercover for Narcotics. Word is out on the streets that the Bloods, Crips, and BGD want to have a summit meeting with someone from Seattle PD. Preferably Chief Rankin here himself."

That caught me completely flat-footed. After all I thought we were going to discuss something else entirely. And I wasn't the only one who was surprised. Chief Rankin's eyes bulged. "With me? All of them at once? What about?"

"About Ben Weston," Freeman answered. "They say they aren't responsible for killing Ben Weston and his family. They want to help us find the cops who did."

You could have heard a pin drop in that room. Sue and I had been gradually collecting our own set of suspicions, but to hear them come ricocheting back at us, uttered with Captain Freeman's unsmiling, dead certainty, made the hair prickle on the back of my neck.

Chief Rankin was the first to find his voice. "Did you say cops?" he croaked. "You're saying that a fellow police officer or officers killed Ben Weston and all his family?"

"That's what they said — cops, plural not singular," Tony Freeman answered grimly. "That means two or more."

"And the gangs, all of them together, are offering to help us catch them? I've never heard of such a thing. That's preposterous."

"I've never heard of anything like it before, either," Tony Freeman agreed. "But that's the message. They say they'll help, but only on the QT. Word of this temporary truce is not to go beyond this room, is that clear?"

For several moments we were all too thunderstruck to even open our mouths. I was the one who finally managed to ask a question. "How's this all going to work?"

"One step at a time," Freeman replied confidently. "By the way, Larry, as of now and until further notice, Detectives Beaumont and Danielson are working for me."

Powell nodded his acquiescence, and Captain Freeman turned to us. "Any questions?"

"No, sir," Sue Danielson replied. "Just tell us what you want us to do."

CHAPTER 16

I've never actually been in a horrible hurricane, but it must be very much like the meeting that went on in Captain Freeman's office that day as late afternoon changed to evening. In Seattle the Weston family murders dominated the local news. As a consequence, the room was charged with an almost electric tension. Anthony Freeman took control and issued orders to everyone involved, Chief Rankin included. There was no doubt in anyone's mind that the commander of IIS was running the show.

Most of the time Internal Investigations deals with specific allegations against specific officers, police brutality in the course of making an arrest being one of the most common, although drug use, domestic violence, and job-related alcohol problems show up with a fair amount of regularity. In all of these instances, the identity of the officer isn't so much in question as is the propriety of his actions. Here, we were faced with a far more difficult and complicated problem because not only were the identities of the officers and their actions totally unknown to us, there was a reasonable possibility that one or more of them might be actively involved in some aspect of the Weston Family Task Force investigation.

Captain Freeman began the meeting by laying out for all of us the situation as he saw it. "At the moment, there's no way to tell whether or not what our informant has told us is true and that the gang warlords really will cooperate with us on this. I've been around Seattle PD for a long time, folks. So have most of you. Anybody here ever hear of the gangs making this kind of offer? I'd be less surprised if Santa Claus or the Tooth Fairy dropped in to pay a personal visit."

Most of us shook our heads. "It could be a trick," Chief Rankin suggested.

Freeman disagreed. "I don't think so," he said somberly. "I think we're going to have to operate on the assumption that the intelligence we have been given is correct and that fellow police officers are somehow responsible for the murders of Ben Weston and the others. For a change, the gangs don't want to be blamed for something they didn't do."

Freeman allowed his gaze to wander slowly around the room while the weight of his words sank in. If he was expecting objections, no one made any. Even Kyle Lehman, who was doubtless the least affected, paused for a long moment before biting thoughtfully into an apple which had appeared from the same jacket pocket as the diet Pepsi.

"These people," Freeman continued, "however many of them there are, constitute a cancer on the body of the Seattle Police Department — a cancer I'm determined to eradicate. How do you get rid of a cancer? By taking it out, by cutting it out, by destroying it before it destroys you. This is the preliminary biopsy stage, that critical time where early detection is the key to survival. We're going to find out who these people are, and we're going to take care of them. We're going to do it the same way a surgeon would — by making the smallest possible incision.

"To that end, my intention is to limit the number of people who actually know what's going on to a mere handful, specifically to those of us who are in this room at this very moment. If it becomes necessary to add more — and it probably will — those additions will be handpicked by me and nobody else. You are not to include anyone else in this part of the investigation without my express permission. Do I make myself clear?"

This time a response was definitely in order. We all nodded in turn, including Chief Rankin. His was probably the most heartfelt of all. Rankin, one of a vast number of unappreciated and much maligned California transplants, was fairly new to Seattle. Coming from Oakland, he brought along with him a reputation for being both a consummate politician and an ace delegator — two prime prerequisites for being the chief of police in any major metropolitan area. Rumors that he was also a closet racist had followed him to Seattle, but as far as I was concerned, they had yet to be proven one way or the other.

Rankin's ability to delegate, however, was without question. The people I knew who'd been handed assignments by him respected the fact that Rankin hadn't second-guessed them. When he put someone in charge, they stayed in charge. I could see that myself as Tony Freeman continued to run the meeting as a one-man show.

"We have a slight advantage," he said, "in that no one on the task force, other than Detectives Beaumont and Danielson, has any knowledge that we've been tipped off. As I mentioned before, it's possible that one of the crooks is actually connected to the task force operation. We'll have a much better chance of nabbing him if I don't have to send up a red flag by transferring in one of the current crop of IIS investigators."

"If you ask me, that's not any advantage at all," I put in. "We got our information from the street, so chances are the crooks will too. Informant loyalty always goes to the highest bidder. What's to keep the beans from getting spilled in the other direction?"

Freeman considered for a moment before replying. "I guess we'll just have to see to it that the information that's on the street, including some of the information that goes through the task force itself, is wrong information."

Sue Danielson had listened quietly to this exchange. Now, she spoke up. "That's fine as far as it goes, but what about the boy?" she asked.

"What boy?"

"Junior Weston. He's an eyewitness. To my knowledge, he's the only one who can possibly identify the killer. Everyone who attended the task force meeting this morning knows Junior was moved from his grandfather's house to Reverend Walters's home. If someone on the task force . . ."

She didn't complete the sentence, and she didn't have to. Her words landed another haymaker in the pit of my stomach. Thanks to me, Junior Weston was still at risk and so were Reverend Homer and Francine Walters. I personally had come up with the brilliant idea of having him stay there.

I started out of my chair, determined to take some kind of precautionary action.

"Where do you think you're going?" Freeman demanded.

"To call Reverend Walters, to warn him."

"No," Captain Freeman said.

"No?" I yelped. "What do you mean, no? People's lives are at stake."

Freeman's calm eyes met mine and held them. "I'm well aware of that, Detective Beaumont. Sit down and tell me about your partner."

"My partner. About Big Al? You know Big Al Lindstrom, Tony. You know him as well as I do."

"My understanding is that he was removed from the case by Captain Powell here. Is that true?"

Captain Powell himself started to interject something, but Tony Freeman waved him to silence. "I was asking Detective Beaumont," he said. "Tell me what you personally know about Detective Lindstrom being removed from the case."

"Ben Weston and Big Al were friends, damnit. Good friends. I guess Captain Powell thought there might be a potential conflict of interest if Allen was investigating the case, that emotion might cloud his judgment."

"Would it?" Freeman asked.

"I don't think so. He's the one who found Junior Weston hiding in the linen closet after the murders were discovered, and he did a hell of a job interviewing that little kid, of getting him to remember what he saw, of helping him open up and talk to us about it. You should have been there."

"I wasn't. Were you?"

I was fast losing patience. "What is it you want me to tell you? Are you asking me if I think Big Al is one of the crooked cops? Are you asking me if I think he did it? The answer is no, absolutely not, no way. I'd stake my life on it."

"Would you stake Junior Weston's life on it?"

Like any good investigator, Captain Freeman doesn't ask questions if he doesn't have a pretty damn good idea what the answers will be. Questions for him are always a means to a specific end, not a device for use in casual conversation. It took until then before I realized where his questions were going, what he was really asking.

"It's risky as hell," I said. "For all concerned, but, yes, I'd bet Junior's life on Big Al Lindstrom in a minute."

"Do you think he'd do it?"

"Damned right he would!"

Captain Freeman picked up his phone. "What's his number? We'll call him up and ask."

Freeman waited with his finger poised over the number pad while my mind went totally blank. I couldn't remember my own phone number right then to say nothing of Big Al Lindstrom's.

"Just a second here," Sue Danielson interrupted. "I don't understand. What's going on?"

"Seven eight five . . ." I started.

Now Captain Powell leaped into the fray. "Wait a minute. You can't pull Detective Lindstrom back into all this. I already threw him off the case."

Freeman put the phone down. "That's exactly why I want him," he returned mildly. "Because he's off the case. No one's going to think of him as a source of information. I asked Detective Beaumont for his opinion, but I happen to be of the same mind. I know Allen Lindstrom, have known him for a long time. Of all the people at Seattle PD right now, if I can only have one cop to guard Junior Weston, Big Al Lindstrom is the one I want."

"Who said you can only have one, Captain Freeman?" chimed in Chief Rankin. "You can have as many as you want. All you have to do is ask."

"Remember what I told you? This is going to be a limited incision," Freeman reminded them, "an operation conducted with limited assets. If Big Al Lindstrom is the one guard on duty, one will be more than enough. I'm going to dial his number now and put you on the phone, Beau. Tell him you've just started worrying about Junior and ask him if he'd mind doing something about it overnight, unofficially, as a favor to you, but armed and with a bulletproof vest. We can take care of paying him overtime for it later, right, Larry?"

Captain Powell nodded glumly. "Right," he said.

"Now what was that number?"

I gave it to him. In the intervening seconds, it had miraculously reappeared from my memory bank. When Freeman finished dialing, he handed the phone over to me. There's an old Ogden Nash poem that says something about how one becomes a capable liar. If ever I wanted to be proficient at lying, this was it.

Molly Lindstrom answered the phone. "Is Al there?" I asked innocently.

"He is," she said, "but he's not feeling so good. He said he was going straight to bed."

I heard the wariness in her voice, understood her wanting to protect her husband from any further hurt. "Get him up, Molly. He'll want to talk to me."

She slammed the phone down on the table. It was several long minutes before Big Al came on the line. In the interim, no one in Captain Freeman's office said a word.

" 'Lo, Beau," Big Al said finally. "Whaddya want?"

"I'm worried about Junior," I said.

"Junior? What's the matter with him?"

I heard Big Al snap to attention. It wasn't necessary to lie. All I had to do was express my own legitimate worries and let Detective Lindstrom draw his own conclusions.

"He's still our only eyewitness," I said. "What if the killer hears where he is somehow and tries to take him out? I just realized everyone at the task force meeting knows where the boy is staying. If one of them happened to make a slip in front of the wrong person . . ."

"Gotcha," Big Al said. "Ja sure you betcha. I can be there in twenty minutes flat. Does Kramer know anything about this?"

"Are you kidding? That schmuck would shit a brick if he even suspected I was talking to you about it."

"Don't tell him then," Big Al said. "I'm on my way in my own car on my own time. No one needs to know about this but you and me."

"By the way, Al, do me a favor. Wear your armor."

"Right, Beau. And don't you take yours off, either."

He hung up and so did I. In the meantime, Kyle Lehman had rolled his apple core up in the empty potato chip bag and was looking around for a garbage can. Freeman took the bag and tossed it into a container under his desk.

"This is all very interesting," Kyle was saying, "but what the hell am I doing here?"

He's such an obnoxious little twit, I couldn't understand how Freeman could tolerate him, but he did. "I was just getting around to that. I want you to do an analysis of all the blue-and-whites in the department. I want to know their locations, their usual drivers, who else may have checked them in and out. I want you to look for any discrepancies in mileage. If one has consistently more than one of the others, I want to know about it."

Lehman nodded. "I can do that. It'll take a while and some work, but it can be done. Anything else?"

"Yes," Freeman said. "There is. You know that PC down in the gang unit?"

Kyle nodded again. "What about it?"

"I want you to take charge of it. Personally. Physically remove it if necessary. Say it crashed or something. Do it now before anyone else has a chance to touch it. My understanding is that as long as no one has written over a deleted file, it may be possible to retrieve the information. Is that right?"

"Pretty much. It'll be hell on wheels finding it is all," Lehman returned. "It'll take time, lots of it. Why? What are we looking for? And why can't we get the information from one of the back-up floppies?"

"The night of the murders, someone got into Ben Weston's directory. Whoever it was went through all his files. My guess is that the critical one, the one no one wanted us to see, is missing."

"The floppy's gone too?"

For the first time in the entire meeting, Kyle Lehman was on his toes, both interested and irate. "You're saying that some-body broke into one of *my* secured comput-ers? I'll break the SOB's neck. How'd he get the password? How'd he get verified?"

Freeman smiled. "I thought you'd be interested in knowing about this. We are too. How long will it take?"

Lehman looked at his watch. "I don't know, but I'll get started right away. Which one do you want done first, the car analysis or the missing files?"

"The files."

"Good. I would have done that first any-way."

Without waiting for Freeman to call a halt, Kyle Lehman careened out of the room. The senseless slaughter of five people didn't bother him one bit, and the fact that Seattle PD was infected with crooked cops had made no visible effect either, but the idea that someone had broken into his pre-cious computer system lit a fire under Kyle Lehman's scrawny butt.

Freeman turned to Captain Powell. "Larry, I want you to run interference for Beaumont and Danielson, and I want you to help me sort the misinformation we'll be feeding to the task force. Detective Daniel-son, you're to check with Kramer, visit the Crime Lab, the M.E.'s office, and anywhere you can think of. Your assignment is to gather up any new information that may have come in during the course of the day. I want the information regathered by you rather than taking whatever Kramer has at face value. What's going into the Weston Family Task Force may very well have been tainted somewhere along the way. See what I mean?"

Sue nodded, and Freeman turned to me. "As for you, now that you've delivered Detective Lindstrom, I need you to do something else. You're the one who hangs around the Doghouse Restaurant so much of the time, aren't you?"

My reputation for having that particular home away from home has long been cause for departmental teasing. The Doghouse is a downtown Seattle twenty-four-hour hangout with a reputation for deep-fried everything and a flock of old-fashioned waitresses who would most likely deck anyone who had balls enough to try calling one of them a wait-person.

In the middle of the night the Doghouse attracts late-night carousers of all varieties, as well as a fair selection of the city's good guys and bad guys who tend to congregate there. Inside those four walls, everybody knows who's who, and, believe me, they all mind their manners. The Doghouse is neutral territory, and the rules are simple. Inside, good guys don't bother bad guys and vice versa, and nobody but nobody hassles the waitresses.

"What about it?"

"Don't they have a funny little back room down there? A relatively private room?"

"Yes. The back room, where ham radio operators meet occasionally and every once in a while a group of cartoonists."

"Good. I want you to set up the summit meeting there for Chief Rankin and the official emissaries from each of the gangs. I want to know what those creeps have to say, and I want to know tonight."

"Tonight? How the hell . . ."

"I'm sure you'll be able to manage it. As soon as you get it set up, let the chief here know what time. He'll be up in his office, waiting for your call."

Captain Freeman peered around the room. "Everybody have a handle on their task assignments?"

"I've got a question," Chief Rankin put in. "I've got police departments from all over the state calling to say they're sending official representatives to the funeral on Saturday. What do I do about them?"

"Nothing. Let them come," Freeman replied.

"What if Weston was one of the bad apples —"

"Then we find it out after the funeral and not before," Freeman interrupted. "Because if Ben Weston gets anything other than a hero's burial, we've blown our own cover. Any other questions?"

There were none. With general nods of agreement, people took the hint. Rankin and Powell left together, followed by Sue and myself. Before I made it through the doorway, though, Freeman called me back.

"You were raised in Ballard, weren't you, Detective Beaumont?"

"Yes."

"Not too many Jewish people in Ballard, would you say?"

"Hardly any."

Tony Freeman got up and came around his desk. He stopped only a step or two away from me. "How much do you know about Jews?" he asked.

"Not much. I've met a few over the years, but . . ."

"Detective Beaumont, the Jewish religion passes from mother to child. I may not look Jewish to you, but I am because my mother is. Do you have any idea what the word

271

'schmuck' means?"

"No-good jerk, I guess. Why?" I couldn't figure out what he was driving at.

"Not in Yiddish," Captain Freeman said without a trace of a smile. "In Yiddish it means something else entirely, 'penis' to be exact. My mother is a gentle woman, Detective Beaumont. I only remember her hitting me once, and that was when, as a smart-mouthed twelve-year-old, I used the word 'schmuck' at the dinner table. I would appreciate it if you didn't use that word in my presence. I find it offensive. Thanks."

With that, he ushered me out the door and closed it behind me. Sue Danielson was waiting for me by the elevator. I was blushing beet red and hoping she wouldn't notice.

"What was that all about?" she asked.

I shook my head. "I could be wrong," I said, "but I think I've just had my ass chewed."

CHAPTER 17

When I got back down to the fifth floor, I picked up my phone and heard the stuttering dial tone that meant I had voice-mail messages. Two of the three calls were from Ralph Ames. As he was my houseguest, it seemed to me I owed him some kind of explanation, at least enough to let him know that duty called and that work had overtaken my responsibilities as host. I figured he was a big boy, fully capable of rustling up some suitable evening's pastime including some suitable evening's companionship as well. As far as I could tell, he was doing fine on the companionship score without any help from me.

I dialed home, wondering if the phone would work this time or not. Ralph answered after the second ring.

"Don't wait up for me," I told him. "Things are heating up around here. It looks like it's going to be another long one again tonight."

"Too bad. Curtis Bell is here right now. We finally managed to touch bases late this afternoon. I told him to come on over, that you'd be home eventually. He was hoping to see you. In the meantime he's been giving me some preliminary figures. I'm finding them quite interesting."

Captain Freeman's painful vocabulary lesson was still ringing in my ears, so I didn't call Curtis Bell what I might have called him a mere half hour earlier.

"Look," I said, "I'm up to my eyeteeth in a case right now. How come he has so much free time when nobody else does? Anyway, I don't have time to see that pushy bastard, and I wish he'd lay off."

Ralph Ames laughed. "Give him a break, Beau. He's a salesman, working on commission. What do you expect?"

"Maybe if he'd bust his butt down at the department more, he wouldn't need to moonlight. Not only that, I more than halfway expected him to make the appointment at a time when we could both see him."

I probably sounded almost as disagreeable as I felt, but as the alleged owner of the money that was about to get spent, it didn't seem like asking too much that I be consulted right along with Ralph Ames. And since I was already in a complaining mode, I moved right along to the telephone situation.

"By the way, Ralph, what's all this about a fax machine on my phone? I tried calling home earlier today and couldn't get through. The operator said I must have left my fax hooked up to the phone. Have I missed something, or do I own a fax machine?"

Ralph laughed. "Actually, you do," he said. "I bought it for you the other day as a surprise, a sort of bread-and-butter gift, and had the woman who sold it to me come and install it yesterday at noon. I was afraid you'd show up and catch us in the act. I'll bet you still haven't had time to go into the study to see it, have you? It's a real beaut, Beau."

"But why do I need a fax, Ralph?" I countered.

"Once you get used to having it, you won't know how you got along without it. I used it today to get some background information on Curtis Bell's company. He seemed to be quite impressed."

A fax installer? That's who Ralph had escorted into the apartment when I thought he was bringing home a noontime something else? If so, when had he had time to pick up the lady who loved Bentleys, and how did she fit into the picture?

"You never fail to surprise me, Ralph, and that's the truth. Get what you need from Curtis. We'll talk insurance later. And by the way, thanks for the fax. I think."

He was still laughing when I hung up. The other call was from my favorite criminalist, Janice Morraine. She had left two numbers, both in the Crime Lab and one at home as well. The Crime Lab said she had gone home for the day, so I tried reaching her there.

"Beaumont here, Janice," I said when she answered. "What's up?"

"I wondered if you'd had a chance to see my analysis of the hair you found. I gave it to Detective Kramer late this afternoon. Since you and Big Al were the ones who discovered the hair in the first place, I thought you might be interested in seeing the results."

"I haven't seen them yet," I told her. "I've been tied up in meetings until just a few minutes ago. If Detective Kramer's been trying to find me to hand over a report, he hasn't had any luck."

Of course, there wasn't much likelihood of Kramer looking for me for any reason other than to tell me to drop dead. I figured hell would freeze over completely before he would voluntarily pass along any information at all, but I couldn't very well say that to Janice Morraine.

"It looks as though he's gone home, so why not tell me about it yourself?"

"It's a plant," she answered at once.

"A plant?" I repeated dubiously. "It sure as hell looked like hair to me."

"Don't joke around, Beau. This is important. The hair you found stuck between Shiree Weston's fingers was placed there on purpose after she was dead. I've checked it out. The hairs don't all match. My assessment is that the hair was taken from somebody's brush, a brush several different people had used. Black hair," she added, "as in race, not color. All of it. It could match up with hair from the family members themselves. I'll be checking on that tomorrow, but I doubt it."

I was barely listening to her. Instead, I was remembering how Junior Weston had described the man he had seen struggling with his sister. He had said that the man was a white man with skin tones very much like my own, that Bonnie Weston's killer was a white man wearing gloves.

"That means whoever did it meant for us

to go looking for a black perpetrator, doesn't it?"

"Right," Janice replied, "and with feelings in the city running so high, I didn't want to risk not letting you know about this."

"That's what they were counting on," I mused, "that everyone in Homicide would be so strung out that we wouldn't pay close enough attention, that we'd go after any kind of slipshod evidence just to make an arrest."

"Wrong!" Janice Morraine returned. Her single-word vehemence made me laugh.

"Right," I said.

Whoever the killers were, they hadn't taken the likes of Janice Morraine and Tony Freeman into consideration. Or me either, for that matter.

"Anything else interesting come up on your end?" I asked.

"Not really. I spent the whole afternoon working on the hair problem. Once I finish checking the Weston samples, I'll probably be doing something else tomorrow."

"Same case, though?" I asked.

"Are you kidding? Word filtered down from George Yamamoto. For right now, the Weston case is the only game in town. Everything else takes a backseat."

"You'll keep me posted?"

"What do you think?" she replied.

That's what's nice about having a working history with someone. Janice Morraine's and my relationship, rocky though it may be at times, goes well beyond the official guidelines people like Kramer would like to impose. In fact, that was probably precisely why she had called me in the first place.

"Thanks, Janice. I appreciate it."

"No prob," Janice said. "If anything important comes up, I'll be in touch."

I put down the phone. A plant, I thought. The kinds of people who blow one another away over a line of heroin or a lump of crack cocaine don't usually bother leaving behind a trail of manufactured evidence. Most of the time, people routinely involved in those kinds of crimes are already so well versed in the criminal injustice system, they could probably give the state bar exam a run for its money.

Habitual criminals know full well, from vast personal experience, that it doesn't take much effort or even a particularly good lawyer to beat almost any rap we cops may manage to lay on them. Why bother with leaving behind a trail of phony evidence when a well-placed plea bargain makes that whole charade unnecessary?

As far as I was concerned, in the case of

the Weston family murders, planted evidence turned the process into a whole new ball game. If we had renegade cops, including at least one white one, they were going to great lengths to point suspicion at black suspects, and parts of the task force investigation were probably exploring those very possibilities. If the street gangs all knew that none of their people were responsible, no wonder they were in an uproar and wanted a summit meeting with Chief Rankin. Their turf was being invaded, their supremacy challenged.

I sat staring at my telephone and wondered how to go about setting up that meeting. The gang unit probably could have given me a hint — maybe even a phone number or two — but Captain Freeman had issued strict orders not to involve any other personnel without his advance approval. Chances are, my friendly neighborhood gangs had their own voicemail arrangements and probably even fax machines, but I couldn't reach out and touch them since I didn't happen to know their numbers.

After several minutes of wishing I had a Ma Bell phone directory for crooks, I realized that maybe I did. Or at least, I had a friend who did. That very afternoon I had held in my hand Ron Peters's hardcopy pages of Ben Weston's preliminary gang member data base. I considered going to see Kyle and asking him for a look at Ben Weston's most recent data base, but I reconsidered. Why bother him and take him away from what he was doing for Tony Freeman when Ron Peters could probably give me exactly what I needed?

As soon as the thought crossed my mind, I called Ron at home. Heather answered. "Hello, Uncle Beau," she said, sounding very grown-up and businesslike. I missed the gap-toothed, lisping way she used to say "Unca Beau" before her newly sprouted permanent teeth came in. "Just a minute," she said. "I'll get my dad."

Ron Peters came on the phone a moment later. "Hey, Beau, I was looking all over for you this afternoon but Margie said you never came back after lunch. Amy came up with a great idea."

"What's that?"

"She did her preliminary physical therapist work over at Central Washington University in Ellensburg. One of her girlfriends married a guy who's the assistant registrar at the university there. We thought we'd take a run over to Ellensburg either tonight or early tomorrow morning, talk to them, and see what we can find out. We should be back in plenty of time to make Ben's funeral at two. What do you think of that?"

"Don't ask me," I told him, trying to keep the enthusiasm out of my voice, obeying the letter of Tony Freeman's law but not the intent. "What I don't know can't hurt me, can it?"

Ron laughed. "Gotcha," he said. "Mum's the word, but if we could locate even just one of those missing kids, I'd feel like I was doing something real again and not just marking time. So why did you call, Beau? What's up?"

"Do you still have that copy of Ben Weston's project?"

"I sure do. I own it. He gave it to me months ago. Why?"

"Does it have names, addresses, and telephone numbers on it by any chance?"

"I think so. Hang on. I have it right here with me." The sound of rustling papers came through the phone. "Some of them do. Not all, but some. What do you need?"

"Phone numbers."

"Phone numbers?" Ron echoed. "Why the hell do you need gang members' phone numbers, Beau? You planning on selling these guys tickets to the Bacon Bowl maybe?"

The Bacon Bowl is a once-a-year, old-timers' football game, a fund-raising rivalry played between teams of police officers from the Seattle and Tacoma areas who are really frustrated, over-the-hill jocks. I've got brains enough not to play football anymore, but I'm reasonably good at selling tickets.

"Not likely," I replied, "but I need those phone numbers all the same. I'd like even representation of Crips, Bloods, and BGD, as many numbers of each as you can give me."

"You don't want much, do you. Why not try Directory Assistance?"

"Why not give me a hard time?" I returned. "Just read me the damn numbers, would you?"

In the end, I wound up with a list of fourteen names and telephone numbers — five Bloods, five Crips, and four BGD. I wasted no time working my way through the list and calling them all. Naturally, several of the numbers were no longer in service. Two people who answered sounded genuinely mystified and said the telephone number had only been assigned to them in the course of the last few months. Some of the others, however, seemed to know all too well what was going on.

Each time someone answered, innocent-sounding or not, I left the same message:

"Your top guy wants a meeting with our top guy," I told them. "Have someone call this number to set it up. We want to schedule the meeting as soon as we can, tonight if possible."

Once I placed all the calls, I went back to my voicemail number and changed my answering announcement, deleting all the parts of my recording that revealed anything at all about my name and profession. I wasn't much looking forward to shepherding Chief Rankin on this little excursion in the first place, and I especially didn't want the guys we were meeting to know who was attached to that particular Seattle PD extension number.

While I sat waiting for someone to call me back, I started creating a small mountain of reports. Captain Freeman had made it clear that the work Sue Danielson and I were doing for him was in addition to whatever we were doing for the Weston Family Task Force. That meant regular reports would be required in two different directions.

Half an hour passed, then an hour. I was beginning to think I had struck out completely when the phone rang.

"Yes," I answered.

"You're on," said a voice. "Where? When?"

"The back room at the Doghouse," I said.

"Eleven o'clock."

"Who all's gonna be there?" the guy asked.

"Chief Rankin and myself," I answered. "That's all. Just the two of us. How about you?"

"If there's two of you, then there's two of us. We be six altogether."

"You're calling for everybody?"

"That's right, man. RSVPing, as they say. You got a problem with that?"

I just didn't expect the gangs to be quite that well organized. "No. No problem at all. We'll be there by ten-thirty or so. That way, we won't all show up at once. That might make quite a stir."

"You gots that right. Just us being there will cause a stir as you call it. If somebody notices the chief of police, all those television stations will send out their Minicams, turn it into a media event."

"I wouldn't want that to happen," I said, "and neither would the chief."

"Not my chiefs, neither," he answered. "We all play it real cool. Right?"

"Right." We all do.

The idea of sitting down in the same room with the ad hoc leadership committee of several warring street gangs didn't sound cool to me. Chilling was a lot more like it. Already I could feel the rank-smelling, fear-drenched sweat gathering in my armpits. I picked up the phone and dialed up to the chief's — my chief's — office. He answered before the end of the first ring.

"What is it?"

"An appointment. We go to the Doghouse early, at ten-thirty. The others come later. I'm going to go home, grab a shower, and pick up my car. It's probably best if we don't show up in a city-owned vehicle."

"Yep. You're right about that."

"Are you going to go home first, or do you want me to come back here to pick you up?"

"Here," he said. "I'd rather wait here."

I got to the house about nine-thirty. I hoped Curtis Bell would be long gone. I was in no mood to talk to him, and I was right.

"You're home early," Ralph commented.

"Not to stay. I'm going to shower and leave again. Did you and Curtis get everything ironed out?"

"No. Not really. He left right after you called, but I think we may want to do something about single-premium life policies for your kids. It's a way of passing them a substantial amount of money without them having to pay inheritance or gift taxes."

"I thought you said I'd have to pay a rating."

"Only if we buy insurance on you. If we buy it on your children, then it's no problem."

"Right now, I'm going to shower, then I've got a hot date."

"Really."

"It's hot all right, a regular *Who's Who* of street gangs in Seattle."

"Sounds fascinating," Ralph said, sounding for the world like everyone's favorite Vulcan, good old Mr. Spock from *Star Trek*.

"Fascinating?" I echoed. "I just hope it won't be fatal."

CHAPTER 18

Chief Rankin was not the least bit happy.
While I had been busy writing reports and
taking a shower, he had been reading tear
sheets from newspapers and magazines all
over the country regarding the Seattle Police
Department's handling of the Ben Weston
murders. To hear him tell it, most of the ac-
counts were written by a bunch of bleeding-
heart liberals who laced what they wrote
with an undertone of implied bigotry. The
assumption was that the (predominantly
white) officers of Seattle PD were doing
precious little to solve the tragic murders of
this now highly visible African-American
family.

Rankin's grousing about the slanted stories surprised me. I know what comes out
in newspaper stories usually grates on my
nerves — most reporters are a bunch of
bleeding-heart liberals — but I always assumed the brass had tougher hides than us

mere mortals, that they, as political animals, could take all that media crap with a grain of salt. Evidently not.

Once the chief finished complaining about the media, he went on to look a gift ride in the mouth and gripe about my Porsche. According to Rankin, his personal car is a two-year-old Buick Riviera. Without knowing any of my history, he seemed offended by the very existence of my aging and much repaired guard red Porsche, and I wasn't inclined to enlighten him. By the time we got to the Doghouse parking lot, I was wishing I'd left him to walk, but that was only the beginning. It got worse.

I opened the front door of the restaurant to let him go first. He stepped inside, then turned back to me. "My God, it's so smoky in there how can anybody see?"

The Doghouse, smoke and all, is a Seattle institution, but Rankin, as a relatively recent transplant, had clearly never set foot inside the place. Diana, the hostess, came up to me smiling her usual welcome. "Hi, Beau. You're in the back room tonight?"

I nodded, and she led the way past the usual line of hopefuls waiting to do their bit for the state coffers and buy their weekly collection of lottery tickets.

"There'd better be a nonsmoking section," Chief Rankin was saying under his breath.

I almost choked, and not because of the smoke either. If you want to sit in a non-smoking section, don't bother going to the Doghouse. Period. Because they are mandated by law, there are two designated nonsmoking tables in the middle dining room, but the entire rest of the restaurant is so totally permeated with residual smoke that it doesn't make much difference.

The back dining room, with seating for a maximum of fifteen, is used primarily as a day-to-day club room for ham radio operators whose faded collection of QSL cards, showing contacts and call signs from around the world, decorates the equally faded walls. Here, too, stale cigarette smoke lingered heavily in the air. On the far side of the room is the only window in the entire restaurant that actually opens. Rankin hurried over and yanked it open, allowing in a whiff of fresh air. Chilly fresh air.

"How many will there be?" Diana asked me.

"Eight altogether."

She deposited a set of menus on the table and retreated, leaving Chief Rankin and me alone. Moments later Lucille, one of the nighttime waitresses, popped her head into the room. "Chili burger, Beau?" I nodded. "Want me to take your order, or wait for the others?"

"We'll eat now," I said. "There may not be time later."

"How about you?" she said to Chief Rankin, who had picked up a menu and was regarding it with obvious distaste.

"What do you recommend, Detective Beaumont?" he asked. "You must know your way around the menu. You seem to be on a first-name basis with everyone in the place."

It was bad enough being the chief's guide dog here to begin with. I wasn't about to stumble into the trap of suggesting anything. "It's all about the same," I told him.

Rankin scratched his head. "I guess I'll try the salmon," he said grudgingly, "if it's not too greasy."

In the Doghouse, at that hour of the night, them's fightin' words. Lucille peered at me over her glasses as if to say, "Where'd you find this live one?" "You bet," she said aloud, and disappeared.

The back room isn't big, so Rankin paced back and forth in front of the open window. "Do you think they'll show?" he asked.

"They'll be here."

"I wouldn't do this in Oakland in a million years," he continued, "not without a whole squad of sharp-shooters to back us up. Coming here by ourselves is irresponsible, crazy. I never should have let Freeman talk me into it."

Lucille came in to deliver Rankin's dinner salad. She set the bowl of semi-wilted lettuce on the table. He looked at it but didn't sit down. "Are there sulfites on that salad?" he asked.

Lucille smiled at him with a benevolent, sixtysomething, peroxide-blonde smile. "Honey, I couldn't tell you. They only pay me to deliver this food. I never see what goes into it before the cook hands it over."

I'd never seen Lucille put on her dumb-blonde act before. She's a savvy lady who can work her way through a racing form in ten minutes flat. Rankin didn't have sense enough to quit while he was ahead.

"I'd better not eat any then," he said. "I'm allergic to sulfites." Lucille swept the offending salad bowl off the table and marched from the room.

Rankin sat now, looking dejectedly at his hands. "I came up here hoping to get away from gangs, you know. My wife doesn't want me having to work around them. She'd have a fit if she knew I was waiting here in a dive, meeting a bunch of them for dinner, without even any kind of bodyguard."

"I won't tell if you don't," I assured him.

We sat quietly for a few minutes. It seemed to take forever for the minute hand on my watch to move from one slash mark to the next. Eventually, Lucille reappeared laden with two platters of food. She set the chili burger in front of me and slung the other one onto the table, where it came to rest in front of Chief Rankin. He stared down at it, dismay written on his face.

"This doesn't look like salmon," he said.

"It's ham," Lucille told him firmly. "We're out of salmon."

With that she flounced from the room before a stunned Chief Rankin had a chance to reply. It was all I could do to keep from laughing aloud. Rankin had violated one of the prime unwritten rules of Doghouse behavior — offending a waitress — and Lucille had seen to it that he was suitably punished.

I think he would have gone after her, but just then the door opened again, and our guests sauntered into the room.

I've been told all my life that America is a melting pot. The Hispanics may have given rise to the general theme of cool macho dudeness, but urban blacks have elevated it to an art form, and these six dudes were the coolest of the cool.

They came wearing the uniforms and colors — blues, reds, and blacks — of their three diverging armies. They wore leather and gold chains and three-inch Afros with shaved spots over some ears. They stalked into the room, but there was no elbowing, no jabbing or jibing or trading of insults. They filed in silently with all the solemnity of young men attending a funeral. Behind veiled eyelids, they sized each other up, but no one said a word.

Our guests were a disturbing-looking bunch, and the dead silence made it even worse. It got scarier still when the last to arrive peered into the room and then went away, returning with a large leather briefcase, a Hartmann. He set the case on the floor near the door with a resounding thump. The case was big enough to hold a whole arsenal of handguns and other death-dealing weapons. My tie suddenly felt a full inch and a half too tight.

Lucille followed the case into the room, order pad in hand, no-nonsense mask on her face. "Who all's eating?" she demanded.

One of the six seated himself directly across the table from Rankin. Staring at the chief with undisguised, malevolent hatred, he assumed the role of spokesman. "Depends on who's payin'," he said.

Despite his premeeting case of nerves, Chief Rankin seemed to have recovered his equanimity. He met the young man's gaze. "I am," he said. "Have whatever you want."

Lucille turned to the person closest to her. He may or may not have been twenty-one. Unlike Rankin, he had obviously been a guest of the Doghouse on numerous previous occasions. Without needing to consult the menu, he ordered a Bob's Burger and a beer, but the spokesman squelched the latter.

"No drinkin'," he rasped, aiming his smoldering gaze on the offending henchman. "No beer. We're here to take care of business."

No one spoke while Lucille continued taking orders. At last she left the room. "It might be nice if we started with introductions," Chief Rankin began. "I'm Chief of Police —"

"No introductions," the leader interrupted. "We don't need no introductions. We don't need no nicey-nice. We're here to talk business."

"What kind of business?" Rankin asked.

"Look, I got me a business. I go to work every day. It's a capitalist business. Sometimes I got merchandise to sell. Sometimes

I buy. It's a free country, and my business is s'posed to make me a profit, but I'm in this squeeze play, man. I'm gettin' it in the shorts from both ends. I don't mind payin' protection. Like I said, it's a free country. Cops got to make a profit too. What I do mind is gettin' squeezed even after I pay my protection. That's not cool, brother. That is not the American way."

Rankin looked at him in amazement. "You've been paying protection money to officers in my department?"

The leader leered back at him. "I sure as hell ain't been payin' it to the United Way!"

"Who are they? I want their names!"

"Whoa now, I tell you that, I'm breakin' my word, and all that money I spent on protection goes down the drain."

"If you're not going to name names, why are we here then? What's the point?"

"The point is, I want to stay in business. Most black folks leave us alone and most white folks do the same. Some of 'em get in our way, and we kill 'em, but most of 'em leave us alone, and that's cool, man. That's good for business. Except now, everybody's thinkin' we did this murder thing, that we killed Ben Weston and all those little kids."

He paused and snapped his finger. "Ben Weston? I coulda smoked that mother in a minute, but I didn't — not him, not his woman, and not those kids, neither."

For the first time, he looked away from Rankin and stared hard at me. "I give orders. I say shoot to kill. They kill. I say scare the shit out of 'em. The bullet hits the mirror. Understand?"

I understood all right. It was as blatant a confession as I've ever been given, yet I knew there wasn't a damn thing I'd ever be able to do about it. Still, it wasn't a time to back off.

"Who were you trying to scare?" I asked. "Ben Weston or me?"

"Ben Weston busts my homeys. I been paying One-Time for protection so me and my boys don't go down, but he's doin' it anyways, hidin' 'em, makin' 'em forget what they's s'posed to do. So I'm gonna scare Ben Weston, scare him real good, excepten he's dead already and my homey's too damn dumb to figure it out."

Lucille came into the room and delivered the food, studiously ignoring Chief Rankin. By mutual unspoken agreement, all discussion ceased until she went out, once more closing the door behind her. When she left, Rankin resolutely picked up his knife and began attacking the cold ham steak solidifying on his plate. When no one else spoke, I finally put in my own two cents' worth.

"You said you were going to help us," I said quietly. "Do you know who killed Ben Weston?"

My counterpart lifted his hand and the young man nearest the briefcase hefted it onto the table. My heart skipped a beat as I wondered if now was when the guns would come out and the shooting would start, but no one made a move to open it.

"You know a homey named Knuckles Russell?" the speaker asked.

I nodded. "I know him."

"You see this case here? It's his, but somebody stole it. Been gone two maybe three months, and Knuckles is all pissed off 'cause it's from his mother. Then yesterday morning it shows back up at the place where Knuckles use' to live. Like magic, now you see it now you don't."

"He must have brought it back."

My opponent shook his head. "That motherfucker walks on my turf, I'd smoke him, and he knows it. But it's his all right. His bag and his shit." He shoved the case down the tabletop, stopping it when it was directly in front of me.

"Open it, One-Time," he said to me. "Open it and see for yourself."

I flipped the latches on the case and lifted

the lid. The only thing visible inside was a pair of sweats, red sweats, that had been crammed into it. But there was something else in there as well. It came out and wafted heavily through the room. Homicide cops smell that smell all the time — the sickeningly overpowering odor of rotting dried blood.

In a roomful of menacing Bloods, Crips, and BGD, there are some words you don't say if you want to leave the room alive. "Blood" is one of those words. Keeping my mouth shut, I closed the lid on the briefcase and looked back at the spokesman, who was regarding me levelly across the table. When I didn't look away, he picked up his Bob's Burger and took a huge bite.

"You say the briefcase showed up where Russell used to live. Does that mean he doesn't live there anymore?"

"That's right."

"Where does he live now?"

The leader shrugged. "Who knows? Ask Ben Weston."

"Ben Weston's dead," I pointed out. "Did Knuckles Russell kill him?"

"Knuckles didn't dis Ben Weston."

"So who did?"

"That's your job, One-Time. You find that out, 'cause most folks thinks we did it, and that makes it tough to do business. Understand?"

And then I understood why the gangs had called for a meeting. It all boiled down to public relations. Most of the time they operated with impunity, without direct, active, or vocal opposition from the African-American community at large. The slaughter of Ben Weston's family, with the accompanying media presumption that street gang activity was somehow ultimately responsible, had galvanized the black silent majority into being not nearly so silent.

"May we take the case?"

"Yo, man. Take the case if it'll help you do your funky job. That's what we all want."

Just then, Chief Rankin's pager went off. He excused himself and hurried out of the room to answer it, leaving me alone with our six guests. He wasn't gone long. When he came back and stopped in the doorway, I could see from the look on his face that something was terribly wrong.

"Come on," he said. "There's a problem. Grab that bag. We've gotta go. I've got the check."

He dashed away again while I picked up the bag, aware that my every action was being studied by six separate people, five of whom, other than ordering their food, had not spoken a word since entering the room. Only the single representative had acted as spokesman for the entire group.

It amazed me to think how the idea of arousing the ire of the entire African-American community had posed enough of a threat to force these young toughs into an unprecedented show of solidarity, but there was no hint that the truce would last any longer than the time it took to vacate the room.

Six pairs of cold eyes stared at me, and I stared back, examining each face in turn, knowing that some of them would show up on the fifth floor eventually, coming under the scrutiny of Homicide either as perpetrator or victim. I didn't want to say thank-you to this bunch of murderous thugs. The very word would have stuck in my throat, yet I owed them something.

"Somebody here knows someone who has himself a late-model Lexus," I said quietly. "The driver is wanted in connection with the attempted murder of a Seattle police officer. I'd get rid of them both, if I were you, send them back where they came from."

With that, I turned and walked out of the room carrying the briefcase with me. I found Chief Rankin at the counter, dancing from foot to foot, arguing heatedly with the cashier.

"What seems to be the matter?" I asked.

"They don't take plastic here," he protested, waving his credit card in the air. "Not even the city credit card. There are eight meals on this bill. I don't carry around that kind of cash, and I don't have my checkbook with me, either."

"How much is it?"

I took out my wallet and extracted the hundred-dollar bill I've taken to carrying there in case of emergencies. I paid the bill, including a double tip for Lucille, and wrote the entire amount at the bottom of the receipt.

"This is going to show up on my expense account," I said. "And nobody better question it."

"They won't. Come on. Hurry."

"What's the matter?"

"There's been a shooting on Beacon Hill. Officer down."

"Where on Beacon Hill?" I asked as we raced for my car, but I didn't have to listen for an answer. Before he told me, I already knew. The location was the home of Reverend Homer Walters, and the downed officer had to be Big Al Lindstrom.

CHAPTER 19

I drove like a maniac, but nobody pulled me over. Chief Rankin hinted that he would have preferred to stop by the department and pick up his own car. He hinted, but he didn't issue a direct order. It's a good thing too. If he had, I would have been forced to disregard it.

Now it was my turn to be where Big Al had been the night Ben Weston was murdered, my turn to deal with the anger that rose like bile in my throat, my turn to agonize over the part I had played in positioning Big Al in the way of that bullet. How could I have done such a thing?

Chief Rankin and I were back in my Porsche, so we were out of departmental radio contact. Luckily we did have my cellular phone. I picked it up and dialed directly in to Dispatch.

"Detective Beaumont here," I announced. "I have Chief Rankin in the car with me.

We'll be at that Beacon Hill location in five to seven minutes. What's the status?"

"Medic One is on the scene. There's a doctor there as well. They're trying to stabilize him enough to transport him to the hospital."

"Since when does Medic One send out doctors?"

"They don't. Evidently this one just happened to be on the scene when it all went down. Hang on a minute, Beau. I have to take another call."

He was off the phone for some time.

"How's Lindstrom doing?" Chief Rankin asked. "Is he going to make it?"

As soon as Dispatch came back on the line, I asked him that same question. "It's too soon to tell. He took a bullet at point-blank range. It hit him below his vest. Evidently there's lots of internal damage."

"Has anyone gone to tell Molly?"

"Not yet as far as I know. Would you like to handle that? You probably know her better than anyone else here."

"Sure," I said, my voice cracking. "As soon as I drop the chief off, I'll go pick her up and take her to the hospital. Which one, the trauma unit at Harborview?"

"They're the local Roto-Rooter-of-choice for bullet extractions. When it comes to that kind of thing, it pays to use people with experience."

Before I signed off, I gave the dispatcher my phone number in case he needed to get back to me, then, after I hung up, I prayed that the phone wouldn't ring again because I was afraid of what the caller might tell me if it did.

"I can't believe this," Rankin was saying. "Has the whole city declared open season on cops?"

I knew the answer to that question was no, and so did Chief Rankin. The whole city wasn't killing cops, and neither were street gangs. Cops were killing cops, crooked cops killing straight ones.

"Do you have Captain Freeman's number?" I asked.

"Which one, home or office?" Rankin asked.

"Both," I told him. "We'd better call him so he'll be in on this case from the beginning. It may be that nobody else has thought to call him. They wouldn't necessarily know there was a connection between this and IIS."

Chief Rankin reached inside his jacket and removed his pocket-sized Day-Timer. He took out the tiny telephone directory notebook and consulted that. As soon as I saw it, I thought about Ben Weston's Day-Timer, lying there on the bedroom floor, the pages filled with appointments — some kept and some forever unkept — and the elusive numbers he couldn't remember without writing them down.

The sad truth about homicide is that most people are murdered by people they know. For that reason, a victim's calendar in the days shortly before his death becomes a prime starting point in tracing his activities and connections. More often than not, the perpetrator will be found among those final few social or business contacts. For that reason alone, Ben Weston's Day-Timer should have been right at the top of the task force's concerns. I didn't remember Paul Kramer assigning it to anyone, so I assigned myself.

By then Chief Rankin had managed to locate Captain Freeman's number and was dialing it. Tony Freeman's wife answered the phone and told him her husband had just left the house. She said someone had called a few minutes earlier and that Tony was on his way back downtown to his office, although it was still too soon for him to be there. Knowing Freeman was on his way made me feel better. It meant someone besides me was making the same connections and drawing the same conclusions.

When we turned off Columbian Way onto Fifteenth and again onto Dakota, we were thrown into what was almost an instant replay of two nights earlier. Law enforcement vehicles and flashing lights abounded. Traffic was being rerouted. No one on the force expected Chief Rankin to show up at all, to say nothing of having him appear as a passenger in a Porsche 928. It seemed as though every few feet another traffic cop waved us over and tried to divert us in a different direction.

It took time to work our way through the crush to a parking place in front of the Walterses' house, but we made it eventually, stopping only a few feet away from the Medic One van. I had yet to bring the Porsche to a complete stop when Chief Rankin hopped out and began pushing his way through the crowd surrounding the truck. I got out myself and walked up to where a grim-faced Major Phil Dunn, the night commander of Patrol, was conferring with an equally somber Captain Powell.

"How's it going?" I asked.

Captain Powell shook his head. "Not good," he said. "Not good at all."

"Was anyone else hurt?" Only during the last few minutes of the drive had I finally had brains enough to worry about Junior Western. I asked the question with a good deal of dread.

"No. Big Al evidently surprised someone trying to climb in a basement window."

"Man or woman?"

"Man."

"He got away?"

Powell nodded. "So for, but we're working on it. We've brought in two of the K-nine units, but they haven't found anything yet."

"What I want to know," Major Dunn was saying, "is what the hell Big Al was doing here in the first place. I thought you pulled him off this case, Larry, but that's Junior Weston over there in that car or I'll eat my hat."

"Junior Weston?" I asked, my heart flooding with gratitude. "Where is he? Is he all right?"

"He's fine," Major Dunn answered. "He's over there in one of my patrol cars with a two-person guard."

Under most circumstances, that would have been good news, but Major Dunn didn't know we were looking for a crooked cop whose identity we had yet to uncover. Our bad guy could just as easily be from Patrol as from anywhere else.

"Let's go check on him," I said. "I'll feel better once I see him."

Major Dunn shrugged as if to say who can understand these crazy Homicide dicks anyway, but he set off at a rapid pace while I tagged along behind. We found Junior Weston huddled in the far corner of a Seattle PD patrol car once more clutching his precious teddy bear. The two cops with him were doing what they could to reassure him, but they were understandably outraged by everything that had happened to the poor little kid, and they were frustrated by their inability to offer him any real comfort.

I turned back to Major Dunn. "I know the boy," I said. "Tell your guys they can go."

"But —" Major Dunn began.

"Please," I interrupted. "Let me talk to him alone."

"All right," Dunn said, giving in. He turned to his men. "You can go now. We'll take care of the boy from here on out. Go on over to the command van and get reassigned. I'm sure there's plenty to do."

The two patrolmen climbed out of the car, and I got into the driver's seat, closing the door behind me, shutting out the night and the rest of the officers, including Major Dunn.

"Remember me?" I asked.

Junior looked up, nodded, and immediately buried his face in his teddy bear.

"Are you okay, Junior?" I asked. He nodded but this time he didn't raise his head.

"Are you worried about Big Al?"

Another nod. "Is he going to be all right? Is Adam's mom going to be able to fix him up?"

"Adam's mom? Was she here?"

"Yes."

That was news to me. If Dr. Emma Jackson was there, I hadn't seen her. "I don't know if she'll be able to or not. I didn't get a chance to talk to her or the Medic One guys either. They're working on him right now."

"It was the bad man, looking for me again, wasn't it? How come? Why can't you stop him?"

The simultaneous accusation and cry for help cut to the quick. "We're trying," I said. "We're doing our best."

"It's all my fault," Junior Weston whimpered. "It's because of me Mr. Lindstrom got hurt."

"It isn't your fault, Junior. None of it is."

"But what does the bad man want? Why's he still looking for me then?"

"Because he knows you saw his face," I

answered quietly. "He's afraid you can identify him."

Junior Weston raised his head then and looked at me, his small chin set in staunch defiance. "And I can, too," he said determinedly. "I will."

"But until you do," I cautioned, "we've got to make sure you're safe. I thought you'd be safe here, at this house with the Walterses, but the bad man found you anyway. What would you think of coming home with me for a day or two, Junior? I live in a downtown high rise with a swimming pool and a hot tub and a rooftop garden."

"A garden on the roof? Are you kidding? Gardens don't go on roofs. The dirt would all fall off."

"The dirt doesn't fell off this one because it's flat. And there's a duck that lives there, too. Her name is Gertrude and she has five little ducklings. We even put out a wading pool for her so she could teach them how to swim."

"Are there any other kids?"

"Some. Two anyway. Their names are Heather and Tracie. I'm sure they'd be happy to play with you."

Junior grew quiet and seemed to be considering my offer. "What would Reverend

Walters think?"

"More than anything, Reverend Walters wants you to be safe," I answered. "I'm sure he wouldn't mind."

Junior frowned. "It sounds okay, but I really want to go home. To my home."

"You can't go there, Junior. Nobody can. And you wouldn't want to, either, not right now. It's a crime scene."

Tears welled up in Junior's eyes. "But what about all my stuff?" he demanded. "What happens to my toys — my dad's matchbox cars and the old transformers Dougie gave me and the baseball I won signed by Ken Griffey and his dad? What about those?"

"I'll tell you what, Junior. In fact, I'll make you a promise. When it's time to go back to your house, I'll go with you and so will Big Al, if he's well enough. We'll help you get all your stuff gathered up and other things as well, things you should have from the rest of your family, mementos. They may not mean that much to you right now, while you're young, but they will later, when you're older."

"So I won't forget?" Junior asked.

I felt a catch in my throat and tears blurred my own eyes. "You won't forget, Junior. Don't worry about that. No matter what, you'll never forget. Will you come stay with me?"

"Okay."

With a warning squawk of siren, the Medic One van eased down off the curb and began nudging its way through the crowd. While everyone busily focused on that, I smuggled Junior back to my car and belted him into the passenger seat. As I did so, I caught sight of Knuckles Russell's briefcase still sitting in back where I'd left it.

Captain Powell came up behind me. "What's going on, Detective Beaumont?"

"I'm taking Junior here home with me for the time being. Go let the Walterses know, would you? They can tell old Mr. Weston if they want, but under the circumstances, the fewer who hear about this the better."

"What's Child Protective Services going to say?" Powell asked.

"Screw Child Protective Services!" I growled. "If Big Al couldn't handle it, what the hell do you think CPS would do?"

"Not much," Powell agreed. "Go ahead, Beau. I'll back you up on this one."

I paused long enough to drag Knuckles Russell's briefcase out of the car and handed it over to Captain Powell. "Here's this," I said.

"What is it?"

"A present from our Doghouse summit meeting. It needs to go down to the Crime Lab. You might ask Janice Morraine to take a look at it. She's close enough to the case to know what's going on. And one other thing. If you could, try to find out who on the task force if anybody is working on Ben Weston's Day-Timer."

"Day-Timer? I don't remember anything about a Day-Timer," Powell said with a frown. "Where is it?"

"It *was* on the floor of Ben Weston's bedroom the last I saw it, but I don't have any idea where it is now. I'd like to talk to whoever's working on it, and I'd like to see it if it's at all possible."

Powell nodded and stepped away from the car while I climbed into my seat, fastened my own belt, and started the engine. "Can we stop long enough to get my Nintendo?" Junior asked. "I could show you how to play."

"No," I said. "Not tonight. We'd better get you home and into bed." I didn't want to voice my real reason for not wanting to stop — the need to limit the number of people who saw me with Junior Weston and who might guess where he'd been taken.

If Junior was disappointed about leaving the video game behind, he didn't complain.

On the drive into the city, he stayed mostly quiet. I wondered how this tough little kid was managing to cope with the chaos that had suddenly descended over his entire life, leaving him nothing to hold on to but a soon-to-be-scruffy brown teddy bear.

We had come up the I-5 corridor and were about to turn off on the Mercer/Fairview Exit when Junior sat up straight and peered out across me at the myriad lights that make up downtown's nighttime skyline.

"You live in one of those tall buildings?" he asked tentatively.

"Yes."

"Which one?"

"The tall one nearest the Space Needle."

"Which floor?"

"The top one, the twenty-fifth."

"Does your house have a basement?"

I knew at once why he was asking that question, and I didn't blame him. "Yes," I told him, "the building does, but you can't get into it without either a garage door opener or a key to the building."

"Oh," he said, sounding relieved.

When we reached Belltown Terrace, I let Junior punch the button to open the garage door. Then, I let him work the numbered combination lock that controls the door into the elevator lobby on P-1. I thought it was

315

important that Junior Weston know for sure that someone couldn't just walk into the building anytime they pleased. On that particular night it was important for J. P. Beaumont to know that too.

On the way upstairs in the elevator, it dawned on me that maybe I should have called ahead to warn Ralph Ames that I was bringing home company. After all, he might have been entertaining guests of his own, but I needn't have worried. When we walked into my condo, we found Ralph rousing himself out of a sound sleep, floundering to his feet from my rehabilitated but comfortable leather recliner.

"Junior, this is Ralph Ames," I said, introducing them. "He's a good friend of mine. Ralph, this is Junior Weston. I'm going to have to go back out again for a while, but the two of you will be all right here together."

He may have been groggy, but Ralph Ames is always quick on his feet. He reached down and shook the boy's hand. "I'm glad to meet you, Junior," he said gravely, "but I'm very sorry to hear about what happened to your family."

"You know about that?" Junior asked wonderingly.

"It's been in all the newspapers," Ralph

replied. "I've been reading about it."

"Junior's going to stay with us for a day or two," I interjected matter-of-factly. "I thought we'd fix up a bed for him on the window seat here in the living room."

"Sure," Ralph said. "I can handle that. What's going on?"

"Big Al's been hurt. I've got to go get Molly."

"Hurt badly?" I nodded. "You go do whatever you need to do," Ralph said. "Junior and I will be fine."

He turned to Junior Weston with the kind of ease and rapport that only people without children of their own can possibly hope to maintain. "Do you like chocolate?"

Junior Weston nodded.

"I think there's some double fudge chocolate ice cream in the fridge," Ralph said, leading the child away by the hand. "Let's go check. Does that teddy bear of yours have a name?"

I left the apartment knowing that Junior Weston was safe and sound and in truly capable hands.

CHAPTER 20

Police officers live with the possibility of death every single shift of every single day. So do police officers' wives. It goes with the territory.

Molly Lindstrom had been a police officer's wife for more than eighteen years when I drove over to Ballard to get her and take her to Harborview Hospital. When she came to the door of their working-class-neighborhood home, she was wearing a long flannel nightie with a terry cloth robe thrown hastily over her shoulders. She turned on the porch light and peered out briefly before opening the door. A stricken look passed over her face as soon as she recognized me.

"It's Allen, isn't it!" she exclaimed. "Is he all right?"

"They've taken him to the hospital, Molly," I said as gently as possible. "I've come to take you there."

For a long time she stood staring at me uncomprehendingly, saying nothing. "Oh, well then," she said finally. "Come in. Wait right here while I go get dressed."

She hurried away, leaving me standing in the vestibule of their small two-story bungalow. The place showed the benefits of having a full-time Scandinavian housewife on the premises. For one thing, it was spotlessly clean, scrupulously so. The hardwood floor gleamed in the muted light of a small, cobweb-free, entryway chandelier. The gently enticing scent of a mouth-watering home-cooked meal lingered somewhere in the background.

Molly Lindstrom was a full-time housewife because that's the path she and Big Al had chosen together long ago. Now, after years of scrimping to put their second son through college, Molly and Big Al were just beginning to indulge themselves a little. They had talked of shopping for a new couch and chair set for their living room, and Al had asked for my expert opinion on what Molly might think of a surprise Alaskan cruise on the occasion of their thirty-fifth anniversary late in the summer.

All that was in jeopardy now. Big Al, seriously wounded, lay on a hospital gurney when he should have been safe at home and in bed with his wife. He had been off duty, for God's sake. I was the one who had called him up and put the bug in his ear about Junior Weston possibly being in danger. And I had been right, damnit, but I couldn't help wishing our places had been reversed, that I had sent myself instead of my partner — my partner and my friend.

"I'm ready," Molly announced, hurrying in from the bedroom, pulling on and buttoning a heavy hand-knit sweater. "Where is he?"

"Harborview," I said.

We stepped out onto the porch, and I waited while she locked the dead bolt. "How bad is it?"

"Pretty bad, Molly. He was shot below his vest at very close range. They tell me there's lots of internal damage."

She took a deep breath and then straightened her shoulders. "Okay," she said. "I'm all right now. I promise I'm not going to cry. Let's go."

I helped her into the car, helped her fasten the unfamiliar seat belt, wondering why she thought I'd think less of her if she shed tears. I felt like crying myself.

"Do you think I should call the boys, Beau?" she asked as I settled into the driver's seat beside her.

Plucking the cellular phone out of its holder, I handed it over. "Do it," I said.

"But shouldn't I wait until I have some idea of his condition before I call them?"

I knew Gary Lindstrom was working for a truck-leasing company down in California, and Greg, after several months of waiting, had lucked into a job with a prestigious downtown Seattle architectural firm. Of the two, Gary had by far the greater distance to travel.

"I'd call them both, but especially Gary. It's spring break in several of the school districts right now. He might have trouble getting plane reservations."

Molly stared blankly at the telephone receiver in her hand. "How do I work this thing?" she asked.

"Punch in the number, just like you would on your regular handset, then punch 'send.'"

She did. I could tell from the number of beeps that she was taking my advice and calling Gary in California. "It's late," she said. "He'll be worried sick when he hears the phone."

He ought to be, I felt like saying. This was exactly the kind of worst-case scenario that goes through people's heads when a ringing telephone jangles them out of a sound sleep in the middle of the night.

"Hello, Gary. It's your mom. Something's happened . . . Yes, it's Dad. He's in the hospital. He's been shot . . . No, I don't know how bad it is. I'm just on my way to the hospital right now . . . Harborview, that's right. No, I don't know any of that yet. I'll call you again as soon as I find out. I'm with Detective Beaumont. Yes, he came to get me. Well, all right. Just a minute."

She held the phone away from her ear and covered the mouthpiece. "Gary wants to know if you think he should come home."

"On the first available plane," I replied at once.

She looked at me for a long moment before taking her hand off the receiver. "He says for you to wait until you hear from me. There's no sense wasting money on a plane ticket and rushing home if it isn't really necessary. Flying is so expensive."

I wanted to contradict her, but mothers have some inarguable prerogatives, especially ones in her precarious position. "If it's really bad," Molly Lindstrom was saying calmly to her son, "I'll call you back and then you can get a reservation. I'll talk to you again later."

I already knew it was bad. Molly would have to learn that for herself in her own good time.

She disconnected and handed me back the phone. "What about Greg?" I asked. She tried a second number, the one in Seattle, but no one answered.

I hung up the phone for her, and we rode for a while in silence. Overcome by guilt, I could have handled her yelling at me a whole lot better than her enduring, stoic silence.

"I never should have called him," I said at last. "I should have gone there myself and left Al out of it completely."

"What happened?" she asked.

"Someone tried to break into Reverend Walters's house, tried to get in through a basement window. Al evidently caught him in the act and got shot in the process."

"The guy was trying to get to Junior?"

"We believe so, yes."

"Is Junior all right?"

"Yes. He's fine."

"Thank God," she breathed. There was a pause and then she added, "Allen never would have forgiven himself if anything more had happened to that little boy. I'm surprised he let the guy get off a shot. I would have shot him myself if I'd had half a chance. Don't blame yourself, Beau. Allen won't, and I don't either."

We wheeled up to Harborview's emergency entrance. I paused long enough to let Molly out of the car. "You go on in," I urged. "I'll find a parking place and be right there."

I found her a few minutes later upstairs in a surgical floor waiting room. By then Big Al had already been in surgery for almost an hour. We were told it could be as long as two more while they repaired the damage the bullet had done to his intestinal tract.

Molly took that piece of dire news with good grace. "At least he's still alive," she said.

Hospital waiting rooms are terrible places. They're not places where you see the people *in extremis.* What you do see there is the collateral damage, the people whose lives have been thrown into upheaval and concision by whatever is happening to the person behind the closed door of the operating room, the person under the knife.

They say that with long-married couples, if one partner undergoes surgery, they both do. Molly Lindstrom was quiet and seemingly unruffled, but her usually ruddy complexion was unnaturally pale, her breathing sounded shallow, and she gave every appearance of being in physical pain. I worried about her.

"Don't you think you should go ahead and call Gary now?" I asked.

She shook her head stubbornly. "Not until after I talk to the doctor and know what's really going on."

Sue Danielson showed up about one forty-five A.M., bringing with her two very welcome cups of reasonably fresh coffee.

"How's it going?" she asked. We had stepped outside the waiting room into the hospital corridor where we could talk with some semblance of privacy.

"He's still in surgery," I said. "What are you doing here, besides bringing coffee?"

"Captain Powell wanted me to let you know that as soon as he called her, Janice Morraine came right back down to the Crime Lab and is personally taking charge of the briefcase you and the chief picked up earlier. That's the good news. The bad news is that Ben Weston's Day-Timer is nowhere to be found. Neither is his floppy. They never got logged into the evidence inventory."

"But I saw the Day-Timer myself. Right there on the floor of Ben's bedroom. It even had his initials on it. How could it disappear like that?"

"Somebody took it. That's simple enough."

"Who?"

"Somebody who was there that night along with all the rest of us — one of the investigators, someone from the Crime Lab, who knows?"

I shook my head. I knew most of those people personally, had worked with them for years. "But I don't want it to be one of them," I argued. "I don't want it to be someone I've worked with and respected."

"Too bad, buddy," Sue Danielson said. "You lose."

"What are you going to do now?"

"Me? I'm headed home for bed. Captain Freeman wants me back in his office by eight A.M. sharp with a complete report on everything I've managed to pick up along the way. Considering the commute, eight o'clock isn't a helluva long time from now. What about you?"

"I'm here for the duration," I said. "I brought Molly down, and I'm staying until she decides to go home or spend the night or until someone else comes to get her."

Sue left. After I finished my coffee, I went back into the waiting room. Nothing had changed. I found a quiet corner and settled in to wait and think. What the hell had become of that missing Day-Timer? And where was the floppy disk with its backup files? They had both disappeared for good reason, I decided. Was it because of the computer access code, the one Ben Weston never should have written down at all? Or did the killer's name appear damningly in one or the other? It didn't take a genius to figure out that the missing information was vitally important, or it wouldn't have become necessary to run the risk of making it disappear.

I had no idea where the disk might have been, but I knew for certain that the Day-Timer had been on the bedroom floor, and only a finite number of people had had access to Ben Weston's bedroom on the night in question. Either the person or persons who had taken the calendar were involved in the murders or they were closely connected to the murderer. Police officers or not, I intended to find them.

With motive a given, who had opportunity? Of all the people on the scene the night Ben Weston died, the Crime Lab people themselves, the ones charged with protecting the chain of evidence, were the ones with the most latitude. After that came the Homicide detectives, followed, in descending order, by everybody from the police photographers right on down to the beat cops.

I was starting to make a mental list when the waiting room door swung open and a doctor walked into the room. He looked around. "Mrs. Lindstrom?" he asked, spying Molly sitting on a couch with her eyes closed and her head resting against the wall behind her.

Instantly she sat up, fully alert. "Yes," she responded.

"We're finished. He's down in the recovery room right now."

"How is he?"

"Lucky. Very lucky. We've repaired the damage as well as we can for the time being. The biggest danger now is that infection will set in. We'll have to leave the incision open for several days to assure that doesn't happen, but I think he's going to be all right."

"Really?" Molly asked.

"Really."

Molly smiled weakly and shook her head while tears sprang to her eyes. "I think," she said slowly, "that now I will cry." And she did.

Molly stumbled back to the couch, leaving the doctor, who seemed to have something more to say, standing there in the middle of the room, waiting and looking uncomfortable.

Finally he said, "Excuse me, Mrs. Lindstrom, but do you happen to know someone named Beauford, Borland, something like that?"

"Beaumont?" I asked.

"That's it," the doctor announced, snapping his fingers. "Beaumont. I'm terrible with names."

"I'm Detective Beaumont," I said.

"I have a message for you. I couldn't believe it. This guy is going to die if we don't get started doing surgery, but he won't let the anesthesiologist or anybody else touch him until we promise to take a message. I told him, 'I'm a doctor, not Western Union,' but I don't think he thought it was very funny."

I didn't either. "You have a message for me?"

"Sort of. I hope I have this name right. Sanders, Sanderlin? It's close, but I didn't have any way to write it down."

"That's all? Just a name?"

"No, there was something else too. The name, whatever it is, and the word garage. Does that make sense to you?"

"Not really."

"Did he maybe leave his car at a garage someplace with someone by the name of Sanders? From the way he insisted on my taking the message, I thought for sure you'd know exactly what he was talking about. He acted like it was a matter of life and death."

And then, just like in the comics, the light-bulb came on in my head. It was a matter of life and death. Big Al Lindstrom had recognized his assailant and was trying to get word to me as soon as possible. He hadn't wanted to wait however many hours it would take for him to make it through surgery and out of the recovery room.

Meanwhile, with his message more or less successfully delivered, the doctor had re-turned to Molly. Gently, he took her by the arm. "If you'd like to come with me, Mrs. Lindstrom, you can see him for just a few minutes."

They left and I stood there in that mean little waiting room trying to decode Big Al's message. I couldn't think of anybody named Sanders in any garage. Like me, Big Al often uses the bus so he doesn't have to hassle with downtown parking. So it wasn't a park-ing garage. And he usually serviced his own cars, so it probably wasn't a mechanic either. It had to be the department's garage, the motor pool, but who there was named Sanders?

My first instinct was to go roaring down the hill, crash into the garage, kick ass, and take names later, but that wouldn't work in this case. And it didn't make sense, besides. How could a grease monkey from Motor Pool be the mastermind behind a plot that had the entire street gang population of Seattle up in arms? No, I needed to consult with a cooler head on this one, most likely Captain Anthony Freeman himself.

But I was torn. Whatever I did, I couldn't very well take off and leave Molly Lindstrom stranded there at the hospital. She was only gone for a few minutes. When she returned to the waiting room, she was alone but beaming.

"He's going to be fine. I'll call the kids now."

"Do you want me to take you home?"

"No. I'll stay here. They said they'll be moving him out of recovery and into intensive care in a little while. It's a different waiting room, but they said there are couches where I can sleep if I need to."

"You're sure?"

"Of course I'm sure," she replied. "He might wake up and need me. Don't tell him I told you so, but Allen's really a big baby when he's sick."

"My lips are sealed," I told her.

Big Al's dirty little secret was safe with me.

CHAPTER 21

By the time I left the hospital, there was no sense in going back by the Walterses' home. Whatever was happening with the on-site investigation would have been well under way and assigned to someone else. Instead, I headed down the hill to the department with one overriding question still reverberating in my brain. Sanders. Who the hell was Sanders? Try as I might, I couldn't think of anybody.

Even though it was three o'clock in the morning, press vehicles were a visible presence around the Public Safety Building. What Chief Rankin had called "open season on cops" continued to be the biggest story in town that week. I couldn't blame the media for chasing after it, but I sure as hell didn't want to end up being trapped into talking to any of them.

"What's going on?" I asked the officer stationed in the lobby.

"Press conference," he answered.

"At this hour of the morning?"

He shook his head. "Why not? All those people are up anyway — Chief Rankin, Detective Kramer, and all those crazy reporters. They could just as well keep each other company and stay out of everyone else's hair."

I nodded sympathetically. My sentiments exactly. Luckily, I made it into the elevator without running into anyone. But then, when it came time to push the button, I took a wild notion to go upstairs and see if Captain Freeman was still around. I skipped 5 and punched 11 instead.

When the elevator door opened, I saw that the receptionist's desk was empty, but the door into Freeman's office was propped open with a chair. A reading light glowed from inside.

"Who is it?" he called as I stepped into the lobby.

"Detective Beaumont," I answered.

"Come on in."

I stepped to the inner door. Captain Freeman didn't bother to get up. With his tie loosened and shirt sleeves rolled up, he sat at his desk, laboring over that same, much-used yellow pad I had seen earlier. In a world that has gone overboard for comput-ers, I have to respect a guy who hasn't jumped on the latest technological bandwagon.

As I walked in, he put down his pen and rubbed his eyes. "Good to see you, Beau. How's Detective Lindstrom?"

"The doc says he thinks he's going to make it. He came through the surgery all right."

"Great."

"By the way," I said, easing myself into one of the several chairs that still littered the office. "I didn't log in. Do you want me to?"

Freeman smiled wearily. "Hell with it. I didn't either. That's a good piece of work on the Day-Timer and the floppy, Beau. I'm following up right now, as a matter of fact."

"You found them?"

"No, but I'm working on a list of possibles — all the people I've been able to verify who were actually there in Ben Weston's house the night of the murders. Unfortunately, it's a very long list."

As far as I'm concerned, making lists and checking them twice is a line that has nothing to do with "Here Comes Santa Claus." They're words to live by in the crime-solving business.

I nodded. "Good. I would have done that

myself eventually, but I've been too busy. While you're at it, I've got another name for you. The doctor who performed Big Al's surgery gave it to me while Al was in the recovery room. He said that crazy Norwegian bastard wouldn't let them start doing surgery on him until one of the doctors agreed to bring me the message."

Captain Freeman sat up and picked up his pen, holding it poised over the paper. "Who?"

"That's the thing, I'm not sure. The doctor couldn't quite remember the name. He said it was something like Sanders or Sanderlin. Those were his two choices, and I don't recognize either one. And I don't know how accurate the doctor is. He thought my name was Beaufort. Whatever the name is, the guy supposedly has something to do with a garage, maybe even Motor Pool."

Freeman frowned. "Sanders? Sanderlin? Neither one of those rings a bell." Nevertheless, he wrote both names down on his list, tying them together with a two-line parenthesis.

"I want this guy," he said quietly. "I want him in the very worst way. The people of this city are all up in arms. In fact, I just got a look at tomorrow morning's . . . this morning's *Post Intelligencer*. Maxwell Cole is raising the roof because, according to him, Seattle PD is doing nothing to put a stop to the gangs that are running rampant in the streets and endangering the lives of the ordinary and innocent citizens of this community. As a matter of fact, I seem to remember a quote from Detective J. P. Beaumont in the article."

"More likely a misquote," I said.

He smiled ruefully. "What I'm getting at, is they still don't know the half of it. Once the people of Seattle hear rumors to the effect that Ben Weston may have been tainted and that we're investigating fellow police officers in regard to the Weston murders, there's going to be hell to pay, but I say bring it on and let's get it over with.

"Whatever is behind it — payoffs, protection — may have happened on my watch, Detective Beaumont, but I'm telling you it's going to get fixed on my watch as well. I've spoken to Ken Rankin. From what the gang members said, this protection racket must have been going on for some time, since long before Chief Rankin came on the scene. But at least now we know about it, and I want it stopped. I want everyone connected with it brought to justice."

He stopped speaking suddenly and stared

up at the darkened ceiling above his head. "No," he said. "That just doesn't make sense, not any at all."

Freeman is one of those rare people who has mastered the art of mental time-sharing and can think about more than one thing at a time. I had trouble keeping up.

"What doesn't make sense?"

"The Motor Pool. Someone who worked there wouldn't have enough connection with the department's day-to-day investigative activities to be able to provide that much valuable information. In order to make a protection racket pay off, you have to offer valuable and accurate intelligence. So maybe someone there is involved, but we have to look for someone else as well, someone higher up in the departmental hierarchy who would have some idea of what was happening on the various squads in different parts of the city. They'd need to know that in order to warn the gangs away from locations targeted for increased enforcement."

"So you're saying someone in Patrol or perhaps in Investigations?"

"At least. Here's the list so far. Take a look at it and see if I left anybody off."

Freeman's list was a *Who's Who* of the Medical Examiner's Office, the Crime Lab, and the Homicide Squad of Seattle PD. The names were there, all of them glaringly familiar.

"It makes you sick to think about it, doesn't it?" he said, as my eyes traveled slowly down the list.

"Yes," I agreed. "It certainly does."

"So what are we going to do about it?"

"Can we get a list of everybody in Motor Pool?"

"Good idea," Tony Freeman said, "I should have thought of that myself."

He picked up the phone and dialed a number. "Hi, Kyle. How's it going?" He listened for a moment before saying, "Good work. Keep after it. How are you doing on the car question?" Again there was a pause. "Sure, I understand that one's tricky, but we may have a way around it. Can you get me a printout of everyone assigned to Motor Pool? Right, mechanics, clerks, everybody. Sure, if the other one is taking too much time, bring this one down as soon as you can. We'll work on that in the meantime."

Freeman put down the phone. "Kyle Lehman's working on Ben's hard drive, but he says it's not all straightforward. He's having to plow through a lot of junk to see if he can find that deleted file. He says he can bring up the Motor Pool list in just a few minutes."

Within fifteen minutes Kyle himself appeared in the office door, bringing with him a hard copy of the Motor Pool list which he dropped casually on Tony Freeman's desk. The captain picked up the list and began studying it while Kyle lounged against the doorjamb, alternately munching another bag of chips and yet another apple. The guy must have a tapeworm.

"What I want to know is how someone got into Ben Weston's directory in the first place," Kyle muttered. That was his area of responsibility, and his feathers were still ruffled that someone had managed to crack his supposedly secure system.

Tony Freeman looked up at him. "My guess is that whoever killed him found Ben's computer access code in his Day-Timer. Then, if they could lay hands on a copy of Ben's personnel record, say, they'd have the answers to many of the possible verification questions, wouldn't they?"

"But he wasn't supposed to write the damn number down anywhere. I tell everybody that, over and over."

"Have you ever looked at Ben Weston's file?" Tony Freeman asked mildly.

"When would I have had time?" Kyle Lehman returned. "I've been running my ass off ever since I left here."

"The man was evidently mildly dyslexic," Freeman continued. "He did a good job of compensating for it, but remembering random letters and numbers was something he couldn't do."

"Oh," Kyle grunted, and left abruptly, taking his apple core with him. Freeman returned to the computer printout of the people in Motor Pool. He had started with the last page first because that was the one that contained the part where I calculated the *S*'s should have been, and he passed the page along as soon as he finished. There was no Sanders, Sanderlin, Sanford, or Saunders. The Motor Pool's alphabetized list skipped directly from Rudolph to Simms without anything in between.

"Looks like we struck out," I said, giving up.

But Captain Freeman is a lover of lists as well as a maker of same. He went to the very beginning page and hunkered down over it, reading through it name by name from square one. His finger moved steadily down the page, then suddenly he stopped and looked up at me.

"How does the name Sam Irwin grab you?"

I shrugged. "It's not Sanders, but the doctor said he was terrible with names. I, for one, happen to believe him. Sam Irwin sounds good to me."

Freeman picked up his phone again. "I need a set of personnel records," he said. "The guy's name is Samuel V. Irwin, and he's a mechanic in Motor Pool."

Secretarial types aren't exactly plentiful in the middle of the night and it was almost four o'clock in the morning, but Freeman had his ace in the hole, Kyle Lehman, who could, at the drop of a keystroke, present him with a copy of almost any piece of paper churned out by the police bureaucracy. Suddenly, I had a far better understanding of how Tony Freeman could continue using his outdated yellow pad. With Kyle's expertise available at a moment's notice, Tony had the best of both worlds.

Once more Kyle showed up, bringing along a several-page document. He tossed it onto Freeman's desk. "I'm getting a little tired of being a messenger service," he complained, but Freeman wasn't listening. His eyes were already scanning down the top page. They stopped halfway down.

"Got him!" he breathed.

"What is it?"

"Look at this."

He handed me the papers, and I looked straight at the part where it seemed Tony Freeman's eyes had stopped scanning, and there it was in black and white in a section headed Previous Employment. The words said United States Marines, Hand-to-Hand Combat Instructor.

"Silent kills," Tony Freeman said grimly. "The United States Marines wrote the book on those."

"Why's somebody like that working as a mechanic in Motor Pool?"

"That's the next thing you and I are going to find out," Freeman told me. "You, actually. Use Connie's phone." Obligingly, I stepped outside to the other desk.

When Pacific daylight time hits Seattle early in April, it takes away big chunks of our hard-earned mornings and turns them back into night. In exchange we receive longer evenings that are great for Little League baseball and not much else. However, on that particular morning when I started my phone search at four-fifteen A.M., I was glad to find that the East Coast was already up and running.

I don't know how Ralph Ames does it, but he always manages to ease his way through incredible tangles of bureaucracy and come out unscathed and victorious on the other side. I guess I ought to sit down with him and take lessons. My style tends to send me butting up against all manner of officialdom — in this case with representatives of the United States Marine Corps.

The young clerk I wound up talking to eventually was unfailingly polite. He did tell me that after eight years in the military, Samuel V. Irwin had been dismissed with a general discharge. A general discharge isn't as bad as a dishonorable one, but it isn't so very good either, and after eight years of service, the infraction must have been pretty bad for the Marines to toss Irwin out on his ear.

"How come?" I asked, wondering if knowing that would explain why Sam Irwin was working in Seattle PD's Motor Pool and not someplace else. "What did he do?"

"I'm not allowed to divulge that information, sir," the clerk replied. "Not without a court order."

"But this is a homicide investigation," I objected.

"Yes, sir. I'm sorry, sir, but the rules are very explicit."

Arguing made no difference, and neither did my going over his head. Frustrated, I headed back into Captain Freeman's office, where he, too, was just finishing a telephone call. "Look at this," he said, pushing his yellow pad across the desk so I could see it. Most people scribble notes to themselves. Freeman printed his in a rapid but letter-perfect style.

"That's from Motor Vehicles," he said, pointing at the bottom notation. "Sam Irwin owns a 1989 Toyota Tercel. What do you think of that?"

"Bingo," I said.

He nodded. "Bingo," he repeated, but he didn't sound the least bit happy.

I couldn't understand it. If Irwin's Toyota Tercel proved to be white, it might provide a pretty convincing link to the Weston case, especially if Irwin ended up matching the physical description of the driver Bob Case had seen skulking around the Weston neighborhood.

"What's the matter?" I asked. "This looks like progress to me."

Freeman got up and paced to the windows, where he stood looking out at the cleaning crew working away in the high rise across the street.

"At this point, I usually turn a case over," he said thoughtfully. "So far, everything we have is entirely circumstantial. There certainly isn't probable cause to make an arrest right now, but there is enough to prompt further investigation. The problem is, nobody from Motor Pool was at Ben Weston's house the night of the murder. That means, if Irwin is in it, he's not alone."

I nodded. It made perfect sense to me.

He drew a deep breath. "So for now, it's you and me and Detective Danielson. Let's go."

He rolled down his shirtsleeves and started putting on his jacket.

"Where?" I asked.

"We're going to pay a call on Sam Irwin's residence. He's not working tonight. I already checked. Where are you parked?"

"On the street."

"Good. We'll take your car. I'm in the garage."

Which is how my 928 got drafted into service for the Seattle Police Department one more time. Neither one of us thought to check with Kyle Lehman before we left the building. In fact, we probably passed each other in the elevator.

He was coming to bring us printed copies of all the deleted but still retrievable files in Ben Weston's computer. If he had bothered to track us down at the time, it might have helped, but now that the mystery of his broken security system was solved, we had lost both Kyle's sense of urgency and his

345

interest. He could have reached us by pager, if he had tried. He could have called us on my cellular phone. But he didn't.

And maybe it's just as well.

CHAPTER 22

At five o'clock in the morning, the sky was beginning to brighten over the Cascades as we made our way out of the Public Safety Building. While we had been preoccupied with tracking things down on the eleventh floor, Chief Rankin's early-morning press conference had evidently concluded, sending both the reporters and their quarry to ground and leaving my Porsche parked in lonely splendor on the street.

Sam Irwin's address was on the east side of Lake Washington. I don't subscribe to the common downtown Seattleite's notion that intelligent life ceases at the entrance to the Mount Baker Tunnel, but I do know better than to venture into the wilds of the Eastside without a precautionary map. Once in the car, we flipped on the reading lamp and pored over my latest edition of the *Thomas Brothers Guide.* Irwin's address seemed to be within the confines of Beaux

Arts, an exclusive little enclave on the banks of Lake Washington. I had never been there, but I knew it to be a separate governmental entity located entirely within the boundaries of its much larger neighbor, the city of Bellevue.

We headed out. After putting in another almost round-the-clock shift, I should have been dead on my feet, but we were on the scent now, circling ever closer to some real answers. That knowledge kept me energized, focused, and alert, carrying me forward as surely as did the powerful engine of my 928.

With me driving and with Tony Freeman in charge of navigation, we headed east toward a recently opened stretch of I-90 — the new Mercer Island floating bridge. Lights and siren weren't an option, but we were making good time until we hit the tunnel. There eastbound traffic was coned down to two lanes, making way for construction vehicles and equipment parked in the far right-hand lane of the new bridge in support of the crews of workmen busily sandblasting guardrails and pavement off the old bridge deck. Now, in preparation for bringing out an additional piece of oversized equipment, a flagger brought traffic to a complete stop.

In typical type-A fashion, I fumed and

pounded the steering wheel while Tony Freeman remained seemingly unruffled.

"So who's the mastermind behind all this?" I asked. "And was Ben Weston in on it and one or more of the others decided to get rid of him?"

"Ben Weston wasn't in on it," Tony Freeman said quietly.

It was one of those times when somebody jolts you, but it takes a second or two to get the message. "You sound pretty certain about that."

"Ben was working for IIS."

I'm sure my jaw dropped a foot. "He was?"

"He came to me last summer when he started hearing word on the streets about the payoffs. He was the one who suggested he transfer into the gang unit."

"But you engineered it?"

"That's right."

"So he wasn't really in trouble on Patrol?"

"We made it look like it. We were both hoping the crooks would invite him to join them. It just didn't work out that way."

A sudden burst of anger left me shaken. "What the hell!" I exclaimed. "If you knew about the payoffs all along, why the hell are you just now getting around to letting anybody else know?"

"It was a one-man investigation, Beaumont. Ben Weston's investigation into crooked cops. He didn't know who could be trusted, and neither did I."

"Goddamnit, you left him hanging out to dry."

"Not knowingly," Tony Freeman returned sharply. "Ben must have been a whole lot closer to nailing these bastards than he was willing to let on. Either that, or he himself didn't know how close he was."

I felt like I was on a damn emotional roller coaster. If Ben Weston was working for IIS, then I could stop being sick about him being crooked, up to a point, anyway. "What's all this bullshit about student loans? What's that all about?"

Tony Freeman sighed. "Beats me," he answered. "The student loans were news to me. The first I heard about them was when Kramer turned up the applications in Ben's desk. Those hit me from way out in left field, and I can't for the life of me see how they fit into the rest of the puzzle."

"But I thought you were the guy who was supposed to have all the answers."

He laughed ruefully. "I wish I did," he said. "I wish to hell I did!"

We were still stuck in the Mount Baker Tunnel, and I was beginning to feel downright claustrophobic. It was early Saturday morning. Traffic shouldn't have been that bad, but crossing Lake Washington is always a crapshoot. We inched forward, car length by slow car length. Modern-day road construction flaggers seem to have lost sight of the idea that their main job is to see to it that traffic keeps moving. For some of them, getting the chance to hold up other people's lives offers them their only possible power trip.

While I gnashed my teeth with impatience, Captain Freeman was still focused on the case. "Have you ever had any dealings with Sam Irwin?" he asked.

"Not many," I replied. "I've talked to him a couple of times when I've been stuck with a broken-down car. He struck me as a surly son of a bitch, and not much of a mental giant."

Tony Freeman nodded. "Right. That's how he struck me, too. Not that smart and not really a cop either. Everything we keep hearing about this case says real cops are involved, not some renegade mechanic from Motor Pool. My guess is that Irwin will be a minor player, but maybe we can convince him to help us nail the others."

"How?" I asked.

"I can be pretty damn persuasive when I

want to be," Tony Freeman declared.

Suddenly the dam broke and eastbound traffic began to move again. Once we were under way, it was only a matter of minutes before we turned off I90 onto Bellevue Way. A half mile later we headed back west toward Beaux Arts.

In the dawn's early light, we were hard-pressed to read street signs on the twisted, barely two-lane streets that wound through the village. Beaux Arts doesn't have its own police force. The town council rents police and fire protection from King County and the city of Bellevue. For traffic control, villagers rely on a series of car-eating speed bumps. An unwary speeder may hit one of those too fast once, but he won't do it twice, not if he has half a brain.

Reading fine print on the map would have driven me up the wall, but Freeman directed us unerringly through the tree-lined maze. "Take this one," he said, pointing out a twisting ribbon of rain-wet pavement that led down to the water and to what had to be, by any estimate, a million-dollar piece of real estate perched on the pricey shores of Lake Washington.

Freeman whistled when he caught sight of the impressive roofline. "If a guy from Motor Pool can afford digs like this, crime really does pay. No question."

I had pulled into the paved driveway and was puzzling about what to do next when the front porch light snapped on, the door opened, and a sweats-clad woman trotted down the stairs. Before I could turn around and retreat out of the roadway, she jogged up to the car and motioned for me to roll down the window.

"Can I help you?"

"We're looking for Sam Irwin," Tony Freeman said.

"Oh," she said. "Sam's my renter. His house is over there." She pointed to a much smaller house, little more than a cabin, off to the side of the main house.

"He must be up already," she added. "His lights are on. See you later." With a congenial wave the woman darted away from the car and jogged up the hill and out of the driveway.

I turned to Freeman. "What now, coach?"

"Block the road with your car," he said. "Then we'll go have a chat with the man before any other early-morning joggers are up and about. Keep your gun handy, Beaumont. Irwin's résumé says he's a trained killer, and I for one believe it."

Tony Freeman didn't say shoot to kill, but that's what he meant, and I knew it.

I didn't like the idea of using the Porsche as a roadblock, but Freeman didn't give me any options. With considerable misgiving, I moved my car to a spot directly in the middle of the narrow driveway, effectively cutting off the possibility of vehicular flight. I switched off both the lights and the motor. Closing the doors as quietly as possible, we started toward the house.

Halfway there, Freeman motioned frantically toward the side of the house. My heart went to my throat, but finally I understood why he was pointing. There, parked in a small lean-to, sat a white Toyota Tercel. I gave Freeman a thumbs-up acknowledgment. If either one of us had been entertaining any doubts, that was the end of them. The presence of a car that matched one of Bob Case's suspicious vehicles pretty much corked it.

Automatic in hand, I followed Captain Freeman onto the small wooden porch. Boards creaked ominously underfoot. From inside came the sound of a radio station playing soft rock music. The door itself stood partially ajar. There was no doorbell.

Freeman stepped to the door and pounded on the casing. "Sam," he called. "Sam Irwin. Are you in there?"

There was no answer. None. But the radio

continued to play. Freeman knocked again. Still no answer.

Cautiously, moving the door aside with his foot, Freeman shoved it open. Across the room a man sat in front of a glowing computer screen.

"Sam?" Freeman asked again tentatively.

There was no answering movement, no sound. The man's hands hung down limply on either side of the straight-backed chair. His head lolled crazily to one side.

With two long, quick strides, Tony Freeman covered the distance between the door and the chair. I stood in the doorway with automatic at the ready, just in case, but that wasn't necessary.

"You'd better go call nine-one-one on that cute little cellular phone of yours," Tony Freeman told me. "This one's already dead."

Summoned by 911 dispatchers, cops from the King County Police Department arrived within minutes, followed by a pair of longtime homicide detectives named Edwin Hammer and Tom Crowe. Over the years, passing in and out of courtrooms, we've all developed something of a nodding acquaintance. I stayed with them while Tony Freeman hustled off to talk with the commander in charge of the arriving contingent of officers.

For a change, I was shuttled into the background, answering questions only when called upon to do so, giving information that would show up in other people's reports as well as in my own, eventually. When they put me on hold while awaiting the appearance of someone from the Medical Examiner's Office, lack of sleep caught up with me. I was sitting on the couch dozing when Detective Crowe happened to read the words written on the computer screen.

"Get a load of this!" he gloated to his cohort Detective Hammer. "We've got this one sacked and bagged, and we've barely been here twenty minutes. Hey, J. P. What'll you give us if we solve your case for you?"

Far too worn-out to get a kick out of their teasing, I willed my tired legs to move and forced my butt off the couch to go see what they were talking about. I had already seen the selection of drug paraphernalia on the table next to the computer, had already observed the bandage on Sam Irwin's wrist which I assumed probably concealed a set of Spot Weston's teeth marks, but I hadn't spent a whole lot of time examining the body. In my business, if you've seen one drug overdose, you've seen 'em all. It doesn't take a whole lot of imagination to fill in the blanks.

Detective Hammer pointed me toward the computer. The screen itself was filled with text. I had glanced at it briefly in the beginning, and it seemed to be some kind of building fund report, but in the ensuing hubbub, neither Tony nor I had finished reading it.

I did so now, however, starting from the beginning, squinting down at the amber letters, and wondering if it was time to have my eyes checked. Halfway through the screen, layered in with the other text, was the following: "To Whom It May Concern: I can't live with what I've done. Tell my mother I'm sorry. Sam."

I wasn't particularly impressed. "That doesn't say much," I said to the two King County cops. "So it was a deliberate overdose rather than an accidental one. What's the big deal?"

Hammer grinned at Crowe and jabbed him in the ribs. "He still hasn't seen it. Not this case, stupid. Yours. The one that's got the whole city of Seattle turned inside out. Look again."

Again I struggled to read the text. At last Hammer could stand it no longer. "What are you, blind? Look at the metal plate glued to the bottom of the CRT."

I saw it and read it and felt like somebody had jabbed me in the ribs. "Property of Benjamin Weston, Sr.," the plate said, followed by Ben's complete address and phone number.

"So what do you think?" Hammer gloated. "Have we found the killer for you or not? You guys are always rubbing our noses in it, but this time we've got the drop on you. What say we go over to the Pancake Corral when we finish here and have a cup of coffee. You buy."

"Buy nothing!" I headed for the door.

"Wait a minute," Tom Crowe said. "Where do you think you're going?"

"To call Sergeant Watkins. He's head of the Weston Family Task Force. He needs to know about this on the double."

Freeman met me in the doorway. "Needs to know about what?"

I pointed. "That's Ben Weston's computer. It's got an ID plate on the CRT."

The head of IIS went over to the computer and looked for himself. "I'll be damned," he said under his breath. He turned around and faced Detectives Hammer and Crowe. They were grumbling back and forth about me being your basic spoilsport.

"Do you two know who I am?" he demanded. The question and the way it was asked cut through the comedy.

"Yes, sir," Detective Crowe said respectfully. "We certainly do."

"Good," Freeman returned. "Now I'm going to tell you to forget it. Not just tell you to forget it, *order* you to forget it. Do you understand?"

The two King County detectives exchanged puzzled glances.

"There's a whole lot more at stake here than a simple murder investigation," Tony Freeman continued. "It is absolutely vital that no one — no one at all — knows that Detective Beaumont and I were here this morning."

Detective Hammer looked as though he was building up to say something cute, but Freeman cut him off. "I've already spoken to your superior about it. He understands the seriousness of the situation. You are to say that the body was reported by person or persons unknown. I'll get the nine-one-one operators to back you up on that for the time being. No way is word of Detective Beaumont's or my participation in this to be leaked to anyone inside or outside your department. Is that clear?"

"You bet," Detective Hammer returned, but his reply sounded less than halfhearted.

Captain Anthony Freeman was not amused.

He moved a foot or so closer to Edwin Hammer. "You may think," he said softly, "that as a King County police officer you are immune from an Internal Affairs officer at Seattle PD, but let me assure you, if word of Beau's or my presence here leaks out, I will hold you both accountable for whatever happens, and I'm prepared to make it stick."

Tony Freeman may have been SPD's regular straight arrow, but it didn't pay to piss him off. Detective Hammer finally got the message. He swallowed hard and took a step backward.

"Yes, sir," he responded. "I understand completely."

Freeman did not smile. "Good," he said. "We'll be going then. Come on, Beau. They're holding the media at bay out front. I have it on good authority that once we make it to the street, someone can lead us out of here by a back way. That red car of yours is a little too distinctive."

Moments later we were back in the Porsche and threading our way through Beaux Arts. "So that's what you meant earlier when you told me you could be persuasive?" I asked.

Tony sighed and leaned back against the headrest, closing his eyes. "Whatever

360

works," he said wearily. A moment later he was sound asleep and snoring.

CHAPTER 23

Captain Freeman didn't wake up until I pulled to a stop in front of the Public Safety Building. "My brains are scrambled," he said. "Detective Danielson's probably already here for our eight o'clock meeting, but I'm going to have to cancel on her. I've got to go home and get some sleep."

Those were my sentiments exactly. It was somehow reassuring to realize even the resident Eagle Scout of IIS, the original iron man himself, needed sleep occasionally. I was in good company.

"You'll be coming to the funeral, won't you?" he asked as he climbed out of the car.

"I'll be there," I said.

"Good. The three of us — you, Sue Danielson, and I — will have to get together and strategize sometime later on today, but probably not until after the funeral, considering the way I feel right this minute."

"You're the boss," I told him.

Tony Freeman smiled and nodded. "Thanks, Beau. It's been a hell of a night, but you do good work. Go home and get some sleep."

It's a good man who can remember to compliment someone else when he's too tired to keep himself upright. Tony Freeman's stock was already pretty high in my book, but it went up a little more right about then.

He closed the car door and started away, but he turned and came back before I could pull away from the curb. I rolled down the window.

"Remember," he warned, "not a word of this to anyone. No one is to know that you and I were anywhere near Sam Irwin's house in Beaux Arts. When you hear the news that he's dead, it had better be news to you. Understand?"

"I got the message," I told him. "I figured it out at the same time you were telling Hammer and Crowe."

"Good," he said. He waved me away and hustled into the building. I arrived home right around eight o'clock, staggering into what I expected to be a quiet house. Wrong. The apartment reverberated with the clatter and rumble of electronic warfare. In the den I discovered Heather Peters and Junior

Weston happily ensconced on the floor, deeply engrossed in some kind of two-player video game.

I wanted to interrupt, to tell Junior that I thought we had found at least one of the men responsible for the murders of his family members. I would have liked to be able to tell him that I was almost certain the bad man who had killed Bonnie was dead himself, but Tony Freeman had given me marching orders to the contrary. There were far too many other loose ends in the investigation for me to risk speaking out of turn and revealing IIS involvement.

Stifling my loose-lips impulse, I left the kids where they were and went looking for Ralph Ames. I found him in the kitchen, bemoaning the fact that I didn't own a waffle iron. Someday in the far distant future I may have a kitchen that will measure up to Ralph's expectations.

"Where'd you get the video game?" I asked, pouring myself a glass of orange juice from a pitcher of freshly squeezed that had appeared mysteriously in my formerly empty refrigerator.

Ralph shrugged. "I called Reverend Walters and asked him. When he said no problem, I sent a messenger over to his place to pick it up. It was a present to Junior from Big Al, you know. The poor kid was really upset that he couldn't bring it along last night. As much as he's been through the past few days, I wanted it here first thing this morning."

Ralph Ames is the only person I know who's a softer touch than I am, especially when it comes to little kids. "And how did you go about locating Reverend Walters?" I asked.

He grinned at me. "It's an old Indian trick," he told me. "I used the phone book."

On that note, I headed for bed. "By the way," I said, pausing in the doorway, "did Homer Walters say anything about what arrangements have been made for Junior to attend the funeral?"

"The way I understand it, the limo from the funeral home will pick up Emma Jackson first and then stop by here for Junior around noon."

"Good. Wake me up no later than eleven so I can get ready."

"You're going along in the limo?"

"You bet. I'm not letting that kid out of the building without me along as a bodyguard. What about clothes for him? I didn't think to bring along anything but the pajamas he was wearing when I picked him up."

"It's already handled. Homer Walters's

wife had clothes for him there, and the messenger brought them along when he picked up the Nintendo," Ames said. "I figured that was one less thing we'd have to worry about later on today."

I should have known that if Ralph Ames was in charge, all those pesky little details would get handled in a totally seamless fashion. Gratefully mumbling my thanks, I stumbled down the hall and fell into bed. I don't even remember lying down. It seemed only a matter of minutes later when Heather Peters brought me a cup of coffee and announced it was time for me to get up.

Settling cross-legged on the foot of the bed, she regarded me seriously while I sipped coffee and waited for my head to clear.

"Is it hard to tie a tie, Uncle Beau?" she asked.

Heather seems far more mature than I like these days. I still haven't adjusted to the relative size of her new permanent teeth which seem totally out of proportion with the rest of her small, round face. And I miss that damn toothless lisp.

"Not too hard," I told her, "but it's tricky until you learn how. You're a girl. Why do you need to know about tying ties?"

"I don't, but Junior does. Ralph's helping

Junior tie his right now. He can't do it himself."

"I'm sure Ralph doesn't mind."

"But if Junior's daddy is dead," Heather pointed out solemnly, "who's going to teach him about ties and all that other stuff kids are supposed to learn?"

Heather's matter-of-fact question struck smack at the heart of Junior Weston's newly problematic existence. Who *would* teach him all those necessary things? I wondered. Tying ties is only one of the mysteries of the adult universe that must be mastered in those fragile years between five and twenty-five. I had grown up without a father, but not without a mother. Junior Weston would be growing up without the benefit of either one. How would he manage? Thinking about it made my heart ache.

"I don't know, Heather," I told her.

"Well," she said seriously. "I've been thinking about it. Why can't he live here with you?" She waited for my answer with cheerful confidence.

"With me?" I choked, misswallowing a mouthful of coffee. A dozen coughs later, I was able to continue. "It sounds like a good idea, Heather, but it probably wouldn't work."

"Why not?" she pouted. "You have lots of

room. If he lived here, I'd have someone closer to my age to play with. Tracy always acts like I'm just a little kid. And Junior's fun. I already took him downstairs and introduced him to Gertrude."

"You can't just decide where a child is going to live," I told her. "Those kinds of decisions are usually left up to the family."

"But Junior doesn't have a family," Heather insisted. "They're all dead."

"He has a grandfather."

"He's old," Heather sniffed.

"And he probably has aunts and uncles, too," I added. "Scoot, now. If I'm going to be ready on time, I'd better climb into the shower."

Once dressed, I called down to Harborview to check on Big Al. Molly wasn't in the ICU waiting room, but her son Gary, the one from California, took my call. He assured me that his father was sleeping right then but doing as well as could be expected. Gary told me that his brother, Greg, had just taken Molly home to change clothes in preparation for the two o'clock funeral service at Mount Zion Baptist Church. He said Molly wouldn't be returning to the hospital until after the funeral.

"Give your dad a message from me the minute he wakes up, would you? Tell him it's been handled."

"What's been handled?"

"Just give him the message. He'll understand. Tell him I'll stop by later to fill him in."

"Got it," Gary said. "I even wrote it down."

By the time the doorman called to say the funeral home limo was downstairs, I was properly dressed in a suit and tie, and so was Junior Weston. As we rode down in the elevator together, he put one hand trustingly in mine. The other held his faithful companion, the teddy bear.

When Emma Jackson saw that I was coming along, I expected her to voice an objection. Instead, she seemed almost happy to see me and greeted both of us with a tentative smile. "Did you get some sleep?" she asked Junior.

He nodded. "And I got to see the ducks. I even got to feed them. The mama duck's name is Gertrude."

"How can someone have ducks in a high-rise building?" Emma asked disbelievingly.

"Don't ask me," I told her. "Ask the duck. She comes here every year and lays her eggs on the recreation level."

"In a downtown condo?"

"Gertrude must be an upscale duck," I

told her.

I was under the impression that we were headed directly for the church. When the limo driver took us down to Columbia and up the entrance ramp onto the Alaskan Way Viaduct, I didn't understand what was happening. "Where are we going?" I asked.

"To West Seattle," Emma replied. "To pick up Harmon."

I shook my head. "He's not going to be thrilled having me along for the ride."

Dr. Jackson pulled Junior Weston close to her and held him protectively under her arm the way a mother hen shelters her helpless chicks.

"He'll understand," she said. "He may not like it, but he'll understand."

I settled in for the ride, surreptitiously glancing over my shoulder now and then to make sure we weren't being followed. Just because Sam Irwin was dead didn't mean that was the end of all our difficulties. It would take time to figure out whether or not Sam Irwin had taken his own life, but in any event I was fairly certain Sam was the knife-wielding killer Junior had seen on the night of the murders. I was also convinced that, whatever his involvement, Sam wasn't operating alone. The other killers had no way of knowing whether Sam was all the child had seen.

We sped south along the viaduct. The previous few days of clear skies had given way to heavy clouds. Puget Sound lay slate-gray beneath a dark and lowering sky. I'm sure both the weather and fatigue contributed to my growing sense of gloom and despair. So did the fact that I was on my way to a five-person funeral. If we couldn't save innocent people like that from the bad guys, I berated myself, what the hell was the point of being a cop?

For a few minutes, Junior was content to sit there cuddled against Emma Jackson's breast, but finally he pushed himself away.

"Is Mr. Lindstrom all right?" he asked.

Emma looked to me for an answer. "He should be, Junior," I replied. "But he wouldn't have been if Dr. Jackson hadn't been right there to help when it happened."

The boy nodded. "I'm glad he's going to be okay," he said. "I was afraid he'd die too."

I caught Emma Jackson's eye. "Thank you for reminding me, Junior. I should have remembered to thank Dr. Jackson myself as soon as I got in the car."

She gave me a half smile and shook her head. "You don't have to thank me, Detective Beaumont," she returned. "You're not the only one around here with a job to do."

Considering the previous fireworks between us, the matching antagonisms, conversation between us in the limo was surprisingly cordial, and it lulled me into a false sense of security, made me think maybe things were starting to get a little better.

We crossed into West Seattle on the Spokane Street Bridge and meandered south, stopping at last in front of a small, carefully maintained bungalow on Southwest Othello Street. Harmon Weston must have been watching through the window. As soon as the driver stopped the limo, the front door banged open, and the old man came hurrying toward the car. I moved to the jump seat to give him a place to sit.

"The killer's dead!" Harmon Weston declared animatedly as he clambered into the limo. Then, seeing me, a curtain seemed to fall across his features.

"What's he doing here?" Harmon Weston demanded.

"Got who?" Junior was asking excitedly. "Who'd they get? Tell me."

"What's happened?" Emma asked.

Harmon Weston looked hard at me. "Ask him," he said. "I'm sure he knows all about it."

Three pairs of questioning eyes turned on me, but I was under strict orders to keep my mouth shut. Tony Freeman had told me that when I heard the news I'd better be surprised, but I've never been known for my propensity for role play.

"Knows all about what?" I asked ingenuously. "Who's dead?"

Harmon Weston's smoldering eyes drilled into me. "My son's killer, that's who. They found him somewhere over in Bellevue."

"Is he dead for real?" Junior asked. "Did the cops get him? Did somebody shoot him?"

Suddenly accusatory, Emma Jackson turned on me as well. "You knew about this, didn't you?"

"No," I said, trying for total innocence. "I had no idea."

My acting ability will never win an Academy Award. Emma shot me a withering look. "You expect us to believe that you, one of the detectives on the case, didn't know a thing about this?"

Emma turned from me to Harmon Weston. "What happened?"

"A drug overdose," he answered. "They think he committed suicide."

She looked back at me, shaking her head disparagingly. "So the police didn't even catch him." She turned away from me and stared out the window while an uneasy silence settled over the car. No one spoke for several minutes while Junior Weston looked questioningly from one adult face to another.

Finally he caught my eye. "I'm glad he's dead," the child said. "I wanted him to be dead."

I nodded, but I didn't say anything else. I figured I was better off keeping my mouth shut.

We arrived at the Mount Zion Baptist Church a full hour and fifteen minutes before the two o'clock funeral. Already the neighborhood was dogged with traffic, including an ever-growing contingent of law enforcement vehicles from all over the state. They lined one side of Nineteenth Avenue for three full blocks.

The limo stopped in the front courtyard of the church behind a collection of gray hearses. Emma, Harmon Weston, and Junior Weston were whisked away into the church by three solicitous funeral attendants. They probably would have let me come along too, if I had pushed it, but I felt I had intruded enough. Undecided as to what to do next, I started toward the street to join forces with some of the other police officers who were scattered here and there on the sidewalk, talking together in small groups.

Halfway across the courtyard, a young black male sidled up to me. Staggering drunkenly, he was dressed in ragged, disheveled clothing. A battered baseball cap, worn sideways, was pulled down low on his forehead.

"Hey, man," he whimpered to me. "You gots a dollar for a cuppa coffee?"

Before I could answer, a formidable African-American man, much older and dressed in an impeccable black suit along with spotless white gloves, appeared from nowhere.

"You get out of here now," he told the kid firmly. "These folks are here for a funeral. We don't need the likes of you hanging around begging."

"I ain't beggin'," the boy whined. He caught my eye for a fraction of a second, then dropped his gaze and stared at my feet. "I'm jes axing my friend Beaumont here if he gots 'nuff money to buy me some coffee."

The deacon frowned, looking hard from the kid to me. "You know this young man, mister?"

He did seem vaguely familiar, and although I couldn't place him right off the bat, he obviously knew me. I don't make a habit of giving money to bums on the street, but then most bums don't know me by name either. I reached for my wallet. The deacon shrugged and shook his head.

"You get away from here now, boy," the deacon said firmly as he walked away. "I don't want to see your face around here anymore."

I handed the kid a dollar bill. "Don't spend it all in one place," I told him.

He pocketed the money, staggered a little, and grinned, but the urgency in his voice belied the drunken leer.

"Ron Peters says for me to talk to you right away. Only to you, and away from here. Down the hill on Madison at the deli in ten minutes."

He shambled off in the opposite direction, meandering unsteadily from side to side and heading for the corner of the building that would allow him to avoid the growing collection of cops. I was still watching his slow progress when Sue Danielson materialized beside me.

"Don't you know better than to give money to bums?" she demanded.

Maybe it was the sound of her voice that jogged the memory department of my brain. I knew then where I had seen that face before — on a rap sheet. My drunken bum was none other than Knuckles Russell minus his trademark four-inch Afro.

With no advance warning, one of Ben Weston's missing student loan cosigners had magically reappeared, found by none other than Ron Peters, who had directed him straight to me.

"I've gotta go," I said to Sue, backing away, heading for the door of the church.

"Where? I thought we could sit together."

By rights, I should have invited her along, but Knuckles Russell had been very specific about that, and so had Ron Peters.

"To see a man about a dog," I told her. "Don't go away, Sue. I'll be back."

CHAPTER 24

I went into the church itself. There I met another black-suited, white-gloved man — a deacon presumably. I asked him for directions to the nearest rest room. There, after allowing a suitable interval, I ducked out through a back door that opened on to another parking lot. Hurrying over to Madison, I half walked, half jogged down the hill, knowing that eventually my bone spurs would exact a terrible price for such rash folly.

As I approached the appointed place, I wondered if the whole thing might be some kind of trick or if Ron Peters really was behind the mysterious message delivered by Knuckles Russell. If the news was that important, surely Ron would have come to convey it himself, wouldn't he? Why trust a street-toughened gang member or even ex-member to carry missives back and forth between us? The closer I got to the deli in the swale at the bottom of the hill, the dumber I felt and the more tempted I was to call a halt and go back the way I'd come, but then I spotted Ron Peters's K-car with its distinctive wheelchair carrier perched on top. It was parked on the street directly in front of the deli.

Inside, I found Ron Peters and Knuckles Russell seated in the far corner. Ron, alert and keeping watch, had positioned himself facing out. Knuckles, with his disheveled clothing straightened and minus the baseball cap, sat with his face averted and shoulders hunched, nursing a cup of coffee. Ron waved and motioned for me to join them. I stopped by the counter and picked up my own cup of coffee along the way.

"What's going on?" I asked Peters as I sat down at the table. "I don't have much time. I don't want to miss the funeral."

"I know you two have met before," Ron Peters said, "but I don't believe you've been properly introduced. Beau, this is Ezra Russell. Ezra, this is Detective Beaumont."

I held out my hand. Ezra "Knuckles" Russell looked at it for a long moment before taking it. He nodded and shook hands but said nothing.

"What seems to be the problem?" I asked.

"Go on," Ron Peters urged. "Tell him."

"My friend's dead," Knuckles blurted, "an' I can't even go to the funeral 'cause if I do, they'll smoke me too."

"Who'll kill you?" I asked.

He raised his eyes and looked at me, unveiled distrust written on his face. "You maybe? And maybe this dude too? Ben says for us not to come back, no matter what. He says this be . . . this is our one chance to get away. But this One-Time here" — he motioned to Ron — "he says I gotta help. That otherwise Ben's killer walks."

I knew Captain Freeman had warned me to keep quiet, but if Harmon Weston already knew about Sam Irwin's death, why shouldn't I?

"Word's out on the street that Ben Weston's killer's dead," I told them.

Ron's jaw dropped in surprise. "Really?"

"Who?" Knuckles Russell demanded.

"His name's Sam Irwin."

For a moment or two after I spoke it was quiet at our table as the news soaked in. "You mean Sam Irwin from down in Motor Pool?" Ron asked.

I nodded. "One and the same," I said.

Maybe word about traitors in our midst was news to people like Ron Peters and J. P. Beaumont, but clearly Sam Irwin's name was no surprise to Knuckles Russell.

"So?" He spat in disgust. "You think that motherfucker's the only one? All he knows is cars and knives and cuttin' people. Sam Irwin's not the brains. He ain't runnin' the show."

"Who is then?"

Knuckles shrugged. "I dunno."

"I've heard rumors that Ben Weston was in on it," I said tentatively, just to see what kind of reaction the comment would elicit. The result was far more explosive than I expected. Ezra Russell half rose to his feet until his face was barely inches from mine, his features contorted into a look of sheer hatred.

"Don't you dis' my friend, One-Time. You say that again, and I'll smoke you sure!"

I took Knuckles Russell at his word. No disrespect for his dead friend Ben Weston would be tolerated.

"Tell me about Ben," I said, backing off, modifying my tone. "What made him tick?"

Unexpectedly, Ezra Russell's eyes clouded with tears. He wiped them away angrily with the back of his hand. "Ben Weston was the onliest real friend I ever had," he said despairingly. "The only one." He broke off, his voice choked with raw emotion.

The whole time, I had been wondering how Ron Peters had managed to overcome

Knuckles's entirely understandable distrust and antipathy toward cops, how he had talked him into coming to talk to us. Now I knew the answer. Something about Ben Weston had engendered a powerful loyalty in the boy.

"How did that happen?" I asked. "How did you two become friends?"

He shook his head. "I dunno. Not exactly. I didn't want it. Ben shows up at my door one mornin' and says he wants to talk to me. I say I don't wanna talk to no cops. He says we talk anyway, he says he knows my uncle from church and my mama and Mrs. Davis, my fourth grade teacher. He says he knows I be . . . he knows I'm smart and do I want to be somebody's smart homeboy and do their dirty work and get myself killed or do I want to have a life?

"I say to him you can't come in here. My friends'll say I'm turnin' on 'em, and Ben says that's right, that's the way it's gonna look. He says he's puttin' the word out on the street that me and him is good buddies, so if I doan wanna get my ass killed, I better be. And so he come almost every night and we talk. He talks 'bout my mama and my uncle and how family's the most important thing of all. And he talks 'bout how bein' somebody's homeboy's no better'an bein' their slave.

"So word gets out that me an' him hang out together. The BGDs all say I'm spyin' for him. Ben laughs and says that's right, that's the way it looks. So what'm I gonna do now? He axs me if I know Harriet Tubman. He says she run the Underground Railroad back in the old days. He says he's startin' one of his own — a railroad to out, away from gangs and drugs. He axs me if I want to be on that train or be dead. I say that's not much choice and he and says, boy, that's the only choice you gots. And so I took it."

Knuckles's words had tumbled out in an almost breathless rush. Now he stopped and waited.

"Where did the railroad take you?" I asked.

"Ellensburg. Ben Weston worked some kind of deal to get me an' this other kid in over at Central. We both be . . . we're both in this special English class. He helped me sell my car for this quarter and he was gonna get me student aid for the next one. All I gotta do is promise not to come 'round here, not to get involved. He says my family can't even know 'bout what I'm doin' 'cause they might tell the wrong people. He says

383

he ain't tellin' anybody, not even his woman, neither.

"And so I'm over there workin' my ass off. I doan read no papers, doan see no TV. So when this One-Time here wakes me up at six o'clock in the mornin', I think maybe some of my ex-friends're lookin' for me to cause trouble. Instead, he tells me 'bout Ben and all those poor little kids."

"You've been in Ellensburg the whole time?"

He nodded.

"What about your briefcase?" I asked. "The one you got from your mother for your birthday?"

His eyes narrowed. "What about it? How'd you know 'bout that?"

"It was found on what used to be your doorstep the morning after the murders. Some of your former associates from the streets turned it over to us. The clothes inside — red sweats — were soaked with blood."

"I be a BGD," he announced defiantly. "I don' wear red sweats. Ever!"

As soon as he said it, the frame-up was so obvious I felt stupid for falling for it even momentarily. The color red and BGD do not go together.

"Okay." I nodded. "I understand that, but

somebody wanted us to think you did it. They went to a lot of trouble to make it look as though you had something to do with what happened to the Westons. Maybe they figured that if we didn't get you for the murder, maybe some of your ex-friends would take care of you just on general principles. So you tell me, who did it, Ezra? Do you have any idea?"

"You already know one name," he said. "Sam Irwin. If I say the others, I be breakin' my word to the Black Gangster Disciples and to Ben Weston both."

"As far as the BGD are concerned, you're a marked man anyway. They already told me that. And after talking to them, I can understand why Ben wanted you to stay out of it, to keep your mouth shut. We'll try not to use your word alone to build our case, Ezra. There'll be other evidence as well. In fact, there probably already is. Did Ron tell you about Junior, Ben's son, that somebody tried to kill him again last night?"

"Yes," he said with downcast eyes. "That's why I'm here."

"Don't you owe Junior Weston the same kind of chance his father gave you? If we don't stop these guys, they may try again, and the next time they may succeed. I can't promise that you won't be called on to testify against whatever police officers are behind this operation, because you probably will be, but I can say you'll be given the best protection we have to offer."

He raised his eyes and met mine, but he said nothing. "I'll ask you again. What happened to your briefcase, Ezra?"

"One-Time took it."

"A cop took it? Which one? When?"

"Name's Deddens."

"Gary Deddens? From Patrol?" I remembered Deddens from Ben Weston's house. He had been one of the officers left guarding the crime scene, the guy who, along with me, had gone chasing after my would-be assassin. Talk about leaving the wolf to guard the henhouse. No wonder Ben Weston's Day-Timer had disappeared into thin air.

Ezra Russell nodded. "That's the one."

"How did he get it?"

"He's the bagman. We pay him to let us know where the gang enforcement's gonna be. Me? I'm the treasurer of the Black Gangster Disciples. I take the money to Deddens in that briefcase my mama gave me for my birthday. Deddens takes the money and then he says he likes the case and that he's gonna keep that too. And all the time he's sayin' this, ol' Sam Irwin's standin' off to one side with his knife, sharpenin' it. So I say fine, you keep it. But when people ax me about it, I say someone stole it."

"Did Ben Weston know this was going on? Did he know there were cops on the take?"

"Ben knows."

"Why didn't he do something about it?"

"Don't you understand nothin'?" Knuckles Russell demanded. "He was. He was gettin' the evidence. That's why those mothers smoked him. That's why he be dead."

"You've already named two — Deddens and Irwin. Are there others?"

"Ben says there be at least one more and when he finds him, maybe that'll be the end of it."

"Did he mention a name, give you any kind of a clue?"

"Somebody in the gang unit," Knuckles Russell said softly. "He says somebody who all the time knows what's goin' down."

Somebody in the gang unit? Who could that be? I glanced at Ron, who was studying his watch. "I've got an idea," he said, "It's almost time, so let's go to the funeral. I don't know if Gary Deddens plans to attend or not, but my understanding is that as many people from Patrol as possible are coming as a group. Since Ben worked both places, I expect CCI will be there in force

387

as well. If Deddens shows up, let's cut him out of the herd in public, turn it into a media event. Once we do that, all we have to do is watch for a reaction from somebody in the gang unit."

His suggestion made sense. I suspected that Sam Irwin had been killed as some kind of damage-control measure, in another attempt at pinning the Weston murders on somebody else so business in the protection racket could continue as usual. If we made a big show of picking up one of the remaining conspirators, we would be serving public notice to the contrary.

I stood up. "You're right. We'd better get going."

"You'd do that?" Knuckles Russell asked dubiously. "Just on my word?"

I looked Ezra Russell straight in the eye. "Ezra," I told him, "Ben Weston was your friend. I believe you want us to find the people who killed him every bit as much as we do. Maybe your word alone isn't enough for an actual arrest, but that, combined with other things we've learned, certainly makes it possible for us to ask questions. Just asking may get the reaction we need."

"Can I come along?"

"You bet. Let's do it."

We all piled into Ron's Reliant. The push

of a button sent his folded chair disappearing into the specially designed rooftop wheelchair carrying case that resembles a giant clam shell. We drove back up to the church and parked in an open handicapped zone directly in front of the hearse-filled courtyard.

An overflow crowd had spilled out into the courtyard, where loudspeakers blared a full-voiced choir singing an absolutely mind-blowing version of "Amazing Grace." In my experience most funerals feature a single soloist, but from the sound of it, the Mount Zion Baptist Church had done far better than that. If the choir was already singing, however, there was no time to stand outside and savor it. I left Knuckles with Ron Peters and tried worming my way into the church.

The cross-shaped sanctuary was jammed to the gills. Five white coffins, three large and two small, were ranged across the front of the church, creating a telling spectacle of loss that brought an Adam's apple-size lump to my throat. In the very front pew, the top of Junior Weston's head was barely visible where he sat, statue still, with Emma Jackson on one side of him and his grandfather on the other.

On the far side of the church, a red-robed

choir faced across the altar and the middle, forward-facing pews. Opposite them sat a massed group of uniformed police officers, only half of which were from Seattle itself. The rest were from law enforcement departments all over the state of Washington. Maybe some of the African-American officers had set foot inside the Mount Zion Baptist Church before, but if they were anything like me, most of the Caucasians hadn't, and again like me, they probably felt like foreigners, drawn there only by the unifying tragedy of those five senseless deaths.

As I started down the aisle, a deacon moved forward to assist me, but I had caught sight of Sue Danielson seated near the front in one of the middle pews. Obviously, the empty space next to her was reserved for me. With whispered thanks to the deacon, I made my way up the aisle just as the Reverend Homer Walters stepped to the pulpit. I slipped into the crowded pew beside Sue Danielson. She scowled at me but said nothing.

"This is the day that the Lord has made," he said. "Let us rejoice and be glad in it." A chorus of amens echoed throughout the sanctuary.

The opening prayer was long and moving.

Then, one at a time and with heartfelt measured words, Reverend Walters eulogized each of the slain victims in turn. He spoke of Ben Weston's pride in being a police officer, of Shiree Weston's work with the church credit union, of Bonnie's interest in becoming a teacher, of Adam's hope to follow in his mother's footsteps and become a doctor, and of Doug Weston's sometimes impish gift for storytelling. Finally, though, Homer Walters pounced on the meat and gristle of his message.

"I will not stand here before you today and tell you that what has happened is God's will," he declared. "I will not say that God must have had an urgent need for this man and woman and these three little children and that's the reason He took them home. No, I will not say that. They have been literally cut down in their primes without so much as a chance to live and grow and laugh on this good earth where God put them in the first place.

"Maybe you came here today expecting me to give you comforting words in the face of this senseless tragedy, a tragedy not only for the African-American community but for the community at large. Maybe you expect me to tell you that this too shall pass. Don't you believe it. I want you to get mad and stay that way.

"Take a good look at these children's unfinished lives and Ben and Shiree Weston's unfinished business. Are we just going to wring our hands and say that's too bad, or are we going to do something about it? And I'm not just talking about catching the man who did this. Today I've heard rumors that there's a chance the killer is already dead, that he died last night of a drug overdose. So be it. Let him stand before his Maker and explain himself. I have more faith in the Lord's justice than I do in ours."

This was followed by another answering chorus of amens. Across the center aisle I caught sight of a dry-eyed Molly Lindstrom sitting with her son Greg. She didn't see me. She was listening intently to Reverend Walters, hanging on his every word.

"As a minister of the Lord it is my job to write sermons Sunday after Sunday, and some say I do it better than most. But don't you believe that, either, because when I write one of those real tub-thumping sermons, the kind that makes the rafters up there ring, you can bet the sermon's better than anything I could have written myself. I always figure the Lord Almighty must have a hand in those. And that's the way it was last January when I wrote the first sermon of the New Year. I was inspired to challenge the men and women of this church, and especially the men of this congregation, to do something about the young men in our community, and in other communities as well, who have fallen afoul of themselves, of drugs, of gangs, and of the law.

"By no means are African-American young people the only ones involved in gangs, but I told the men in this congregation that they had a responsibility to the ones who are, that they needed to go out in the world and do something about that particular problem on an individual basis. We can sit here inside these four walls and pray about it, and we need to do that. But we need to do something more. Each of us needs to get off our backside and go out into the streets and do what we can to help.

"That's what the sermon said. Ben Weston heard that challenge and he set himself the task of meeting it. He went after boys he knew in gangs who had some connection to this church. I can tell you that before he died he found four of them. He pulled them out of where they were and he put them on another track. Do you hear me? I'm saying he put them on another track entirely. He brought four young men out of the wilderness and led them into the Promised Land."

Another louder murmur of amens trickled through the congregation. I glanced at the choir. In the front row sat an attractive young woman with a mane of pencil-thin braids. She was listening with rapt attention, and I wondered if she wasn't the undercover cop Tony Freeman had tried to conceal from us as he escorted her out of his office.

Walters continued. "I believe Ben Weston is dead because he was doing the Lord's work, because what he was doing rocked those gangs. They don't want to lose their members' loyalty, but Ben Weston figured out a way to take them away, to set them free. And so today, I want to issue another challenge to those of us who are left. And I'm not talking just to the members of the Mount Zion Baptist Church, either. I'm talking to all you people out there who came here today because Ben Weston and his family died, because Adam Jackson died.

"Instead of just grieving over this terrible loss, I want each and every one of us to do what we can, starting right where Ben Weston left off. Maybe we can't save every one of those boys, because, quite frankly, some of them don't want to be saved. And I'm not talking about throwing money at the problem for more social workers or more jails or more drug treatment centers, either. I'm saying that if each of us goes out and takes one boy or one girl by the hand, takes the time to talk to them and lead them in another direction, we can make a difference. If we do, Ben and Shiree Weston, Bonnie and Doug Weston, and little Adam Jackson will not have died in vain.

"After this service, we will be going to the Mount Olivet Cemetery in Renton. Afterward, there will be a reception here, sponsored by the ladies of the church. I hope as many of you as possible will join us both at the cemetery and here later.

"And now, Lord, in closing, we ask Your blessing upon this day, upon the grieving family members, and upon this community, that we can somehow find a way to turn this tragedy into a blessing. Amen."

A small army of men, none of them police officers, rose as one and moved forward to collect the coffins one by one. As they did so, the strains of "Amazing Grace" once more caught fire in the church. This time, it wasn't just the choir singing, either. The whole congregation was, their voices raised in affirmation. I'm sure I wasn't the only one shedding tears and singing at the same time.

It was that kind of funeral.

CHAPTER 25

The coffins were still being carried down
the aisle when my pager went off, summon-
ing me back from the stirring hymn and Ben
Weston's unfinished business to my own. I
stifled the pager's racket as soon as I could
and glanced at the display that listed Tony
Freeman's extension at Seattle PD. Why was
he there instead of at the funeral? I knew he
had planned to attend.

"Freeman's not here?" I asked Sue in an
undertone.

"I haven't seen him."

"Call him back on the double," I whis-
pered, "and use a pay phone, not a radio.
Find out what he wants, and tell him I've
got another name for him to add to the list
— Deddens, Gary Deddens from Patrol.
Got that?"

Sue nodded, but she didn't move. None
of the rest of the congregation had, and I
knew she was questioning the propriety of

our leaving during the recessional.

"Go now," I urged, "while we can still get out. Meet me out front as soon as you can. We've got work to do."

I had finally managed to spot Gary Deddens sitting near the end of the third row of uniformed officers. He was far closer to the door than we were, and I knew that the slightest delay in our getting out would mean losing him and also losing the opportunity to send a chilling message to any other crooks still left in the group. I wanted to serve notice that we were closing in on them; I wanted to force them into making some kind of strategic blunder.

Shaking her head in disapproval, Sue nonetheless started for the side aisle, leading the way and excusing us to the people whose feet we had to step over in the process. In the vestibule, she asked directions to the nearest phone while I took up a station outside the door just as the last coffin emerged followed by Emma Jackson and Harmon and Junior Weston. They disappeared into the waiting limo while the rest of the people began to trickle out of the church into the courtyard. I looked around, trying to catch sight of Ron Peters and Knuckles Russell, but they were nowhere to be seen.

Sue erupted through the doors and looked around anxiously until she caught sight of me. "How'd you do that?" she demanded.

"Do what?"

"Come up with Gary Deddens's name. Freeman says you're right. Kyle Lehman's copy of Ben's deleted files finally turned up on Tony's desk. He says we've got probable cause. He wants us to take Deddens into custody and bring him down for questioning right away."

"But wait a minute," I objected. "I've got to be here in case . . ."

"Captain Freeman is sending a squad car for us and for Deddens both," she replied. "He wants the two of us there. He was very specific about that."

Just then the first batch of uniformed officers emerged into the fitful sunlight, where they joined the growing crowd milling around the limo and the collection of hearses. I turned my attention on the officers, scanning faces, hoping to see that of Gary Deddens. I examined each one, some of them familiar and some not, and wondered how far the cancer of corruption had spread and how many more officers were involved in the protection racket. The possibility made me sick.

"There he is," Sue whispered. "He's just

now shaking hands with Reverend Walters."

"Who's going to do it?" I asked. "You or me?"

"I will," she volunteered over her shoulder. "You watch for trouble."

Making an arrest of any kind in a crowd situation is always a hairy, volatile proposition. Protecting the lives of innocent civilians must always be the primary consideration for the police officers involved.

Already Sue was moving purposefully toward the door, pulling Flex-cufs rather than a weapon from her blazer pocket. I followed, closing the distance between us so that I was only a step or two behind her when she reached the place where an unsuspecting Gary Deddens stood chatting casually with several of his fellow officers.

Sue stopped directly in front of him. He was saying something to the others, but he paused and half smiled a greeting. "How's it going, Sue?" he said.

"You're under arrest," she returned.

He stepped away from her, but his back was to the wall of the church, and he couldn't go far. "Come on, Sue, that's not funny. Don't even joke about something like that."

Around us the crowd fell strangely silent.

"It's no joke. Face the wall, hands on the

back of your head, feet apart. I'm placing you under arrest in connection with the murder of Officer Benjamin Weston."

Surprise and shock registered on the faces of the men who, moments before, had been chatting amiably with Gary Deddens. Now they melted away from him, opening a circle where the three of us stood in isolation.

"There's got to be some mistake," Deddens said, his eyes darting questioningly from Sue to me. "This is crazy."

"No mistake," Sue insisted. "Turn around."

For an electric moment, he stood glaring and belligerent. Time seemed to stretch into an eternity before finally, with a casual shrug, he started to turn. As deftly as any professional pickpocket, Sue unfastened his holster and removed his automatic which she handed over to me. Behind us the wailing siren of the arriving squad car squawked once and was quickly stifled.

Sue had successfully negotiated the first danger — cornering Deddens and capturing his weapon without anyone being hurt — but the incident was far from over. There was another danger as well, and every cop in the courtyard knew it. As the news of what had happened spread through the crowd, every police officer present realized that outrage over the multiple murders was an open, sucking wound in Seattle's African-American community. I think we all feared that once the grieving people from the funeral realized what was going on, they themselves might very well evolve into a dangerous and potentially lethal mob.

The danger in mobs is that they have no brain and no conscience. They are immune to innocence and equally blind to justice and guilt. You can't talk to them or reason with them. If the searing spark of vengeance is once allowed to erupt into flame, there's no stopping it until the glut of violence has run full course. If the people in the courtyard perceived Gary Deddens to be Ben Weston's killer, if their rage was allowed to get out of hand, they might very well turn on the killer and on whoever was with him as well — Sue Danielson and me included.

Speed was of the essence. Every moment of delay compounded the danger. With businesslike efficiency, Sue patted Deddens down. Other than the automatic, there was no weapon.

"All right, you guys," she barked at the clutch of stricken police officers surrounding us. "Help us get him over to the car. Now!"

For a moment no one moved. An angry

undercurrent of comment rumbled through the crowd as more people spilled out of the church, forcing their way into the now motionless crush in the courtyard. Near the door, someone shoved against someone else, and that backward and forward movement eddied through the entire gathering.

"Let's go!" Sue urged.

Finally the nearby cops shook themselves alive. With me leading the way and with seven or eight officers forming a human shield around Deddens and Sue Danielson, we moved away from the protection of the church wall, past the hearses, and across the courtyard. Professional behavior forestalled the possibility of an unfortunate incident. The officers with us, all in uniforms but from several different jurisdictions, reacted instinctively as a unit. They might have been executing a procedure they'd practiced together time and again.

As we made our way through the sullen but silently watchful crowd, I knew how Moses must have felt as he parted the roiling waters of the Red Sea. A way through the multitude opened magically and silently in front of us, revealing a cleared path that led directly to the patrol car waiting on the street.

At last we were there, opening the door,

shoving Deddens unceremoniously into the backseat. Behind me a car horn blared. It sounded over and over. One of those horn alarm security systems, I supposed.

"You get in front," I said to Sue. "I'll ride in back."

By now the courtyard crowd had spilled over onto the street itself. When the officer driving the patrol car started to move, the way was blocked by fifty or sixty people with more being added all the time.

"Come on. Let's get out of here," I urged the driver. "We're all right so far, but we're not home free, not by any means."

He turned on the siren and started nudging his way into the crowd. Some of the bystanders leaned over and stared into the car, trying to catch a glimpse of whoever was there as we eased by them. And then, just as I thought we were close to breaking out, someone began pounding furiously on the trunk of the car.

I figured it was the beginning of the end and that we were all in for it. Even Gary Deddens seemed concerned.

"We're not going to make it," he whined. "If they get hold of me those people will tear me apart."

"Maybe we should let them, creep," I said. "Maybe I should just open the door and let them have you."

He paled. "No, please. Don't do that."

People in front of the car stopped us again while the pounding on the back of the squad car continued. It was on the back panel now, just behind my shoulder, angry and insistent. Next the hammering started on the window beside my head.

Gary Deddens looked at the window with a sharp, involuntary intake of breath. I turned to see what had caused it.

The distorted angry face of a young black man was pressed against the glass. Abruptly the face was jerked away as someone grabbed the man from behind and pried him from the car. Only then did I recognize the face. Knuckles Russell stood there struggling furiously and gesturing toward the patrol car.

Something had happened, and Knuckles was trying to let me know.

"Stop the car and let me out," I demanded.

"What do you mean let you out?" the driver returned. "You got a death wish or something?"

"Goddamnit," I insisted. "I said let me out!"

Reluctantly, he stopped the car and unlatched the door. Sue jumped out to open it. "What the hell is going on?" she began.

But I didn't reply. Instead, I leaped to where Knuckles still stood, trying to free himself from the unrelenting grasp of the King County police officer who had nabbed him.

"What is it?" I demanded. "What's wrong?"

"Come on," Knuckles answered urgently. "Ron Peters says you gots to come with me."

"It's okay," I said to the officer. "Let him go. I know this man."

The car horn was still sounding, closer now and more insistently. Out of the corner of my eye I saw Ron Peters's Reliant pressing its way toward me through the massed humanity. Taking Knuckles by the arm, the two of us started for the slow-moving car. Without waiting for Ron to come to a complete stop, Knuckles clambered into the backseat while I climbed into the front.

"What's going on?" I asked. "What's happening?"

"Curtis Bell," Ron Peters answered, still trying to escape the crush of people and the endless row of vehicles that was already queuing up to form the funeral cortege. Ron's specially equipped car with all its push-button controls would have been a complete mystery for me to operate, but he drove it with the consummate ease and confidence of a speeding juvenile delinquent.

"Curtis Bell? What about him?"

"You should have seen him. He came through the door of the church just as you were moving Deddens toward the car. As soon as he saw what you were up to, he took off like a dog with firecrackers tied to his tail."

"But I thought he was selling . . ."

"Evidently more than insurance," Ron Peters finished. "No wonder he was so interested in getting appointments with you and Big Al. My guess is he thought one of you would slip and tell him how much you knew."

"I'll be damned. He was trolling for information the whole time."

"You've got it," Peters replied. "Looking for leaks and trying to cover his tracks all at the same time."

We finally negotiated our way through the last of the milling crowd. With squealing tires, Ron Peters sent the car rocketing forward. He turned westbound onto Madison.

"So where is he?" I asked.

"See that blue car," Knuckles Russell

asked, pointing from the backseat. "The one just now goin' over the top of the hill? That's him."

Curtis Bell's blue Beretta crested the rise and momentarily disappeared from view as we sped up the steep grade behind him.

"He's ahead of us," Peters agreed grimly, "but not that far and not for long. You two keep an eye on him, and we'll catch up."

"And what do we do then?" I asked.

"I'm gonna smoke the mother," Knuckles Russell murmured.

Even barreling hell-bent-for-leather down the street, Ron Peters managed to dredge up a shred of his customary sense of humor.

"That's probably a bad idea, Ezra," he cautioned reasonably. "There'll be too many other people in line. You might hit the wrong person."

"What if he gets off?" Knuckles demanded.

"He won't. We'll see to it."

There was no way right then to tell who had done what, but in the state of Washington, regardless of who had been running the show and regardless of who actually wielded the weapons, all those involved would be considered equally guilty. In this state, murders committed by others in the course of a conspiracy to commit a felony offense damn all the conspirators. Not only that, Curtis Bell was a crooked cop besides.

"Killing's too damn good for him," I said heatedly. "Look! He's turning north on Sixth. Where's he going?"

We were turning onto Sixth only a block behind him as the light at Spring turned green ahead of us and he sped in a sharp right-hand turn onto the southbound on-ramp to I-5. Peters followed suit, but dropped back and stayed far enough behind so we could keep him in view without arousing suspicion.

"Five bucks says he's headed for the airport," Ron Peters breathed.

"I never placed no bet with cops before, but you're on," Knuckles asserted from the backseat. His eyes never left the back of Curtis Bell's car.

Previous encounters with Ron Peters had taught me the folly of betting money against him on anything. It was a valuable lesson Knuckles Russell would have to learn for himself the hard way.

"It'll be coming out of your student loan," I told him.

And actually, that was probably fair. I figured it would prove to be an educational experience.

CHAPTER 26

For months now people in the media have complained bitterly about the growing traffic problems in the Puget Sound area. When you live and work primarily in the downtown core, it's easy to ignore the fact that Seattle's freeways often deteriorate into vast parking lots, and not just at rush hour, either.

At four P.M. that Saturday afternoon some major cultural or sporting event must have let out minutes earlier, because the southbound lanes of I-5 were crammed. After merging into traffic, we literally inched our way past the I-90 interchange and the city's perpetual Kingdome exit construction projects. Curtis Bell's blue Beretta was only six or seven cars ahead of us as we crawled along.

"I could probably sprint fast enough to catch up with him," I said, itching to jump out of the car and collar the bastard.

"And what happens then?" Peters returned. "What happens if Bell takes off and you end up causing a chain reaction accident? We'll be stuck here with no backup and no way to send for any. We're better off waiting until we know for sure where he's going."

I might have argued with him, except he was probably right. When you're dealing with that kind of traffic volume, any slight fender bender can result in hours of delay for everyone. Under those circumstances, police and emergency vehicles are only marginally better off than civilian ones.

The good thing about being stuck in traffic was that it was easy to keep track of exactly where Curtis Bell was and what he was doing, without it being blatantly obvious to him that he was being tailed. The bad part was that if he somehow did catch on and start making evasive maneuvers, it might be difficult for us to react. I breathed a sigh of relief when he went straight past the Spokane Street and Michigan exits. I was happy when he skipped Martin Luther King Junior Way as well. It was looking more and more like Sea-Tac all the time.

About then my pager went off two different times in rapid succession. Once the readout gave me Tony Freeman's number and once Captain Powell's, but without a radio or a phone in the car, there was no way for me to respond right then.

"You really ought to have a cellular phone in here," I told Peters. "It would make our lives a hell of a lot easier right about now."

The irony of what I'd just said wasn't lost on me, and Ron Peters didn't miss it either. He glanced at me sideways. "Ralph Ames has created a technological monster out of you, hasn't he?" Ron said with a laugh. "Maybe I should have a portable fax in here as well."

I didn't want to talk about who owned a fax and who didn't, but joking around helped ease the tension in the car. It gave us something to think about besides the grim reality of the coming confrontation.

And grim it was. It's one thing to go up against crooks. They may be armed to the teeth, but they're also like untrained guerrilla warriors who often can be outflanked and outmaneuvered by the strategic thinking of even a much smaller force. Unfortunately Curtis Bell was a fellow police officer. He would be armed, probably the same way I was armed — with an automatic weapon — and he had been trained the same way I had been trained, probably by some of the same people. More important, he was desperate. That made him doubly dangerous.

"What do you think he'll do when he realizes he's being followed?" I asked.

"He's likely to recognize the car," Peters said. "If he thinks I'm alone with no way to summon help, maybe we can trick him into coming after me."

"No way! That's risky as hell."

"Do you have a better idea?"

I didn't. Every mile we traveled was taking us closer and closer to Sea-Tac Airport, but the traffic jam had broken up and the average highway speed had increased dramatically. We were zipping along at an unlawful but traffic-pacing sixty-six. Now there were only two cars between us and Curtis Bell. As I watched, one of them switched on a turn signal indicating a planned exit at Tukwila. Bell moved into the far right-hand lane just past that same exit.

"Sea-Tac it is," Peters said grimly. "You two had better get down. He's bound to notice the car sooner or later."

Peters's rooftop wheelchair carrier isn't entirely unique — I've seen one or two others like it in my travels — but it is very distinctive and through a special dispensation from both the chief and the mayor, Ron

413

is allowed to park it in a specially designated handicapped spot just inside the department's parking garage. Everyone on the force sees it on an almost daily basis.

As of that moment, Peters's plan, risky or not, was the only one available. I did as I was told and scrunched down in the seat, assuming that behind me Knuckles Russell was doing exactly the same thing.

Peters switched on his own signal, and the Reliant swerved slightly to the right. "Southcenter?" I asked.

He nodded. "Hang on. I'm going to narrow the gap now, let him know I'm back here, and see what he does about it."

What Bell did next was obvious in Ron Peters's reaction. He accelerated to warp speed. There's something about riding blindly down a highway in a speeding vehicle with your shoulder seat belt dangling improperly around your neck to give you yet another glimpse of your own mortality. Almost like dodging the bullet in a drive-by shooting. Almost like having a life insurance salesman pay a call, but I kept my mouth shut and didn't tell Peters to slow down. People who can't see the road shouldn't backseat drive.

Overhead, the shadow of an overpass blinked across the windshield while we angled first to the right and then to the left. That meant we were turning onto the private road approaching the airport. Theoretically, that stretch is heavily patrolled by port police. Maybe, with any kind of luck, both vehicles would be stopped for speeding and Peters and I would have some help after all, but of course, that didn't happen. Traffic cops are hardly ever anywhere around when you need them.

"Where's he going?" I asked, automatically starting to slide back up in the seat.

"The parking garage. Stay right where you are," Peters ordered.

I slid back down, banging my knees on the bottom of the dashboard as we screeched to a sudden halt at the wooden control gate that allows only one car at a time access into Sea-Tac's parking area. Peters rolled down his window as the buzzer sounded. He grabbed the ticket. I was glad he'd stopped. Otherwise, the Reliant would have been wearing a hunk of two-by-six Douglas fir as a hood ornament.

"Good, he's headed up the ramp," Peters said, reporting what was going on outside my line of vision like some macabre play-by-play sports broadcaster, but this was no game. In the next few minutes, there was going to be a gunfight and someone was liable to get hurt. Considering the small number of people involved, the odds were pretty damned high that a fast trip to Harborview's Trauma Unit was looming in my future.

We started moving forward again, going up and around the circular ramps. "Ezra," Peters was saying. "Are you listening?" Our passenger had been so quiet for so long, I had almost forgotten Knuckles Russell's presence, but Ron Peters hadn't.

"Yo," Knuckles responded.

"Listen to me. I'm going to throw you out. Run like hell into the terminal and alert security. Have them seal off the garage. Tell them not to let anyone in or out until they hear from Detective Beaumont or me. Got that?"

"Got it!" Knuckles replied.

I felt a surge of elation. It wasn't just Peters and me after all. Knuckles was there. If he could go for help fast enough, there was a chance he could save us all.

On what must have been the inside curve of the next ramp, Peters stopped long enough for Knuckles to leap out. "Get going!" he ordered, but Knuckles paused momentarily outside the door.

Ron pressed the button to roll down the windows. "What is it? What's wrong?"

"What if they doan listen?"

"Make them!" Peters barked. "You've got to."

Moments later I heard the first echoing slaps of Knuckles's retreating Reeboks, then Peters continued two-wheeling us up that gut-wrenching circular ramp.

My heart sank. Every single day, cops make life-or-death judgments based on appearances alone, on how the people they're dealing with look, act, and sound. Ezra Russell looked fine. He wasn't wearing gang-type clothing, but he still sounded like a street tough. There was nothing in the way he spoke that announced he had changed his ways and matriculated at an institution of higher learning as a respectable college student. I worried about what kind of call the port police would make with all our lives hanging in the balance.

"What if he's right?" I asked. "What if they don't believe him?"

"That's a risk we'll have to take, isn't it?" Peters returned. "Hold on. You get out here. It looks to me as though he's on his way up to the top floor."

"But . . ." I objected.

"No buts. This is seven, the end of the line. Come up either the stairs or the elevator. As far as he's concerned, I'll be a sitting duck. I'm counting on you to see to it that isn't the case."

Peters paused barely long enough for me to clamber out of the car. Luckily I landed on my feet. The next thing I knew, I, too, was racing through the almost deserted parking garage. The place was full of cars, but empty of people. Evidently Saturday isn't a primo flying day.

Never before had I noticed how unbearably long those aisles were. They must have stretched forever while behind me I heard the squeal of tires as Peters rounded the last curve that would take him onto the eighth level of the parking garage, the top and unroofed level.

I ducked my head and ran that much faster, dreading with every step the reverberation of a gunshot echoing off concrete that would mean the end of Ron Peters.

Overhead I heard a terrible crash followed by the scraping of metal on concrete. There was no way to tell what had happened. The sound seemed to come from behind me, from what was now the far side of the garage. By then there was no point in running all the way back to the ramps and making my way up from there. I was already far closer to the elevators and stairwells.

Between stairs and elevator, there was no

contest. I knew from bitter firsthand experience that a stairwell can be as bad as a blind alley, a trap, or a box canyon. But at least a stairway exit door wouldn't ring a bell and point an arrow announcing my arrival.

I dashed through the door marked STAIRS. On the first landing I paused for a moment to hear if anyone was headed either down from above me or up from below, but there were no echoing footsteps. The place was empty. Relieved, I pounded up the remaining set of steep concrete stairs, covering three steps at a time. By then, my breath was coming in short, sharp gasps, there was a splitting pain in my side, and one ankle was giving me trouble.

Damn! I still expected my body to respond like it had twenty years ago, but it didn't. Couldn't. Even if I didn't want to accept the idea that middle age was setting in with a vengeance, my body knew it. I had to wait outside the heavy metal door to catch my breath before I dared open it and go on.

Without my consciously being aware of it, the 9 mm automatic appeared in my hand. Taking a deep breath, I pushed the door open a crack.

Level 8 in the Sea-Tac Airport Parking Garage — the uncovered, rooftop portion — is the floor of last resort when it comes to parking cars. Usually it's relatively open. Not so that particular day, and not because cars were parked on it either. Instead, the whole place had become a construction material staging area for the massive expansion of the parking garage. The place was strewn with stacks of lumber and iron rods, rolls of metal mesh fencing, piles of sheet metal, and several parked forklifts.

Where I expected a clear line of vision from the stairs to the ramps, instead the view across the floor was totally obscured. Over the noise of a departing jet, I could hear nothing. The only way to find out what was happening with Peters was to leave the relative safety of the stairwell.

I stepped out onto the concrete rooftop. At that exact instant, Curtis Bell's Beretta came hurtling past my line of vision. Heading toward the exit ramp and busy dodging among the piles of construction material, I don't think he even saw me. Raising the 9 mm, I assumed the proper shooting stance, hoping to squeeze off a shot at him before he disappeared down the ramp, but then I saw Peters.

Nosing his car straight through a stack of fencing, he sent huge rolls of the stuff spinning off in all directions. But the maneuver had accomplished its desired effect, creating a shortcut that took him to the top of the exit ramp and cut off Curtis Bell's only remaining avenue of escape. With a sickening crunch the speeding Beretta plowed into the Reliant's rider's side. The grinding, sheet metal-devouring crash that followed made me grateful that I wasn't sitting there in Peters's car on the rider's side. If I had been, I would have been holding the front end of the Beretta's V–6 engine.

Instead of moving forward toward the melee, I stood as if frozen, still holding my weapon. There was no way for me to pull the trigger. If I had, Ron Peters would have been directly in my line of fire.

The dust settled slowly. At first glance I didn't see either Ron Peters or Curtis Bell. Then, just when I'd almost convinced myself that they were both either dead or too badly injured to move, the clamshell top on the wheelchair carrier shot up and with a whir Peters's wheelchair lowered down beside the car. So Ron was all right. He was getting out, moving himself expertly from car to chair.

Breathing a sigh of relief, I started forward, but then I saw movement in the Beretta as well. Curtis Bell, his head bloodied, crawled out through the rider's side window. There was no need to shout a warning —

they saw each other at precisely the same moment.

Midafternoon sun had finally managed to burn through the cloud cover. I saw the reflected glint of sunlight on metal and knew without a doubt that Curtis Bell had a gun in his hand.

My main problem was one of distance. Physics and reality to the contrary, it seemed as though the eighth floor aisles must have been far longer than those on the seventh, longer at least by half. I tried to shout a warning across the intervening space, but the sound was swallowed up in the roar of a departing jet. My only hope — Ron Peters's only hope — was that I close the distance between us. Knowing I didn't have a snowball's chance in hell of getting there in time, I ducked my head, said a silent prayer, and ran.

It was like running in slow motion or in water or sloughing through deep sand. The vast distance that separated us didn't seem to get any smaller. Partway there, I could see that Ron Peters and Curtis Bell were speaking earnestly back and forth across the hood of Ron's car, but I wasn't close enough to hear their voices. I wondered if they were negotiating about which one would end up having to give up and let the other one go.

With less than a quarter of the distance to go, a blaring alarm began sounding from somewhere inside the terminal itself. Thank God, I thought with relief. Knuckles had done it. He had somehow sounded the alarm and airport security was coming to help, but before that could happen, Curtis Bell swung around and saw me.

He saw me and pulled the trigger all in the same movement. He didn't pause, didn't have to think about it. He aimed and fired, hoping to gun me down without even the slightest pretense of hesitation. A long way from any cover, I hit the ground and skidded along the rough concrete surface just as the first bullet whizzed by overhead.

Curtis Bell was carrying the same kind of automatic I was. There should have been a whole barrage of bullets, but there wasn't. Not exactly. There was a second shot — I heard it — but it didn't hit anywhere near me.

I heard a single outraged screech of pain and I saw Curtis Bell crumple to the ground. Ron Peters may have looked like a sitting duck, but he wasn't. And maybe his aim wasn't all it had been once, before his accident, but it was close enough for government work, close enough to do the job and save my life.

I scrambled to my feet and hurried over to where Curtis Bell lay writhing on the ground, clutching his bleeding gut. Picking up his weapon, I left him lying there and walked past him to check on Ron Peters.

"You all right?" I asked.

"My car's screwed," he answered, "but I'm okay."

"I don't give a rat's ass about your car as long as you're fine."

With a whir of his electric wheelchair, Ron Peters rolled up beside me, and we both looked down at the injured and helpless Curtis Bell. Neither one of us leaped forward to administer first aid.

"He's not, though, is he?" Ron said casually. "Looks as though he's hurt pretty bad . . ."

"You shot him real low," I said. "Looks like you hit him well below the vest."

Ron shook his head and clicked his tongue. "Can you imagine that. Guess I'm still not used to shooting from this angle. Maybe I need more practice."

"I wouldn't want you to change a thing," I told him. "And neither would Big Al."

Chapter 27

The Medic One unit came from Angle Lake. As soon as we gave the port police the all clear, the medics arrived on the scene, where they determined Curtis Bell's condition was far too serious to risk an ambulance ride. Harborview's med-evac helicopter was summoned. Despite the construction debris and wrecked vehicles, it landed right there on top of the garage and the injured man was loaded aboard along with a police officer guard, compliments of the Port of Seattle.

Before the tow trucks finished hauling away broken cars, the garage had turned into a jurisdictional nightmare. Because of the likely connection to the Beaux Arts case, King County wanted to be involved as well as the city of Seattle and the Port of Seattle. Knuckles Russell remained on the fringes of the ever-expanding group, shoulders hunched, hands in his pockets, warily watching the proceedings.

One of the last officers to arrive on the scene was Captain Anthony Freeman. He spoke first to Peters and me, then he asked Ron to introduce him to Knuckles Russell.

"I'm Captain Freeman from Internal Investigations," Tony Freeman told him, shaking hands. "Thanks for all your help, Ezra. We've got them now. Sue Danielson is down at the office working with Gary Deddens right now. He's waived his right to an attorney. He's spilling his guts."

"You shoulda caught him sooner," Knuckles said accusingly. "Then Ben Weston wouldn't be dead."

"You're right. Ben was almost ready to move on this. From looking at the file, I can see what he was doing. Ben didn't want to do anything until he had enough corroborating evidence that he wouldn't have to call you or any of the others back to testify. Even though he had gleaned much of his information from you, he didn't want you to be involved."

A jet took off in the background. No one said anything for a moment while Knuckles Russell's eyes filled with tears.

"You mean Ben's dead 'cause he was protectin' me?"

Tony Freeman nodded. "You and the others," he said.

"Shit, man!" Ezra muttered fiercely. "Shit!"

He walked away from us to the far side of the garage, where he stood hunched and withdrawn, looking down at the traffic below. No one followed him. At that moment, Knuckles Russell needed nothing so much as to be left alone.

I turned back to Captain Freeman. "So how much more cancer is there?" I asked.

He shook his head. "Not much I hope, but I don't know, not for sure. Like I said. Deddens is spilling his guts, hoping it'll go easier on him. If anyone else is involved, he'll tell us. Turns out he's the one who placed the call to nine-one-one, hoping to create enough confusion over the massacre that Curtis Bell would have a chance to get into Ben's office computer undetected and do the deleting. From the looks of the files, Ben was within minutes of bringing me the case. Unfortunately, I was out of town."

"So the deletion almost worked, didn't it," I said.

Freeman nodded. "It might have. If Kyle hadn't managed to bring those files back up when he did, they could have been written over and lost for good. But we've got it now. Gary Deddens can squeal all he wants, but

I've got some bad news for him and Curtis Bell as well. I'm going to convince the prosecutor to go for aggravated first degree for both of them, not only for murdering the Westons but also their pal Sam Irwin."

"They wanted us to turn him into the fall guy, didn't they?"

"Yes, but by then they were panicked and it didn't work. Those two bastards may figure out a way to wiggle out of the death penalty, but they'll never be out on the streets again, either one of them. I'll see to it."

Without our noticing, Knuckles Russell had returned from the other side of the garage and was hovering just outside our circle of conversation. Captain Freeman stepped aside and motioned for him to join us.

"Did you need something?" Freeman asked.

For several seconds the two men stood facing each other, their eyes locked in an unblinking stare — the tall balding white man with his red bottlebrush mustache and the much younger black one.

"Ben Weston tol' me once that a One-Time named Freeman was all right. I can see that be . . . that's true."

It was a moment of understanding that

cut both ways. Freeman nodded. "Ben had a lot of faith in you, too, Ezra. We were on the right track, but it's possible Curtis Bell might have gotten away if you hadn't come forward when you did."

"I din't come forward on my own," Knuckles said, shaking his head. "But for him," he added, pointing a finger at Ron Peters, "I'd still be in Ellensburg."

Tony looked from Ron to me and back again. "Detective Beaumont, I thought I told you specifically not to add any additional personnel to this investigation without my express permission."

"Excuse me, Captain Freeman," Peters interrupted. "I put myself on the case, long before Beau had any idea Internal Investigations would be involved."

"Why? Don't you work in Media Relations?"

"That's my job," Peters conceded, "but what I do on my own time is my business."

"Including tearing hell out of your own car in the process of apprehending a fleeing felon?"

"That too."

Peters and I both stood there waiting for what we figured was an inevitable chewing out. Instead, Captain Freeman nodded. "I see," he said. "Why don't you come talk to

429

me next week some time, Officer Peters. I might have a place in IIS for someone as motivated as you. Seems to me you're wasting your time in Media Relations."

"You name the time," Ron Peters said. "I'll be there."

Freeman turned back to Knuckles. "Where are you going to be staying tonight, Ezra? And how can I get in touch with you once you get back over to Ellensburg? Questions may come up that we'll need you to answer."

Knuckles shrugged. "I dunno about staying here. The Disciples still wants my ass."

"He can stay with me tonight," I offered. "With Junior and Ralph Ames there, too, it may be a little crowded, but we'll manage."

It was beginning to feel as though I was running a hotel. "Good," Freeman said, accepting my answer at face value. "Now. How are you all getting back to town? Should I make arrangements for rides?"

"I called my wife, Amy," Ron told him. "She's bringing the van. There'll be plenty of room."

By the time we finished giving statements to everyone who needed them, Amy Peters had arrived. Afterward, she gave us all a ride back to Belltown Terrace.

"Ralph said we're invited for dinner," she

told me as we drove into the parking garage. "I hope you don't mind."

Actually, I did. I was once more running out of steam — I just can't seem to go without sleep the way I used to. Besides that, my feet were killing me. But if Ralph was doing the cooking, all that would be required of me was to hold up my head long enough to eat.

Knuckles looked at me suspiciously as I held the door for him to go into my apartment. "How come a cop gets to live like this?"

"Don't worry," I told him. "I inherited it. On what I make, I could barely afford the bottom floor in this place."

The house smelled of garlic and roasting chickens and something else, something exquisite, that turned out to be homemade bread. Once inside the apartment, I expected to hear the clattering din of a video game, but the house was quiet. I introduced Ralph to Knuckles Russell, explaining that he was a friend of Ben Weston's and that he needed a place to spend the night.

"Where are the kids?" I asked.

"The girls are down swimming. Junior hasn't come back from the funeral yet, although I expect them any minute. Emma Jackson called to say they'd be by in a few

431

minutes to pick up Junior's things."

"Where's Dr. Jackson taking him, back to West Seattle to his grandfather's?"

"Oh, haven't you heard?" Ralph asked. "Evidently Ben and Shiree Weston named her as legal guardian if anything ever happened to both of them. Emma said they'd come by for the Nintendo on the way. They're going to take some time off. She says she's taking him to the coast for a few days so they can get used to the idea of living together."

The telephone rang and I answered it. "It's Emma," a voice said from downstairs. "Junior said he knew the door code, but I thought we should call and let you know we're here."

"Come on up," I said, buzzing them in.

When I opened the door into the hallway, there were three people waiting there — Emma Jackson and Carl Johnson, that uncommonly tall principal from McClure Middle School. He was holding a worn-out and half-dozing Junior Weston cradled gently in his arms. Junior in turn was holding tight to his teddy bear.

I invited them into the apartment. "Emma," she corrected when I introduced her to Ralph Ames as Doctor Jackson.

"Ralph Ames and I already met on the phone."

Ralph nodded. "I have everything gathered up, but wouldn't you like to stay for dinner?"

"No thanks. I've reserved a room down at Long Beach. It's quite a drive, but I want to go tonight. I probably won't be able to sleep anyway."

Ralph handed her Junior's things, and I followed her to the door. She stopped and held out her hand. "I went by Harborview to check on that detective friend of yours. He's going to be fine."

"Good," I said. "I'm glad to hear it."

"I'm glad we're both good at what we do," she continued. "Maybe Ben was right and I was wrong. The city needs doctors, but it also needs cops. See you around."

With that, she turned and started toward the door only to collide with Knuckles Russell, who was just coming down the hall from the bathroom. Dr. Emma Jackson stopped and studied him with a long, searching glance. It was a moment before she made the connection.

"You wouldn't happen to be Ezra Russell, would you?" she asked.

He nodded.

"I should have figured you'd be here.

Reverend Walters told me about you, Ezra. As soon as you can, you go back to school and work hard, you hear? I'm sure it's what Ben would have wanted."

Knuckles ducked his chin. The gang-induced bravado and identity had disappeared, leaving behind a shy young man who still didn't know who he was.

"And you take good care of Ben's little boy," he said. "You see to it that he doan get mixed up with no gangs."

CHAPTER 28

The next morning I was awakened by a strange scraping noise, one I'd never heard before. At first I thought it was a fire alarm, but when I came staggering out to check, Ralph laughed and told me it was just the fax machine.

"I'm surprised they're sending it this morning, but some people work all the time," Ralph said. "I asked one of my people in Phoenix to get me a Best's analysis of that company Curtis Bell was working for. From everything he said, it didn't seem like he was entirely legitimate. He just didn't know enough, not even for a beginner. The company's not that good either. It's pretty much one of those pyramid schemes, but saying he was in the life insurance business and actually selling a dozen or so policies was a good cover. It allowed him to have extra money that otherwise he wouldn't have been able to explain away."

"It figures," I said glumly, taking a proffered cup of coffee.

"Nonetheless, he did give me some good estate-planning ideas, and we'll have to get together with someone from a better company to get it handled. Do you know any CLUs?"

"Any what?"

"Never mind," Ralph said. "That's insurance talk. I'll find one for you, an insurance agent who actually knows what he's doing."

A Sunday newspaper was strewn on the window seat. I glanced at the headline. "SPD COPS ARRESTED FOR HOMICIDE" it said. I didn't bother to read the article. Regardless of what it said, every honest cop in the Pacific Northwest was going to be dealing with fallout from Curtis Bell and his cohorts for a long, long time.

After rummaging through the paper and locating the crossword puzzle, I took it over to the desk. The puzzle didn't take long, and when I'd finished it, I picked up the phone and dialed Harborview. Much to my surprise, instead of being put through to the ICU waiting room, I was connected directly to Big Al Lindstrom.

"How're you doing?" I asked.

"Better than anybody expected," he returned. "You guys did a helluva job. Thanks, Beau."

"We did what needed to be done," I said.

Call waiting — call interrupting, as Heather calls it — signaled that someone else was trying to get through. I switched to the other line.

"Good morning," said a woman's voice. "This is Alex."

For a moment I couldn't place her, and the stunned silence must have given me away. "Remember me? Alexis Downey from the Seattle Rep."

"Sorry," I said. "The one who likes Bentleys. I guess I'm not quite awake. Did you ever get to go for your ride?"

"No," she said, "I never did. Actually, Ralph had hinted that you might be able to convince the Belltown Terrace syndicate to donate the Bentley to the Rep. We're trying something new this year, an auction. That Bentley would make a terrific auction item. I wouldn't be calling on a Sunday morning, but tomorrow's our deadline."

"Give me your number," I told her. "I'll have to get back to you on this."

I cut short the conversation with Big Al and went looking for Ralph Ames, who had disappeared into the kitchen, where he was

totally involved in starting a new pot of coffee.

"All right, Ralph," I said. "Tell me about
Alexis Downey. We both know that if the
Belltown Terrace Syndicate needs to be
talked into making a charitable donation,
Ralph Ames is a whole lot more qualified to
do the talking than I am."

For the first time in all the years I'd
known him, Ralph Ames looked guilty as
hell. And he couldn't seem to think of
anything to say, either. That hardly ever happens either.

"All right, Ralph. Out with it. Tell me what
the hell's going on."

"She's a nice lady," he said lamely.

"So?"

"I thought maybe, if I set it up, the two of
you would hit it off."

"So this was all a plot to fix me up?"

Ralph sighed. "I keep telling you, Beau.
It's time you got over Anne Corley and went
on with your life."

Naturally, my first reaction was an over-
reaction. "Here's her number," I said, handing him the scrap of paper on which I'd
scribbled Alexis Downey's number. "You
call her back and tell her she can have the
car or not, I don't care which, but leave me
out of it."

The next morning, Knuckles Russell returned to Ellensburg and Ralph Ames went back to Phoenix. On Tuesday Ezra called to say that with Ben Weston dead, the bank wanted him to rewrite his student loan and the other three as well. Which is how it happens that I am now the proud cosigner on four separate student loans. I told Ralph I consider it an investment in this country's future. So far they're all getting good grades.

While I was busy having fun, I called to find out about the Teddy Bear Patrol's annual kick-off fundraiser. They assured me my name will be on the invitation list. I don't know how many teddy bears ten thousand bucks will buy, but it should be fun to find out.

Then, a week or so ago, right after Big Al came back to work on a part-time basis, the phone rang in our cubicle at work on a rare sunny Monday morning.

"I'd like you to be my guest at the Rep auction," Alexis Downey's unfamiliar voice said. "I'm sure the Bentley will go for a ton of money and I'd like you to be there to see it."

I tried to stammer my way out of it, but Alexis wasn't taking no for an answer. Finally, reluctantly, I agreed.

"At the white elephant sale last year I

bought an old picnic basket," she continued. "I was wondering if you'd like to help me break it in? I do great picnics."

It sounded to me as though Alexis Downey should have been in sales. Come to think of it, she is in sales. Before I told her good-bye we had a date for the following Saturday afternoon.

"Who was that?" Big Al asked when I finally put down the phone.

"Trouble, I think," I told him.

"Not bad trouble, I hope," he said.

"No, good trouble."

I went on the picnic with Alex Downey and it rained like hell, but we had a good time. We didn't walk far, because my feet were killing me that day, but she's a fun, interesting lady. For a few hours I was able to forget all about the Seattle Homicide Squad, and that's good for me. Now, I'm even looking forward to the auction. I may rent a tux.

According to Ralph Ames, having fun is something I need to do more often. Maybe I'll fire up the fax and tell him thanks.

ABOUT THE AUTHOR

New York Times bestselling author **J. A. Jance** was born in South Dakota, brought up in Bisbee, Arizona, and now lives with her husband in Seattle, Washington, and Tucson, Arizona. Readers can visit her online at *www.jajance.com*.

We hope you have enjoyed this Large Print book. Other Thorndike, Wheeler, Kennebec, and Chivers Press Large Print books are available at your library or directly from the publishers.

For information about current and upcoming titles, please call or write, without obligation, to:

Publisher
Thorndike Press
295 Kennedy Memorial Drive
Waterville, ME 04901
Tel. (800) 223-1244

or visit our Web site at:

http://gale.cengage.com/thorndike

OR

Chivers Large Print
published by BBC Audiobooks Ltd
St James House, The Square
Lower Bristol Road
Bath BA2 3SB
England
Tel. +44(0) 800 136919
email: bbcaudiobooks@bbc.co.uk
www.bbcaudiobooks.co.uk

All our Large Print titles are designed for easy reading, and all our books are made to last.

BRENT LIBRARIES

Please return/renew this item
by the last date shown.
Books may also be renewed by
phone or online.
Tel: 0115 929 3388
On-line www.brent.gov.uk/libraryservice